AUDETTE
OF BROOKRAVEN

SHARI L. TAPSCOTT

Audette of Brookraven
The Eldentimber Series, Book Four

Copyright © 2016 by Shari L. Tapscott
All rights reserved.

ISBN-13: 978-1540753519
ISBN-10: 1540753514

This is a work of fiction. Names, characters, businesses, places, events and incidents are either the product of the author's imagination or used in a fictitious manner. Any resemblance to actual persons, living or dead, or actual events is purely coincidental.

Editing by Patrick Hodges and Z.A. Sunday
Cover Design by Shari L. Tapscott

Silver and Orchids

Moss Forest Orchid
Greybrow Serpent
Wildwood Larkwing
Lily of the Desert
Fire and Feathers: A Silver and Orchids Novelette

The Eldentimber Series

Pippa of Lauramore
Anwen of Primewood
Seirsha of Errinton
Audette of Brookraven
Elodie of the Sea
Rosie of Triblue: An Eldentimber Novella
Grace of Vernow: An Eldentimber Novelette

Fairy Tale Retellings:

A Marquise and Her Cat: A Puss in Boots Retelling
A Bear's Bride: A Retelling of East of the Sun, West of the Moon
Chains of Gold: A Novelette Retelling of Rumpelstilzchen

The Glitter & Sparkle Series

Glitter & Sparkle
Shine & Shimmer
Sugar & Spice

Just the Essentials

To Mom

Thank you for being my first and most devoted fan.

CHAPTER ONE

Milly rushes through the chamber door and shuts it swiftly behind her. "I can't find it, Audette. Not any-where."

Careful not to wrinkle my gown, I stand. "I must have it."

My lady-in-waiting shrugs, looking both helpless and harried.

"If she can't find it, Audette, there's not much we can do," Barowalt says. "Did you remember to bring it?"

"Of course I brought it!" I whirl toward my broth-er, and my long train catches around my ankles.

I remember packing the ring. I wrapped it and placed it in a leather pouch, and it went right in the trunk.

My brother places his hands on my wrists. "You're working yourself up over this. But I wonder...is it the ring?" He pauses, uncomfortable. "Or something else?"

There's a sadness burrowed in my core, a constant nagging ache that I've managed to lock away for the last six months. But Barowalt's right. This day—my wedding, is causing it to rise to the surface.

"I miss them," I whisper, feeling weak for saying it out loud. "She was supposed to be here for this."

Barowalt's face contorts, and he crushes me into a hug. Tears sting my eyes, but I fight them back.

"I'm here," he says fiercely, and then he pulls back, his hands firm on my upper arms. "We're strong, you and I. Our family is strong. With or without Mother's ring, you will walk down that aisle, graceful and sure, and you will do credit to the family name." Softer, he says, "They would be so proud of you."

Gathering from his strength, I nod.

He's right.

But I can't help but think that if that idiot betrothed of mine could have found a bride of his own in a reasonable period of time, I wouldn't be standing here today.

I haven't seen Irving since we were children, but I've heard rumors. But then, who hasn't heard rumors about the Prince of Primewood? They're so numerous, a person is bound to stumble on at least one or two.

There's a knock at the door, and I blink the last of my tears away. My lady's maid, Ella, has been sitting quietly in the corner, calmly embroidering a handkerchief. Now she rushes to answer the door.

Her Majesty, the Queen of Primewood, sweeps into the room. Her eyes, too, are bright with tears.

"Audette," she says, and then she pulls me into her arms.

I close my eyes, overcome again. Not only is the queen my future husband's mother, but she was my mother's dearest friend. Those memories threaten to take me over the edge.

"You are beautiful," she whispers. When she draws back, she hastily dabs tears from her eyes. "You look so much like Calla."

Drawing in a deep, fortifying breath, I smile. "Thank you."

She brushes her hand over my hair. "Your mother and I dreamed of this day together, but I never dared hope it would truly come to pass."

Guilt eats at me. She's so happy, and I'm...less than happy.

After another embrace, she slips out the door.

I turn to Barowalt and Milly and wave my hand over my face, blinking back tears. "I'm never this emotional. I don't know what's gotten into me."

Milly's face softens, and she says, "It's your

3

wedding—"

"Self-pity," Barowalt interrupts.

Scowling, Milly turns on my brother, not caring a bit that he's her king. "What a heartless thing to say."

I sit and let out a slow breath. "No, he's right."

This marriage alliance teetered on top of so many contingencies, it's ridiculous that it's come to pass. But it was a promise made between our mothers, something our overly indulgent fathers granted them. When I turned twenty, if Irving hadn't found a bride, and if I hadn't yet fallen in love, we would be wed.

My twentieth birthday was last week. Irving hasn't chosen a bride, and, sadly, I've never been in love.

I can't break my mother's promise.

A sense of resolve settles over me, and the tears pass. I rise, already feeling stronger, and head toward the door.

"Where are you going?" Milly asks, aghast.

"To find my ring."

She sets her hands on her hips, and she blinks at me with hazel eyes. "You can't roam the halls in your wedding gown!"

I eye her. We're just about the same size.

"You're right," I say. "Trade dresses with me."

As Milly assaults me with a string of protests, Barowalt raises his hand to his temples, looking harried. Seeing my knightly, stoic brother overcome with

4

wedding troubles finally makes me smile.

Barowalt gives me a wry look, but there's relief in his eyes. I hate that he's worried about me. He doesn't like the rumors any more than I do.

"I'll step out," he says. "Milly, give her your dress."

She meets his eyes, her expression calm, but fire brims just under the surface. "I will not put on Audette's wedding gown."

Barowalt steps toward her, and their eyes lock. "You will, my lady, because I have asked you to do so."

Narrowing her eyes, she pokes him in the chest. "I liked you better before you became king."

A knowing smile graces his face, and then he steps into the hall.

I grin at Milly's irritation and motion to her gown. "All right. Hand it over."

***

Primewood's castle is much larger than Palace Brookraven, and I'm afraid I've lost my way. The wedding will begin any moment, and I have no idea where I am.

My mother's ring is on my finger, though. That's something.

Half-running, I turn a corner and smack right into someone. I yelp and try to step back. "I'm so sorry—" I begin, but the words die in my throat.

The man's hands are on my shoulders, steadying

SHARI L. TAPSCOTT

me, and he laughs under his breath. "Don't be. It's the best thing that's happened to me all day."

I blink at him, flummoxed. The edge of his mouth quirks up in a smile that's more than a little mischievous, and his dark brown eyes are bright with humor.

To my horror, my stomach flutters.

I yank away, irritated with myself and the shameful way I'm reacting to a stranger in the hall—a stranger who is not my intended. "Please, excuse me."

The man gently catches me as I try to brush past him. "I've never seen you before. You must have come with the Brookraven court."

His hair is fair and blond, and he has the look of a man who's just leaped off a horse. Though he was in as much of a hurry as I, he lingers, holding my arm.

I raise my eyebrow. "Yes. I am, in fact, from the Brookraven court."

"I've just seen your princess." The light in his eyes morphs to boredom. "She's lovely."

Seen the princess? He must mean Milly.

I almost laugh.

"She is," I agree, speaking of my friend and not myself. Then I pointedly look at his fingers, which are still on my arm.

He ignores me and absently shakes his head. "I thought it would be easier to have the decision made for me. But now I'm not sure."

6

My stomach clenches at his words, and I tilt my head, studying him. "Who are you?"

Our eyes meet, and that smile returns.

"You don't know me?" he asks.

"Should I?"

He seems to miss the chill in my voice, and he looks at the ornate ceiling as if studying it. "I'm Irving of Primewood. At your service, my lady."

It's him. The man I'm going to pledge my life and allegiance to in mere moments.

"Most men bow during an introduction," I say, my thoughts jumbling and swirling.

He steps closer, and though the flutters increase, my irritation overwhelms the sensation.

"If I were to let you go," he says. "You'd run away."

I jerk my arm hard, and this time, he lets his hand drop. He gives me a mystified look as if he's actually startled I don't want his hands on me.

"The Princess of Brookraven would be most un-pleased if she saw the way you are behaving right now," I say. The anger grows, making my voice increasingly hard.

This man is supposed to be marrying me in mo-ments, and yet he sees no harm in flirting with a ran-dom woman from his betrothed's court.

Irving laughs and steps forward as if he thinks he can soothe my nerves. "I doubt she'll hold a friendly conversation against me."

Milly might not. I certainly will.

I push past him.

"Wait." He jogs to catch up with me. "I've upset you. I'm sorry."

Shaking my head, I ignore him and continue on. He catches my hand, and the contact startles me enough I stop.

There's still a smile on his face, but his eyes are troubled. "Tell me, lovely-girl-wandering-the-halls, do you believe that everyone has one true love? That if you've fallen for someone, you'll never find it again?"

"I don't believe in love at all."

It's a lie, but he doesn't question my answer.

He closes his eyes, and his mask of flippancy drops for just a moment, revealing turmoil underneath. "My love was married at the beginning of the summer. I don't know how I'll ever move past it." He shakes his head. "How can I marry your princess when I don't know if I'll ever feel anything for her?"

"You had years to ask this girl to marry you," I snarl, disconcerted that he's this close. "Perhaps if you weren't so busy flitting from one woman to another, you wouldn't have missed your chance."

Startled by my curt answer, Irving raises an eyebrow. "She's a gypsy." He meets my eyes again and steps closer. "And I did ask—she refused."

He still has my hand, and I try to shift away. "Let me go."

Irving studies me, and that glimmer of pain is forgotten, hidden now under sparkling eyes. "You know that moment you meet someone and your breath catches in your chest? You lay eyes on them, and your stomach twines itself in knots?"

My stomach is knotting right now.

"No," I lie.

"I haven't felt that for two years. Two." He shakes his head. "Not since Rosie. And I had hoped..."

Despite my better judgment, I say, "Hoped what?"

He rubs his free hand over his temples, much like Barowalt did earlier. "That I would open that door, and the princess would be there..." He sighs. "And she'd be the one. The one to bring it back."

"She wasn't?" I whisper.

He shakes his head, torn, and then his eyes focus on mine. "But you..."

Overcome, I grow warm. My hand is still trapped in his, and for some illogical reason, I want to step closer.

But everything he's saying is wrong. He's promised to me, but he doesn't know who I am.

I could be anyone.

And rumor has it he's very good.

"Let me go," I say again.

"Tell me your name, and I will," he promises.

Shaking my head, I refuse.

A cocky smile spreads over his face, making him look more handsome, if possible. "Then leave me with the memory of what it feels like to kiss someone I want to kiss."

I yank my hand from his, ready to slap him, but he catches it before I can raise it, and he twines his fingers through mine.

Something about the sensation makes me pause, and, momentarily, my reason flees.

"Beautiful-girl-in-the-hall-who-won't-tell-me-her-name, grant me a kiss," Irving says. "Leave me with one last fond memory."

He leans in, that smile growing. When I don't immediately resist, he backs me to the wall and pins me in. Gently, he holds our clasped hands next to my head against the stone.

"You don't have to look so torn. I'm not married yet," he murmurs, and his breath tickles my lips. Then he pauses, his eyes teasing. "You're not married, right? I accidentally stumbled down that road once, and it didn't end well."

He's such a scoundrel. I've never met anyone so awful, so detestable...so wrongly appealing.

"Not for another few minutes," I breathe. My bottom lip brushes against his as I say the word, and I gulp.

Irving hesitates and pulls back just enough to look me in the eyes. "Another few...minutes?"

I'm about to answer, to admit who I am, when he's suddenly ripped away.

Barowalt stands over Irving, seething. My brother towers over him, and though the prince of Primewood is built of strong, lean muscle, my brother is a mountain.

Irving's eyes go wide as he takes in the crest stitched in white on my brother's burgundy tunic—the Unicorn of Brookraven. He pulls away from Barowalt, indignant.

"I believe you have a wedding to get to," Barowalt snarls, his anger only thinly veiled.

Ignoring my brother, Irving looks at me, a question in his eyes. His thoughts are displayed in his expression; his confusion is written plainly across his face. But what really makes my heart clench is the hope I see there. The hope that I might somehow be the princess. His betrothed.

Taking me by the arm, Barowalt leads me away. Unable to help myself, I glance back.

No one has ever looked at me like that before.

We round the corner, and I pull away from my brother. "Barowalt—" I'm cut off by a female voice coming from the hall we just exited.

"Irving!"

Unable to help myself, I peek back around the corner.

A pretty young blond woman with bouncing curls hollers again from the opposite end of the hall. She's carrying a plump baby on her hip, but she runs toward Irving. She's obviously not happy.

"Where have you been?" the woman demands.

"Anwen," Irving says, and a huge grin lights his face.

There's so much affection in his voice when he says her name, a jolt of jealousy courses through me.

He takes the baby and coos at her. "How's my beautiful girl?"

I go cold. Surely it's not...it can't be his...

They don't keep mistresses in Primewood. Vernow, yes. Murin, possibly. But not here.

Do they?

The girl clasps her hands together. "You're late. Your mother is frantic, and your father is speaking of disinheriting you." She lowers her voice to a whisper. "People are saying you've left the princess at the altar."

He hands the baby back, and then, his voice reassuring, he says, "Father's all bluff. It's not the first time he's threatened it, and I doubt it will be the last."

"I know you don't want to go through with this," the woman says, "but there is a girl in there, waiting for you. Like it or not, you are getting married today." She looks near livid. "Irving, for once in your life, you're going to do the right thing."

With my heart in my throat, I round the corner, stepping back into the hall where they're speaking.

Startled, Irving jerks his eyes toward me. He looks...guilty.

Anwen glances our way. With a forced smile, she acknowledges me and my brother. Her eyes drift to Barowalt first, and then she pales when she sees the crest. Her eyes widen, and she looks like she might pass out.

"I'm sorry," she says, her voice small. "We haven't been introduced. I'm Anwen of Glendon." She gives a hesitant curtsy. "How do you do?"

Barowalt gives her a curt nod but otherwise ignores her. He casts a last, loathing glance at Irving, and then wraps his arm around my shoulders and pulls me back around the corner.

I feel strangely numb. I don't want to marry Irving. What would make me think he'd want to marry me? And why do I care?

We reach the chambers that were given to me to prepare myself for the wedding, and Barowalt ushers me through the door.

"I don't like that man," Barowalt growls.

Still in my wedding gown, Milly stands. She's

relieved to see us, but at my brother's harsh words, she freezes. "What's happened?"

Before Barowalt can explain, there's a knock at the door. Ella hurries to answer it, and we're all startled when one of our own strides through the threshold.

"Hallgrave," Barowalt says, immediately concerned at the solemn look on the knight's face. "Why are you here? What is it?"

"I wouldn't interrupt if it wasn't Lingard business." Hallgrave hands Barowalt a message and then turns to me. "I'm sorry, Your Highness."

Barowalt's face shadows with disbelief and then shock. "Impossible."

My brother folds the message, and then, overcome, he crumples it in his hand and heaves it across the room.

"What's happened?" I whisper, terror flooding my veins.

The Order of Lingard has one duty—to protect a hunted group of magical beings, and any news to upset Barowalt like this is bad. Very bad.

"Where?" I ask Hallgrave when Barowalt doesn't answer.

The burly knight looks sick. "Ptarma."

"Ptarma's safe...they've never..." I set my hand on the knight's arm. "How many have been...?"

Slaughtered is the correct word, but I can't bring

14

myself to say it.

Hallgrave clasps his palm over mine. "Twenty-three, Princess."

I turn away, trembling. There hasn't been a slaughter this colossal in over three hundred years.

It's my fault. We were here, tending to this ridiculous promise, a promise that meant nothing to the prince of Primewood, when we should have been there.

"We're leaving," I say as I scoop up the note. I look at my brother before I hold it over a candle flame. "Do you need this?"

He shakes his head, and I let the message burn.

Once the note is ashes, I say, "Milly, you'll come with us. Ella, you stay here. Inform His and Her Majesty that we extend our apologies, but I will be not be marrying their son."

CHAPTER TWO

A warm subtropical breeze caresses my face as I step down the gangplank. After the two-week sea voyage, I'm glad to be on solid ground again.

In front of me, Barowalt strides down the plank at a brisk pace with a no-nonsense look on his face. The sailors on the pier send him wary glances and avert their eyes when he passes.

I hide a smile and nod serenely as I go by.

The port village of Vallen Harbor is protected on either side by tall, sheer white cliffs. The turquoise ocean slaps at the base of the rocks, creating white foam on the waves. Palm trees dot the sandy beach, but higher, clinging to shelves in the cliffs, needled evergreens grow. Past the beach, brightly-colored wildflowers grow in clusters amongst the expanse of grass.

Here, it looks like summer. It's impossible to tell we're nearing the end of the autumn season.

It took several days to find a ship willing to sail us this time of year. The storms at sea can be treacherous, and most ships have already taken to land or sailed far south to Waldren and beyond for the winter.

Milly takes in the scenery, gawking at everything with wide eyes.

I haven't been to Ptarma in over five years, and I've missed my mother's kingdom. I would be as giddy as Milly if the reason for our visit wasn't weighing heavy on my mind.

Sometimes, it would be a relief to be as blissfully unaware as she is. Like most subjects of Brookraven, Milly only has a vague idea of what our royal line has been charged with.

Barowalt speaks with Hallgrave on the dock, and we join them.

"Arrange for our things to be delivered to the estate," Barowalt says.

Hallgrave bows his head. "Your Majesty."

The knight nods to both Milly and me, and then he makes his way to a group of ship's men loitering on the pier.

"Stay here," Barowalt commands. "I'm going to hire a carriage." He begins to turn and then hesitates, giving Milly a sharp look. "Do not wander off. I don't have time to track you down today."

Milly gives him a flirty smile. "Of course, Your Majesty. I would hate to cause you any distress."

He stares at her, expressionless, and then turns down the street.

Beside me, Milly grins.

I elbow her. "Behave."

"He's too easy."

"There's a lot on his mind."

My friend looks at me and pushes a strand of blond hair behind her ear. "You have a lot on your mind as well. How are you?"

"I'm fine."

Milly rolls her eyes. "Why do you still bother lying to me? We've known each other too long."

I watch the palm fronds sway in the light breeze. Nearby, a child runs along the rock-dotted shore. She tosses a stick to her small dog, and the people nearby smile at her with affection.

"I feel I've disappointed her," I finally answer.

"Your mother would have wanted you to marry a good man." Milly sets her hands on her hips. "She wouldn't have truly wished you to be with the Prince of Primewood if she'd known what a scoundrel he's become." She pauses, and a smile twitches at her mouth. "An incredibly handsome scoundrel, though, isn't he?"

I let out a breath and allow myself to laugh. "He

has this smile..."

Milly lets out a longing sigh. "And his eyes..."

"But let's not forget the fact that he loathed the very idea of marrying me."

My friend's smile drops, and it's replaced with irritation. "Then he's a fool."

"His loss, right?" I say, attempting to smile again.

"You don't need him anyway." She stands straighter and motions to the street Barowalt just disappeared down. "Not when you have all of them tripping over themselves to serve you."

And there they are—Brookraven's elite knights, my Order of Lingard. Seven men stride forward, Barowalt at their head. With chain mail shining in the bright Ptarmish light and standing as tall as oaks, they're an impressive sight. Each man is handsome, young, and strong—every one of them.

Milly sighs and fans herself. "I just want one or two. You can keep the rest."

I let out a short laugh. "You only want one, and seeing as how he's my brother, he's all yours."

"Honestly," she scoffs. "How can a girl be expected to choose? Just look at those rippling muscles."

It feels good to release the darkness welling in my heart for a moment. I bite the inside of my cheek to keep from laughing. The men are close enough now we must hold our tongues.

One of the knights breaks from the group and steps forward, saying to Milly, "Look who the sea washed up."

She grins. "Miss me, Rogert?"

"Always, my lady." Then the chestnut-haired lord turns to me, and his expression becomes solemn. He drops to his knee and lowers his head. "We've failed you, Your Highness."

I set my hand on his shoulder, giving him permission to rise. "Let's not dwell on our losses but focus on what must be done."

He stands and nods. One by one, my seven knights stand before me, kneeling in greeting. Several of them have been away from Brookraven on missions, and I haven't seen them in months.

These men are my family, my friends, but our reunion is bittersweet.

Several villagers look at us with awe, wondering who we are and what we're doing in their sleepy town.

After the greetings are over, Barowalt turns to me. "They've been waiting for you. Asher's at the estate."

That's nine men, including Barowalt. Hopefully it will be enough.

I turn to Rogert. "Are we expecting any more?"

Rogert shakes his head.

"Did you leave your posts adequately covered?" Barowalt asks.

"Yes, we believe so," Rogert, who's designated himself as the group's unofficial spokesman, answers.

"Perhaps," I say. "But we thought Ptarma was covered, and look at what happened here."

I don't say it to be harsh, but it's true. We must be more vigilant from this point on.

***

"I hate it when you dress like that." Milly lounges on a settee, looking bored.

Giving her a wry look, I slide my sword in its sheath. "You try sparring in a gown."

"Why must you? Can't you let Barowalt deal with whatever it is we're here about?" She sits up. "I want to explore...find a cute fisherman to spend the afternoon with."

I slide a knife in one of my knee-high leather boots. "No one's stopping you."

Milly pouts. "I don't want to go by myself."

"You won't be by yourself." I grin. "You'll have the fisherman to keep you company."

Sighing, she clasps her hands in her lap. "Let me come with you. Let me in on your very secret, very important Guild of Handsome Knights."

My smile drops. "Don't belittle it."

"I'm not." She rises to her feet, her expression earnest. "I just don't want to be in the dark anymore."

For some reason, I hesitate, and her eyes widen

with hope.

Technically, as the only remaining female in our family's line, the Order of Lingard is mine to lead, though I've transferred most of the responsibility to Barowalt. I'm the head, but it's mostly a show for tradition.

And Barowalt would be displeased if I showed up at the meeting with Milly in tow. Not only is she completely worthless for the task ahead of us, but she'd distract the knights.

"Milly, I can't—"

I'm interrupted by a knock at the door. I stride across the room to open it.

Barowalt stands in the hall, looking irked. "You best change into a gown. The Ptarmish court found out we're here."

I groan. "Already? We haven't even had a chance to speak with Asher, and I haven't picked up a sword since we left Elden."

My brother walks into the room. "Well, then, you best make it quick. Aunt Camilla is expecting us for dinner."

Pursing my lips to keep myself from voicing my less than pleasant thoughts, I nod. "Fine. Round the men up, tell them to gather in the courtyard for a quick meeting."

Barowalt raises an eyebrow. "Yes, Your Highness."

I smack him on his rock-hard chest. "Don't mock me."

"Wouldn't dream of it." He holds up his hands in surrender.

I crack a smile, and he returns it.

"So...Ptarma?" I finally say.

Barowalt shakes his head. "Of all the places for an attack, I never dreamed it would be here."

"How are they doing?" I ask.

"They wouldn't meet with Asher. They're waiting for you."

I suspecting as much. "When can we visit them?"

"Soon."

That, at least, is a relief.

After shooing Barowalt out the door, I strip out of my trousers and change into a gown. Since Ella isn't here, and Milly insists on making the laces too tight, I choose a front-cinching gown I can tie without assistance.

Feeling slightly sorry for myself, I toss my sword on the bed.

Milly nods, approving. "That's so much better."

Giving her an ornery smile, I say, "That might be. But I'm not taking the knife out of my boot."

She rolls her eyes and flops onto the settee. "Come get me when it's time to leave for the Ptarmish court."

***

"Audette, my darling." Aunt Camilla draws me into a tight embrace.

I return the hug, pleased to see her even if I'm not pleased to be summoned so soon. She smells overwhelmingly of floral water and the ingermint she uses on her arthritic knuckles.

My grandmother's sister holds me at arm's-length and purses her thin lips. "What is this news I've heard of you running away from your wedding?"

In a most unladylike move, I gape at her. How could she possibly have heard of that yet?

Sensing the question in my expression, she narrows her eyes. "The sailors like to talk, child. And I have a network you wouldn't believe."

I laugh, startled by her answer. "I assure you, it was a much more sensible move than you might have been led to believe."

"Hmmm."

My aunt lets me go and then totters toward Barowalt, who looks at her with something akin to fear in his eyes. I bite my lip, trying very hard not to laugh.

Her Majesty, Queen Clara of Ptarma, steps forward and takes my hands. "We're so pleased to see you, Audette."

"Thank you, Your Majesty, for your hospitality."

Next to the queen, King Edlund beams at me. "Look at you! You're all grown up."

I smile at my mother's distant cousins, trying to keep my mind in the great hall and not brood over the situation we've come to attend.

Clara loops her hand through my arm and walks me down the hall. "You look so much like your mother." She squeezes my arm and blinks several times. "I'm so sorry for your loss."

"It's been a long six months."

The queen stops. "You're welcome here, you know that, don't you? For as long as you want—stay forever if you like."

I look at my feet. "You've also heard about the disaster that was supposed to be my wedding."

She smiles. "You have Ptarmish blood in your veins. We make hasty, rash decisions, but our gut instincts are rarely wrong."

And my gut instincts told me to kiss Irving in the hall. What does that say?

Clara continues, "I tried to convince your mother to betroth you to handsome Javid, but he went and found his own bride a few years ago."

I smile at the couple she motions to. I remember Javid, now the Duke of Marfell. He's several years older than I am, but his wife looks to be closer to my age. She's pretty, tall, and demure, and she's all smiles as the couple speaks with Milly.

Here, at court, my radiant friend is in her element.

25

"Here's someone you have not met." Clara waves to a man and woman who stand toward the edge of the group. "Kent, Giselle."

The two, who look like they were quietly arguing, are somewhat startled to be addressed.

"Audette, you know my nephew, Prince Kent. He and Aldus just arrived back from a hunt this morning."

I give my cousin a polite smile.

"This is his lovely bride, Giselle." Clara turns toward the couple. "Giselle, this is Her Highness, Princess Audette of Brookraven—a dear cousin of ours."

Kent's closer to Javid's age, probably six or eight years older than I am. Giselle appears to be somewhat younger. She's in an immaculate dress that makes me glad I changed. Her hair is dark and thick, and her eyes are a warm, rich brown.

"It's a pleasure to meet you, Your Highness," she says, offering me a small curtsy.

I can't place her accent.

Clara and Edlund's son, Aldus, joins us as I greet Kent's wife. Ptarma's crown prince is tall with brownish-auburn hair that shines copper in the late afternoon sunshine that streams in through the windows. Like his father, Aldus is warm and friendly, and I've always liked him despite our six-year age difference.

"Hello, cousin," he says, giving me a friendly bow. "What a pleasant surprise."

26

Just as I'm about to answer, an announcement is made from the entrance of the hall.

"His Royal Highness, Irving Windom the Third, Crown Prince of Primewood, is here, seeking an audience with His and Her Royal Majesties," the guard calls out, his face expressionless.

"From Primewood?" Edlund says, surprised. "Well, of course, he's more than welcome. Send him in."

My stomach lurches, and I blink, feeling disoriented. Surely, the prince is not here. He would have had to have traveled to Triblue and procured a ship the same day we did.

But I can't deny it's Irving when he strides in the room. There's a warm smile on his face, and he scans the hall, looking to address the king and queen personally, I presume, but his eyes lock with mine. He looks handsome and roguish, and my breath catches.

His warm smile vanishes, and in its place is a look so full of irritation that I almost take a step back.

Milly slips to my side.

The room has gone still. All watch the silent exchange, and I'm sure most wonder why the mood has suddenly turned tense.

Irving gives Milly a smile, but it doesn't reach his eyes. "Ah, my lovely betrothed." His gaze slides to me. "Or is it?"

My heart beats at a frantic pace. His hair is wind-blown from the ride to the castle, and his trousers are dusty. He wears a sword at his side, and it makes him look rather dashing.

How unfortunate that I finally find a man that makes me weak in the knees, and he's a knave.

"So which one of you is Audette?" Irving motions between me and my lady-in-waiting and gives us a tight smile. "Just out of curiosity, you know. It would be nice know which one of you left me at the altar."

CHAPTER THREE

Drawing my courage, I'm about to answer when Barowalt steps between us, blocking Irving from my view.

"You are not welcome to speak with Princess Audette or her lady." Barowalt's hand drifts to the hilt of his sword.

"King Barowalt, I presume?" Irving asks, undeterred. "I'd just like to know which one is your sister."

Barowalt makes to take a step forward in challenge, but I clasp his arm, drawing him back.

"It's all right," I say to my brother. "I'll speak with him."

Obviously more keen on the idea of running Irving through with his sword than chatting, Barowalt mulls it over. Finally, he steps aside.

29

Though it's an intimate gathering, dozens of eyes are trained on us, making me feel like I'm on display.

Irving doesn't look surprised when I step forward. He raises an eyebrow, waiting for me to speak first.

"Let's go into the hall," I say.

He looks like he's going to say something clever and then changes his mind. With a flourish of his hand and a tight smile on his face, he motions me ahead. Before I step out, I glance at Milly over my shoulder.

She widens her eyes, asking me what I'm going to do. I very subtly shake my head. I have no idea.

We reach the hall, and the guards close the doors behind us, giving us privacy. Though not the flighty type, I almost jump when they thunk shut.

Attempting to look disinterested, I glance at Irving. With his arms crossed, he watches me. His expression is far from friendly.

Turning from him, I study a painting on the wall. The silence thickens, growing more uncomfortable by the moment.

"Why did you leave?" he finally asks.

How dare he follow me here and question my decision—especially when I was party to that horrifying conversation in the hall.

I whirl around, my eyes flashing. "Let's start with a question for you. Why would you follow me here? We both know I did you a favor by leaving." I take a step closer. "You're free. Go find a barmaid to complain to. Perhaps she'll jog your memory as to why you didn't want to marry me in the first place."

He narrows his eyes—and what nice eyes they are—and a slow, angry smile curves his lips. "Can you blame me? Why would I want to marry a spoiled, privileged princess who pouts and takes off the moment her feelings are hurt?"

I suck in a breath. No one ever speaks to me like that—usually because I have a sword at my hip. I miss the comforting weight of it now.

"I'll ask you again," I say once I'm sure my voice won't quaver with indignation. "Why are you here?"

He rolls his shoulders and looks away. "I've come to bring you back with me."

A laugh bubbles in my throat, and I don't bother to hold it back. "And this is your idea of wooing me?" Feeling bold when I see another flash of irritation cross his face, I step forward, forcing him to shift back. "I'm afraid the rumors about you are wrong."

His eyes flash, and there's a challenge there. "What rumors?"

Smiling, I take another step closer.

There's really little difference between an argument and a duel. In both, you want the upper ground, and for the moment, I have it.

"That you're dashing and debonair," I purr. "That

you could—and do—seduce any woman you please."
I scoff. "You probably started and spread the gossip yourself."

Suddenly, his hands are on my shoulders, and he twirls me around, pushing me against the wall. He leans down so we're eye to eye, a confident smile on his face. "They're not rumors."

My heart hammers in my chest. Just like that, I lost my advantage.

"It won't work with me," I lie.

Slowly, with maddening control, he brushes my hair behind my ear and leans close. "That, Princess, is because I'm not trying."

Gulping, I ignore the heat in my chest and the flutters in my stomach.

"I don't want your pretty words or your lies," I say. "You sailed a fortnight to speak with me. Be blunt."

Irving pulls back just enough he can look me in the eye, and his anger bubbles to the surface again. "My father blames me for you leaving. If I don't return—with you by my side—he's cutting me off and naming his third cousin's seven-year-old boy as his heir."

Unable to help myself, and feeling wicked, I grin. "I daresay that will put a cramp in your lifestyle."

At the end of his patience, Irving smiles, shaking his head. "No, because you're coming back with me."

I shift away slightly. "I'm not marrying you."

Without a word, his thumb shifts, and he strokes the side of my neck. I freeze, terrified to move for fear he'll realize how much I'm enjoying his touch. Our eyes meet, and his expression changes, softens. Slowly, he shakes his head—more to himself than me—and growls low in his throat.

"What?" I demand.

"You are my least favorite person right now." Irving pauses and makes another soft noise of frustration. "But you're so..."

I hold my breath, unable to even blink.

His hand drifts again to my hair, and he wraps it in the strands at the base of my neck before he breathes, "You're beautiful."

My knees go weak, and I'm barely able to hold myself up. My eyes drift to his lips just to see them curl in a knowing, smug smirk.

Realizing I've been duped, I snarl and shove him away. In response, he raises his eyebrows, crosses his arms, and smiles with triumph.

Storming off, leaving him as I walk blindly down the hall, I seethe. Once I'm a safe distance away, I yell over my shoulder, "I'm not marrying you."

"Don't fight it, Princess," he calls after me. "We both know you find me irresistible."

***

33

I twirl, ducking Rogert's attack, and lunge forward before he regains his balance. He jumps back, barely avoiding my blade, and then attacks again. I whirl to the side, taking him off guard and circle behind him as he staggers. Quick and sure, I knock him in the back of the knees with the blunt sword, sending him to the ground.

Our small crowd roars their approval as I point the tip of my sword between my knight's shoulder blades.

Breathing hard, I say, "I win."

"That was a low blow." Rogert rolls over, his face red with exertion, He grins. "I don't think I've ever been so proud of you."

I match his grin with one of my own and glance over my shoulder at Barowalt, seeking his approval. The remaining seven elite look on, laughing at Rogert.

Grandmother's estate doesn't have a true practice yard, so we gather in the courtyard, sparring amongst the Ptarma lilies. Milly sits in the shade of a tree, not far from us, painting. When our gazes meet, she rolls her eyes. My lady-in-waiting hates to see me hot and sweaty—like a mule—as she so kindly puts it. Then she glances at Rogert, who's still sprawled on the ground, and a smile twitches her lips. She shakes her head and goes back to her properly domestic pursuits.

Barowalt smiles, but he's still not impressed. "You

hesitated."

"I didn't," I argue. "I got behind him, and I took him to the ground."

"Did the princess hesitate?" Barowalt calls to his men.

One by one, the knights agree with their king.

Huffing out a breath, I push a limp lock of hair out of my eyes. "It's not a very sportsmanlike tactic, is it?"

Barowalt gives me a wry look—the same look he always gives me when the conversation comes up—and crosses his arms. "Are you as tall as Rogert?"

Here we go.

"No," I answer.

"Are you as muscular?"

Bored, I slide my sword in its sheath. "No."

"Thank goodness," Milly pipes up, making the men laugh.

Barowalt flashes her a slightly-amused warning look and turns his attention back to me. "What advantage do you have?"

"I'm faster."

"And?" he asks.

"More agile."

"And?"

Rogert leans on a pillar near Milly. "She's prettier."

I hide my smile so Barowalt will finish his lecture and let me silently bask in my win. "I'm a smaller target."

"But all those mean nothing if you hesitate." My brother's eyes bore into mine. "One half-second of indecision could be the difference between life and death."

Letting out a long exhale, I nod. "I know."

He eyes me for a moment longer, nods, and turns back to the group. "Who's next?"

There are days it's easy to forget that Barowalt, at twenty-three, is only three years older than I am. He seems so much older. My brother may be a young king, but he wears the crown well.

Sometimes I wonder if it's hard on him, leaving his kingdom in the hands of our uncle. It's the way it's always been done when the Order is needed, but this is the first he's had to leave for an extended period of time. Brookraven is only as large as a good-sized province to begin with, and it's easily tended by a small number of related nobles. Still, I wonder if he feels like he's deserting our people.

"I want to see you fight, Your Majesty," Milly calls out. She can't say his title without drawing it out, teasing him—flirting with him.

"Against who?" Asher, the knight assigned to Ptarma, asks.

My friend sets her paints aside, taking her time because she enjoys the attention, and rises to her feet.

She taps her lips and walks down the line as if inspecting the men.

Barowalt wears a bored expression, and Milly glances at him, amused. Finally, she stops in front of Keven, a strapping twenty-year-old knight with a mane of blond hair and cornflower blue eyes. Always patient with Milly despite her constant attempts to rile Barowalt, Keven smiles at her.

She taps him on his mail-covered chest, and he steps forward, eager to fight.

My brother's eyes narrow only slightly, but Milly pretends to ignore him as she glides back to her seat. Though she's never admitted it, I know what game she's playing. She thinks if she pushes Barowalt over the edge, eventually his control will snap, and he'll accidentally admit he's in love with her in a passionate and wildly romantic display.

They've been dancing around each other for ten years now. I'm not sure how well her plan is working.

Keven meets Barowalt, and they study each other, circling. Exhausted, I sit on a low wall and accept a ladle of water from Asher.

Barowalt strikes first, as usual. He rarely has the patience to wait. They continue to circle, looking for weaknesses, and I yawn behind my hand.

I didn't sleep well last night. My argument with Irving kept circling in my head, keeping my mind from falling still. He's a fool if he thinks I'll marry him now.

After I drink my fill, I hand the ladle back to Asher. He glances at the men, and then he quietly says, "Can I have a moment with you?"

"Of course." As I stand, my muscles scream out a protest.

I'm going to be sore tomorrow. A fortnight is too long to go without practicing.

I follow Asher toward the well, where he hangs the ladle. Since the Order placed him here, I haven't seen him in several years. He's taller than I remember, his jaw a little more defined. He still wears his dark hair short, but now there's a constant shadow along his jaw. It looks good on him.

Like me and Barowalt, Asher has family here. It's why he was the perfect choice for this post.

Asher leans against the well. "I've been hearing strange reports of rumors from the villages along the coast on the southern side of the kingdom."

"Strange reports?"

"Gossip is spreading that there have been animal attacks..." He shakes his head, looking as if he thinks what he's about to say is foolish. "Dragon attacks."

"A dragon?" I give him an incredulous look. "In Ptarma?"

The beasts rarely venture as far south as Triblue. The thought of them flying over the sea to a subtropical island is absurd. They tend to stay close to their icy lairs in the far north of Elden, especially now that a true alliance has been made between them and the new king and queen of Errinton.

I shake my head, but as I'm about to speak, he cuts me off.

"I know." Asher shrugs. "But it's enough of an oddity here that I thought you should be informed. Especially now."

Thinking, I run my fingers over the rough stones at the lip of the well. "Do you think these attacks are related to ours?"

"I don't know what I think." He passes a hand over his face, looking weary.

Setting my hand on his arm, I ask, "How are you faring?"

Asher was my first kiss, my first young love. Would something real have grown between us if he hadn't been sent to Ptarma? Would he have saved me from that embarrassing sham of a wedding?

It doesn't matter at this point. The feeling is gone, faded with time. I have no desire to resurrect it now.

The knight meets my eyes, and from his expression, I wonder if he's reliving the same memories. "I have the largest loss in over two hundred years on my hands, Audette."

It's longer than that, but I don't think he needs

reminding.

"I don't know how it happened." He lets out a slow breath. "I just don't know."

Our group hollers out, yelling and cheering. Keven is on the ground, and Barowalt stands over him, his sword at the blond knight's throat. With a smile, Barowalt abruptly stands back and offers the defeated man his hand.

Keven accepts Barowalt's goodwill, rises to his feet, and shakes out his glorious mass of golden locks. "I'll win for you next time, Milly."

"I have no doubt," Milly calls back.

As soon as the knight looks away, her eyes drift to Barowalt.

Laughing under my breath, I examine my blade and let my mind drift back to Asher's words.

A dragon in Ptarma? It just doesn't seem possible.

CHAPTER FOUR

Milly and I weave through the streets of nearby Kallert, the largest village in northern Ptarma and the closest to both the castle and my family's estate. It's late afternoon on a market day, and with the good weather, the merchants are thick. They sell their wares, shouting out their value to whoever is willing to listen to them. A few performers sit on corners, playing their flutes and collecting coins. They're not a garish lot, unlike the gypsies on Elden's mainland. Instead, they are the children of fishermen and farmers.

As the sun sets, the streets become busier, lending a festival spirit to the evening. Keven, our guard for the night, follows, silent and intimidating. Without Barowalt here to torment, Milly doesn't pay the poor knight much attention.

"Look at these." Milly stops in front of a stand of brightly-colored flowers.

In addition to the blooms, the woman also has bulbs for sale.

"We should buy some and plant them at home," Milly says.

I shake my head. "Brookraven's winters are too cold. They'd never make it to spring."

Looking disappointed, Milly steps away. "I won't miss that. I'm glad we're here instead."

"We won't be here that long."

I only plan on staying in Ptarma for a month at the very most.

"Are you sure? I wouldn't mind missing a winter." She follows me. "There are flowers on the balcony in my chambers, growing in pots and on the ledges. It's like a tiny hanging garden."

"Mine too." Angling my head toward the sun, I close my eyes. "I do like it here."

"Then why are you in such a hurry to return home?"

Continuing down the street, I say, "I'm not, really. I just don't feel at ease when I'm away."

"You would have been away indefinitely if you'd gone through with the wedding."

She must remind me. My mind, again, drifts to Irving.

He's obnoxious. Self-important. Charming.

Growling under my breath, I push the thoughts away.

We're visiting the village for a reason. Since Asher mentioned the dragon sightings, they've been haunting me. Something is strange about the coincidence of the timing. Still, I haven't mentioned it to Barowalt yet.

A respectable-looking tavern just ahead of us has its windows and doors open to the breeze. Like most of the structures in Ptarma, the tavern is built of various shades of white and ivory stone. Clay tiles line the roof, and iron scrollwork decorates the windows and balconies. A few patrons linger outside, talking, and the smell of baked confections wafts from inside.

"Let's stop here." I'm already walking toward the door.

The tavern is busy, and people filter in behind us. A man accidentally jostles me, and Keven steps forward, silently threatening. The man glances at our trio, murmurs his apologies, and hurries from the tavern.

I glance at the knight and smile. "Don't let that kind of power go to your head."

Keven's blond hair is contained today, pulled back at his neck, but he's still my golden knight. He's only a few months older than I am, and like most of the knights of the Order, we practically grew up together. He comes off as quiet and reserved, but he's incredibly loyal.

I like him immensely, and I prefer to have him on guard duty over flirtatious Rogert.

Keven smiles at me now, and we nudge our way through the crowds and find an empty spot in the corner. A pretty brunette barmaid spots us and immediately makes her way to our table, eying Keven as she sashays through the crowd.

Milly and I share a glance, both of us working to contain our laughter.

This is the way it is with our elite. Women fall at their feet, and men try to emulate them. It's gone to some of their heads, but they all know their mission takes precedence over everything else. My father hand-picked each one. Though many preen like peacocks, they have valiant hearts and level heads.

"I'll have tea, please," Milly tells the girl.

"And you?" the girl asks, looking down at Keven through her lashes. "Mead? Ale?" She leans close. "We even have some of the rum the sailors favor."

"Cider is fine, thank you."

She gives him a hopeful look. "That's all you want?"

He nods, a pleasant but closed smile on his face. "Cider is all."

I tell the disappointed girl I want cider as well, and she disappears into the crowd.

"Fancy meeting you here," a man says from behind me.

Milly's eyes flutter wide and Keven tenses, his smile instantly vanishing.

"What are you doing here?" I ask Irving, not needing to turn to know who the man at my shoulder is.

I'm not sure when I memorized the timber of his voice, the cadence of his words. It's not a good thing.

Irving comes round the table, pulls out an empty chair between me and Milly, and sits as if he's been invited. There's a friendly smile on his face, like the one he wore the day I met him in the hall, and he turns it on Milly.

"We haven't been properly introduced." He takes her hand and bows over it. "I'm Irving, my lady."

Easily swayed by a bit of charm, Milly raises her eyebrows at me and then turns her attention back to the prince. "The pleasure is mine, Your Highness."

"And your name?" He flashes her a dazzling smile. She blinks. "Milly."

He holds her hand a moment longer and then sets her free. When he turns his attention on Keven, Milly presses her lips together, her face filled with glee.

I glance at the ceiling, not impressed, and frankly a little unsettled. Something in me doesn't like the way he looked at Milly, all gallant and debonair. Living deep inside, normally dormant, a nasty green beast reared its ugly head the moment he smiled at her.

Which is a bad sign if Queen Clara is right about gut instincts.

"Hello," Irving says to Keven, friendly.

Keven doesn't say a word. The knight stares Irving down and eventually, after several moments go by, gives him a curt nod.

Irving raises his eyebrows, brushing the knight's cold reception off, and his gaze finally falls on me. "Hello, Audette."

"Irving."

He shifts his knees toward mine, turning his full attention on me, looking at me as if I were the center of his world. His fingers drift over my hand. "I think we got off on the wrong foot."

"I think if you fail to remove your hand from mine, I'll cut off your foot."

Instantly, an amused smile flashes over his face. He makes a show of pulling his hand away. "Do you think we could go somewhere..." he glances at Keven and Milly before he turns back to me, "...a little more private?"

"You are welcome to go wherever you like. I am quite content right here."

After accidentally letting a glimmer of irritation sneak past this nonchalant, friendly veneer he's donned, Irving takes a long breath through his nose.

He glances again at my friends and smiles. "Of course."

"You're welcome to stay," Milly says, smiling brightly. "We'd love more company, wouldn't we, Audette?"

The moment Irving turns to see what I'll think of this idea, my friend flashes me a wicked look of triumph, which she then turns on Keven.

The knight doesn't seem amused with her matchmaking schemes, but he doesn't object. He does, however, look like he's itching to have a go at Irving. If the prince insists on interfering, he better hope he's skilled with a sword.

The barmaid returns with our drinks, and her eyes glide over Irving, assessing him. She must like what she sees because her smile turns feline. She rests her hip against the table, practically sitting on the aged wood as she asks Irving what he'd like to drink.

"Cider," he says, cheerfully dismissing her.

Disappointed for the second time, her eyes linger over him before she leaves.

"So," Irving says, "What brings you to Ptarma?"

"We have family here." I cross my hands in my lap. "My Great-Aunt Camilla is my late grandmother's dear sister. She's getting up in years, and we wanted to visit her."

"I met your aunt, actually." He smiles, challenging me. "She's invited me to stay in her hall of the castle."

47

I grit my teeth, smiling. "Did she?"

"I'm afraid she's taking pity on me." He leans close. "Did you hear? My bride deserted me on the day of our wedding."

"How tragic for you."

He nods. "I'm quite devastated."

Never breaking eye contact with him, I nod in the direction of the bar. "I'm sure the barmaid would be happy to comfort you."

A smile—a real smile—steals across his lips, but he quickly hides it. "Tell me what I have to do, Audette. How can I fix this?"

Uncomfortable, I glance at Keven and Milly.

Milly, misunderstanding my look, grabs Keven by the arm. "It's so dreadfully hot in here, isn't it?" She practically swoons in the knight's arms. "Take me outside for fresh air? I'd go myself, but who knows what villainous sorts may be loitering in the dark shadows."

From the front, just beyond the doors, a child squeals with joy as her father swings her up on his shoulders. Around them, the crowd laughs and smiles at the happy girl.

Keven gives Milly an incredulous look.

"Please?" She yanks on his arm and gives him a radiant smile the moment he reluctantly gives in.

Flashing me a smug look, she pulls Keven from the tavern.

"I rather like your friend," Irving says, somehow closer than he was a moment ago.

Another wave of hot, irrational jealousy courses through my veins.

I meet his eyes. "Disappointed she's not your betrothed? I can assure you, she wouldn't give you nearly as much trouble as I am."

He turns, and a knowing look lights his eyes. "You should have told me."

"Why? Wouldn't it have ruined the moment for you if you'd known you were about to kiss your intended and not a random noble from her court?"

Crossing his arms, he sits back, shaking his head, hiding that smile. "You are something."

Several heartbeats pass before I look at him again. My anger fades, and it's replaced with the sadness that haunted me the day he and I were supposed to wed.

"I didn't want to marry you, either," I blurt out, feeling bad as soon as the words are out of my mouth. I lay my hands on the table, palm up. "It was too fast. We didn't even have a promising ceremony."

At my honest declaration, Irving's face softens. "I didn't remember you."

I shake my head. "Or I you."

We sit in silence for a few moments.

"I'm not that bad, I don't think," he says softly.

I glance at him.

49

"I can even be charming." He offers a small smile that makes my world tilt. "Perhaps we—"

When I begin to shake my head, he claims my hand again. "Give me a chance, Princess. If you still hate me after a few days, send me on my way...but not yet."

Slowly, I pull my hand away. "It's not me you have to convince—It's Barowalt."

Irving flashes me a relieved grin, knowing he's bought himself time. "I'm likable. I'm sure your brother and I will have a nice chat, and after that, we'll get on fine."

Should I warn him that Barowalt "chats" with his sword?

No, let him find out on his own.

"Let's go now." He's already standing.

"Now?"

He tosses enough coins on the table to pay for not only his drink but ours as well. "There's no time like the present, right?"

I rise, feeling like this is a bad idea. I came into town to listen for gossip of the dragon. I can't leave yet.

But how am I going to hear anything here, hiding away at the table with Keven and Milly? Perhaps it would be best to try for another night.

Irving weaves through the crowd in front of me, looking over his shoulder every two seconds to make sure I'm still following. For a moment, I'm stabbed with a pang of guilt that I've given him reason to trust me so little.

Outside, the sky is purple, and the last of the sun's rays glow like a torch to the west. Soon, stars will appear. I glance around for Keven and Milly, but they seem to have wandered off.

There are even more peddlers out than there were before. Many of the carts offer goods, but it seems like most are selling food. Children and adults wander the street with pocket-pies, grouse legs, and crystallized sticks of sugar candy. The smell makes my stomach growl. Why didn't I order something from the tavern?

Oh, yes. Irving showed up and distracted me.

I glance at him from the corner of my eye. He's smiling, greeting people as we pass them. Sometime in the warmth of the day, he rolled the sleeves of his tunic up to his elbows. Everything about him is casual, but there's no mistaking that he's a man of noble blood. He wears it easily.

As I'm studying him, a girl of eight or nine accidentally darts in front of us, stumbling right into Irving. He grasps her arms, keeping her from toppling over. She blinks at him, embarrassed and besotted.

With a flash of a smile, he steps back and bows to her. He extends his arm, allowing her to pass. "After you, fair lady."

She giggles, gives him a youthful attempt at a curtsy, and runs off to join her friends.

A warm and fuzzy feeling settles in my stomach, but I choose to ignore it and continue on.

He turns and catches me watching him. I look away, ready for him to say something obnoxious. Instead, he steps up to me and takes my arm like it's the most natural thing in the world.

Like there's no place for me but on his arm.

Slowly, I look up and meet his eyes. He doesn't seem to realize my heart's in my throat.

"Are you hungry?" he asks, nodding toward one of the merchants.

I'm about to say I'm not, but then I stop myself. "A little."

"Good." He flashes me a smile. "I'm starving."

I let him lead me to a woman manning the cart. He buys two meat pies and a small brown-cloth package of candied fruits. We wander through the streets, eating and watching the performers.

Near the center of the square, at the heart of the market, a stage has been constructed. Three girls spin about, twirling at a dizzying speed as they do a country dance. Their brightly colored skirts swirl about them, and the crowd cheers and laughs.

As we watch, Irving's expression becomes pensive.

"Did you truly fall in love with a gypsy?" I ask.

Instantly he schools the expression and turns to me. "Love's such a strong word."

"You said she married at the beginning of the summer?"

He studies me for a moment, his expressive brown eyes dark in the dim light of the street. "Yes."

"Did you know him?" My voice is soft, but even with the din around us, I know he hears me.

Slowly, he nods. "He's a friend."

My heart twists, but my brain tells me I shouldn't let myself feel something for him.

"Is he still?" I ask.

After a long, slow breath, a small smile creeps up, tilting one corner of Irving's mouth. "Yes."

"Who is he?"

Irving looks at the cobblestones under our feet, avoiding my gaze. "Dristan of Triblue."

I know the prince, have met him briefly a few times at social gatherings.

"What happened?"

With a self-deprecating smile, Irving meets my eyes again. "When she told me to leave, I left." He shakes his head. "She stayed in Triblue and fell in love with one of my closest friends."

"Did you go to the wedding?"

He laughs, a quiet, sorrowful sound. "No."

"I'm sorry." And I mean it.

Studying me, he steps forward. "I learned an important lesson from the experience."

"What's that?" His nearness makes my breath hitch.

He looks me right in the eyes, his gaze so intimate I almost step back. "When you meet the love of your life, don't tell her you're a stable boy and then ask her to marry you."

Unable to help myself, a giggle slips out. He grins, obviously pleased to have made me laugh.

"Tell me the truth," I say, still smiling. "Are the rumors about you true?"

"No," he says immediately and then winces. "Well...not all of them."

We've left the main streets and are nearing the cliffs. Beyond us, the sea glistens in the moonlight, and the landscape has taken on various shades of sapphire.

"Who was the woman who met us in the hall?" I don't tell him I'm speaking of the day of our wedding. He knows.

He smiles, his eyes lighting with that maddening affection again. "Lady Anwen and her very sweet daughter, Galia."

"You're fond of her."

Knowing where this is going, he smiles. "I am fond of Anwen. She is one of my very favorite people."

I nod and stare out at the sea.

"She's also the wife of my good friend."

Immediately, I look back at him. "The little girl... she's not yours?"

He laughs quite suddenly. "What would make you think that? The girl's dark brown curls? Her bright blue eyes?"

Feeling foolish, I refuse to answer.

Gently, he takes me by the shoulders and turns me toward him. "I've made mistakes—probably more than I can count, but I promise you, I have no illegitimate children wandering about."

"That you know of."

His forehead wrinkles, and then he gives me a genuine smile. "I'm about ninety-eight percent certain."

I shake my head, a smile creeping on my lips despite my best efforts to hide it. "And the two percent?"

He grins. "There's a hazy night involving a fairy, a crown of wildflowers, and a grass tunic—but I'm fairly positive I'd remember if something tawdry had occurred."

I shake my head, wondering if he's joking. Surely he is...

Far below, the waves lap at the cliffs. The chaos of the market fades into the background, and the moon shines down on us. Irving's hands are still on my shoulders, and it's as if we both realize it at the same time. His eyes flutter from my eyes to my lips, and my breath catches.

"Normally, I would kiss you now," he says, his voice quiet in the night. "But that wouldn't do much to improve your current opinion of me, would it?"

Slowly, mesmerized, I shake my head. "Not likely."

He shifts closer, and I set a tentative hand on his tunic. Under the cloth, his chest is strong, solid.

"You could kiss me," he whispers. "Then it wouldn't reflect badly on me."

"That day we met in the hall," I say abruptly. "Were you leaving? Your friend seemed to think you were."

Sighing, he rubs his thumb against my shoulder. "I don't know."

Our eyes meet, and I search his. "Is that a yes?"

Irving shakes his head. "I didn't know what I was going to do."

"But you thought about it?"

"Yes." His lips tilt in a ghost of a crooked smile. "But I hadn't met you yet. Remember? You had a decoy...what was that, anyway?"

I smile and step back, glad for his honest answer and for the space I'm putting between us. "Milly wouldn't let me run through the halls in my wedding gown, and I had to find my mother's ring."

Still wearing the ring, I glance at it now. The stone

is a pale aquamarine—worth little in monetary value but priceless to me.

He takes my hand and examines it. "Something blue?"

I nod.

After a moment, he says, "I'm sorry for your loss."

The stone shines in the moonlight. "I am too."

Without a word, he slides his palm over mine and turns toward the cliffs.

Side by side in the moonlight, with my hand in his, we watch the sea.

Soon, Milly and Keven find us. From the not-so-distant street, Milly calls to me, and Irving and I pull apart. My fingers tingle where his skin brushed mine, and I try not to dwell on the light tingling feeling in my chest.

"I wondered where you two got off to," Milly says once she joins us. Reading my thoughts—and knowing me far too well—she smiles at me in a maddening way that's all her own. She turns toward the sea. "Just look at that view."

"It's growing late," Keven says after several moments. "It's time to ride back, Princess."

"I'll escort you," Irving says, eager to meet with Barowalt.

"That won't be necessary." Keven's expression doesn't waver, but his words are cold.

Irving's about to argue, but I shake my head, telling him to be patient. If he wants to prove himself, he's going to have to do it our way.

After a few moments, he relents. Nodding, he steps aside.

"Good evening," I say to him as I step past.

As I walk by, he catches my hand and brushes his lips over my knuckles. "Until tomorrow?"

I nod a silent agreement, and he sets me free.

Until tomorrow.

CHAPTER FIVE

"There's a visitor for you, Your Highness," a maid says from the doorway of my family's small library.

Expecting Irving, I turn to her, a book in my hand. "You may take him to the courtyard. I'll be with him momentarily."

"It's not a 'him,' Princess."

I cock my head to the side. "Who is it then?"

"The young Duchess of Marfell."

"Javid's wife?"

The maid looks uncomfortable at the informal use of my cousin's given name, but she nods.

"In that case," I say. "Show her in here and call for tea."

She murmurs an acknowledgment, and I scan the room, debating which window would be the most pleasant for entertaining.

After only a few moments, the maid comes back, leading the tall, poised young woman behind her. The duchess smiles brightly when she spots me and hurries in front of the maid, not bothering with formal introductions.

"We didn't have a chance to meet the other evening," she says. "I'm Grace."

We didn't meet because I was so shaken after the encounter with Irving, I refused to return to the gathering. Instead, I hid in the gardens, taking comfort in the quiet hum of a bubbling fountain.

"Audette." I needlessly motion to myself.

Grace takes in the well-lit library, and her eyes practically sparkle as they slide over the huge picture windows, potted orchids, and walls of books. Though it's not as large as many estates, my grandmother's library is lovelier than most.

Several servants carry in a small table and chairs, and two maids trail behind—one with linens and a vase of flowers and the other carrying a tea set. With practiced efficiency, they place the table near the open balcony doors and make quick work of the settings.

I thank them, complimenting them on their attention to details, and they slip out of the room.

Grace has wandered to the wall of books, and she browses them, a smitten look on her face as she caresses the leather covers. She turns back. "Your family's library is lovely. I have a feeling we're going to get on just fine."

I laugh, liking the duchess immediately. "I'm happy to have your company. When I told Milly I was spending the morning in the library, she procured one of my knights and deserted me to go shopping." I pour the tea. "Is this purely a social call?"

"Would it be rude of me to say I was hoping to escape from Giselle for a few hours?" Grace joins me at the table and hands me a note sealed with my great-aunt's insignia. Grace laughs when I cringe. "Camilla was hoping you and your brother would join us for the evening meal, and I jumped at the chance to deliver the invitation."

"Giselle is Kent's wife, correct?"

"That's right. And, truly, she's lovely." Grace wrinkles her nose. "In small doses."

After adding a thin slice of orange to Grace's tea, I hand her the cup.

"Everything's so much prettier here," she says as she drizzles honey in the amber liquid. "Even the tea."

"Where are you from?" I ask, recognizing her accent as someone from the southern mainland.

Her smile falters, and she brushes an escaped strand of her very light brown hair behind her ear. "I grew up in Vernow."

"I take it you're glad to be away?"

"I was happy there, for the most part. But those good memories are tempered with unsavory ones." She glances out the window and pauses as she takes a sip of tea. "I much prefer it here."

Changing the subject, she asks, "Doing a little light reading?"

Dragons, A History of Terror, V. 3, sits discarded on a nearby settee.

"Ah...yes."

"You've heard the rumors," she says.

I look up. "You know of them?"

She nods. "Yes, but as far as we can tell, rumors are all they are. King Edlund sent a regiment of knights to both villages that had supposedly seen the creature, but there was no evidence."

"Were the reports of the same description?"

"In both cases, the witnesses only claimed to see a massive figure cloaked in the shadows of night."

"But there were attacks, weren't there?"

Grace shakes her head. "A farmer in Balt lost four sheep, and a family in Marble lost a horse. There was no blood, no sign of struggle. It's more likely to have been the work of a thief."

Brushing the subject aside, obviously not keen to talk of it anymore, she informs me of the plans for the evening's dinner.

***

Milly chatters as I finish dressing for the evening meal. I nod here and there, but she's mostly content to carry on a one-sided conversation about her trip to the village with Rogert.

Irving never showed up. Grace came and left, I browsed through books that told me nothing, and Milly returned home—and all that time I foolishly waited for him.

"Help me cinch this." I turn my back toward Milly.

She clasps my pale beige gown's laces and yanks them snug, nearly jerking me off my feet. "And Rogert said the blue would suit me better, so, of course, that's the one I chose."

"Of course."

She's speaking of earrings or sashes or possibly a gown she commissioned. I'm not entirely sure.

"After that, we had tea at that little tavern with the fountain in front."

"Mmmhmmm."

"And then we stopped at that lovely rustic chapel and were married by the sweetest old bishop."

"How lovel—" I angle my head over my shoulder and give her a sharp look. "What did you say?"

She gives me a wry smile. "I was only checking to see if you were paying attention."

"I was."

63

Milly yanks the laces again as she secures the knot. "Barely. What's on your mind?"

"Nothing." Which isn't true. "I'm simply not looking forward to this evening's dinner." Which is true.

After we're finished, we make our way to the courtyard where the others should already be gathering.

Milly gasps when we walk through the front entryway.

Though we are to be at the castle in less than an hour, the men are gathered in the front, sparring. They're sweaty and dusty, more ready to go to battle than to a formal dinner with the ruling family of Ptarma.

"Barowalt!" I cry out.

My brother turns, startled. I gape at the man Barowalt was dueling against. Irving looks as if he's been dragged by a rope from the back of a horse. He's filthy and his tunic is torn in several places. Resting his sword at his side, he leans forward, grinning, and draws in a lungful of air.

"Good evening, Audette. You look lovely."

"What is going on?" I demand, sweeping toward them in my layers of gauzy, sparkling gown. I turn most of my venom on my brother. "You do realize, don't you, that we're expected to dine this evening with the king and queen of Ptarma?"

Barowalt slides his sword in the sheath at his side and looks at me, unconcerned. "Irving and I were attending to some business."

The knights watch the exchange, some looking guilty and the others amused.

"And are you finished?" I ask.

Barowalt looks at Irving. He nods. "Yes, I believe so."

I cross my arms and tilt my chin in the air. "And what, exactly, has been decided?"

Barowalt turns back to me, his face solemn. "Irving has earned the right to be inducted into the Order."

CHAPTER SIX

I gape at my brother. "That is not your decision to make."

Barowalt sighs, somehow frowning in an indulgent way. "Audette—"

"No," I say, stepping forward. "I am still head of the Order, and I will make the final decision." I'm careful to keep my eyes off Irving and trained on my brother. "There has never been a man who wasn't a product of Brookraven blood in the Order, and I do not believe it's wise to change that tradition now."

These men, my knights, have been trained since birth. Though I'm inclined to cast my hard feelings aside when it comes to Irving, this decision isn't a wise one.

Barowalt crosses his arms. "We'll discuss it after

tonight's dinner."

Frowning, biting my tongue so I won't continue to argue with him in front of our men, I nod. He may be my brother, but he is also my king. I will respect him.

But that doesn't mean I'll let him push this through. The Order is outside the whims of the Brookraven king. It's a ruling entity of its own.

"You best hurry," I finally say. "We're going to be late as it is."

The men scatter, nodding in greeting—and some in apology—as they pass me. As Barowalt steps by, he nudges me with his shoulder. I glance at him, irritated. He wears an ornery smile, and my mood lightens.

"You'll see the wisdom in my decision," he promises quietly.

I study his dark hair, his dark eyes—so different from mine. Where Barowalt looks like our father, with my fair hair and fawn-colored eyes, I've taken after Mother. Yet, despite our differences, we wear the same determined look, the same obstinate tilt of our jaw. That, according to Father, is all from our mother.

Stepping aside and motioning Barowalt to hurry, I say, "We'll see."

Finally, when they've all passed, there's only Irving. Milly mumbles an excuse, claiming she forgot something in her chambers, and she disappears inside.

Irving strides to me, looking a little worse for

wear. "Good evening, Princess."

"What are you playing at?" I ask him.

"It was Barowalt's idea, not mine." He smiles, his eyes teasing. "I was only vaguely aware of Brookraven's secret guild until this evening."

"Then why do you desire to be part of it?"

I want to brush the dirt off his tunic, wipe a smudge from his cheek with my thumb, but I keep my hands still.

He runs a hand through his disheveled hair. "If this is what it takes to prove myself to your brother—to you, then I'll do it."

Stepping past him and into the gardens, I say, "And that's why it's a bad idea. You can't join the Order in hopes of pleasing me. You must believe in it."

Irving matches my pace. "And perhaps I will—but I still have no idea what your Order does, so, for now, it's about you."

I glance at him, meeting his eyes in the moonlight. Why does it seem all our civil conversations take place at night, with the stars and the evening breeze marring my judgment? When did this become so difficult? Irving wasn't expected to join the Order when we married. In the original agreement, my mother already told his parents I would be needed from time to time on Brookraven business with no questions asked.

He knew of the guild, and that was enough.

"Meet me here tomorrow night, just before dusk." Worried I may be making a grave error in judgment, I continue, "I'll show you what the Order is about. After that, we'll decide if you're worthy."

He nods, solemn. Then his expression shifts, and he smiles. "You look lovely this evening."

Self-conscious, I glance at my gown. It's gathered at my waist, and though the skirt is full, the gossamer layers are light. This time of year, at home, I'd never be able to wear a sleeveless dress. Here the evening is just on the side of cool...the perfect temperature to step into someone's arms in hopes of warding off the chill.

But even if I were so inclined—which I'm not—I wouldn't. Irving is filthy. And yet, there's something very male about him and the sweat darkening his hair. The almost full moon shines on his chain mail, and though most of it's dull with dirt, there are places it shines. He looks strong and capable.

"You should go," I say. "You're going to be late for dinner as it is."

As if he knew where my thoughts were trailing, he gives me a knowing smile. "I'll see you shortly."

I press a hand to my stomach as I watch him leave. He disappears into the stable and shortly emerges again with his horse. He mounts, the picture of masculine grace. With a hand raised to me in farewell, he rides down the road, toward the castle.

I hear Milly come up behind me. She stands next to me, watching as Irving's silhouette disappears into the blackness.

"You like him," she says, her voice both teasing and accusing.

"I might."

"It would be all right, you know," she says, tilting her head, "to let yourself feel something for him."

The Ptarma lilies are at the end of their bloom cycle, but a few persistent ones stand tall in their beds. I examine one, carefully brushing its petals with my finger.

"Our marriage was never about an emotional attachment." I glance at her. "I know his kind. He'll get bored, and his affections will shift elsewhere. If I do agree to marry him, it won't be because I'm in love." I look at her. "It would be very foolish to fall in love with that man."

"That's all very logical." Milly glances toward the villa as Barowalt strides through the front. "But we can't choose who we fall in love with. It simply happens."

I straighten. "Maybe it does for you, but I will not let myself fall in love with Irving."

Smiling, she rolls her eyes, turning her attention away from my brother. "You'll have to tell me how that works for you."

Soon the knights are ready, each of them in a light dress chain mail and looking far too handsome for their own good.

I catch Rogert's arm as he walks past. "You'll behave yourselves tonight, won't you?"

"I'm hurt, Princess." He flashes me a grin. "Don't we always?"

***

Barowalt's seated on my right, and Milly's on my left. Irving is directly across from him, and Giselle, who turns out to be the third-born princess of some kingdom in Waldren, sits by his side. Her husband, Kent, has gone off, hunting boar in western Ptarma with his father and Prince Aldus.

I hope she wouldn't behave the way she did if he were present.

"You must take a tour of Ptarma while you're here." Giselle's hand trails to Irving's wrist, and she leans a fraction closer. In her charming accent, she continues, "It's such a lovely kingdom."

In an attempt to ignore the exchange, I carefully pull the bones from the delicate, pink-fleshed fish on my plate. The cattle here is mostly used for milk, and fish is a staple in the Ptarmish diet. Besides the prawns, I'm not overly fond of it.

Irving reaches for his goblet, subtly moving her hand from his wrist. "Perhaps you and your husband will take me on a tour?"

I hide a smile behind my napkin. Grace catches it and presses her lips together, holding back a laugh. Javid's between her and Irving, and, though his attention is on the meal, he doesn't seem terribly impressed with his cousin's wife either.

Giselle gives Irving a knowing smile, and she tosses her glossy hair behind her shoulder. "I'm sure he'd love to, but Kent keeps himself so busy, and I'm often bored to tears." Her eyes travel over Irving, and she wears a telling smile. "But I'd be happy to entertain you."

I look at Grace, shocked. The duchess raises her eyebrows, silently reminding me she'd told me as much.

Giselle continues to make eyes at Irving through the rest of the meal. Unfortunately, the king and queen are at the end of the table, conversing with the elder nobility, and they don't see the shameful display their nephew's wife is putting on.

"Audette," Giselle says after following Irving's gaze to me. "You're from Brookraven, is that right?" She says the name of our kingdom slowly as if she's questioning its existence.

"Yes."

She leans forward, smiling. "I'm not familiar with all of Elden's tiny kingdoms—they are so many on the outskirts, after all. I was curious of yours, seeing as you're family. But when I tried to find it on a map, I'm afraid I wasn't able to locate it."

Brookraven is on the eastern edge of Lenrook, and though it may be small, it's plainly marked on any map of Elden.

I have no answer for her, so I only smile. Unfortunately, next to me, Barowalt is in a conversation with Rogert and didn't hear. He would have had a clever answer for her.

"Primewood, though," she says, turning back to Irving, "looks fascinating."

What map was she looking at? It's nothing but forest.

"I'm rather partial to it," Irving says.

Giselle's hand drifts under the table, and, from the way Irving jumps, likely to his leg. She leans closer. "You'll find that I am very friendly, should you grow homesick."

Irving stands. "Audette, you seem to be finished. Shall we take that walk you promised me?"

I promised him no such walk, but I rise, eager to be away from Giselle. "Of course."

A harpist begins to strum her soft melody as others excuse themselves from the tables. Irving escorts me through the hall and into the gardens. Fire-lit urns dot the paths, lighting the walkways.

"Thank you," Irving says.

"The princess seemed to be rather fond of you." I avoid his eyes, looking instead at the flowers.

He shakes his head. "Persistent, wasn't she?"

"And lovely."

Irving stops suddenly, and since my arm is in his, I'm forced to stop as well. Leaning in, he says, "And married."

I shrug, still not able to meet his eyes.

"There's only one girl I'm interested in." With a finger to my chin, Irving tilts my head toward him, making me look at him. "And I'm looking at her."

The words roll off his tongue in a practiced manner, and I don't doubt he's saying them because he thinks they are what I want to hear. And maybe I do, but I don't necessarily believe him.

"Because you don't want to lose your title," I say.

He smiles, and it's such a brilliant thing, my heart gives an extra thump.

"Telling me I have to marry you to keep my title," he says, "is like saying I must eat dessert before I choke down the fish they're so fond of here."

A smile fights at my lips, and I give into it. "That implies you don't want your title."

Readjusting our arms so they are linked just a little closer, he continues on. "Honestly? I like my position—I like the freedom, and I'd be lying if I said

I wasn't fond of the gold. But crowning me king? It doesn't seem like a sane idea."

Earlier, I'd had the same thought of him being in the Order. But now, seeing the shadow of doubt on his face, I wonder if Irving hasn't drawn himself short.

"Barowalt believes there's more to you than you give yourself credit for," I say.

He gives me an incredulous look.

"I'm serious. He'd never suggest you join the Order if he didn't."

We walk through the meandering paths, past fountains, private nooks, palm trees and weeping willows. Scattered amongst the beds of vibrant flowers, moonstones, artfully arranged in patterns, glow after soaking up a full day's worth of sunshine. Nearby, a night bird calls.

It feels as if we're the only ones out here, but the gardens are so extensive, there are likely more people strolling as we are.

"Speaking of the Order, tell me something." Irving glances at me, smiling. "What exactly flows in Brookraven's water?"

"I'm sorry?"

"Are all the men of Brookraven as huge as your chosen elite, or did you scour the countryside searching for them?" He grins. "Being amongst them is a bit humbling, to tell you the truth."

"Not all of them."

"Is there something in your water that produces such beefy individuals? Fairy magic?" He grins at his joke.

"In a manner."

Startled, he pauses. "Darling, I wasn't serious."

I have no idea why Barowalt suddenly feels Irving should join the Order, but I trust my brother's judgment.

"If you really want to know our secret, be at the villa tomorrow as we discussed."

Suddenly, he looks concerned.

"What is it?" I ask.

He turns toward me and sets his hands on my shoulders. "You're not dabbling in something dangerous, are you?"

Giving in to impulse, I run my hand from his shoulder, down his arm. "Dark magic?"

Solemn and wary, he nods.

I laugh at the thought. "No. We're as far removed from the dark sources as the day is from the night."

"In that case, please tell me you're not actually in league with fairies." He smiles, but there's something in his expression. "I've had my fill of them."

"No fairies," I promise and tug him back toward the castle. "We can't keep avoiding the party. Your lady love awaits."

Irving groans. "Protect me from her."

"I'll do my best."

The prince escorts me through the doors, but as soon as we pass into the hall, I'm cornered by Aunt Camilla. Like a tiger, Giselle sidles next to Irving the moment he's free.

He flashes me a mock horrified look, and I'm forced to hold back a laugh so Camilla doesn't launch into a lecture on proper decorum. Amused, he grins at me over his shoulder as the she-tiger drags him away.

Butterflies flutter in my stomach, making me feel giddy...and then I'm flooded with horror.

What if Milly is right? What if we can't help who we fall in love with?

If so, I might be doomed.

CHAPTER SEVEN

"Why does Irving get to go with you, but I can't?" Milly's hands are on her hips, and her pretty face is scrunched with hurt as she stares my brother down.

Barowalt swallows, uncomfortable. He's not overly fond of female displays of emotion. "Milly—"

"Don't 'Milly' me!" She blinks quickly. "You drag me along with you, but you never explain what it is we're doing."

I edge toward the door, not sure I'm needed for this particular argument.

A maid clears her throat from behind me. "Prince Irving of Primewood has arrived, Your Highness."

"Oh, good." I duck out of the room, hurrying toward the entry hall.

Irving waits for me, dressed in light mail and a

tunic. He studies a tapestry. His back is to me, and I pause, letting my eyes wander over him.

Too quickly, hearing my footsteps, Irving turns. His face lights in a smile when he sees me. "I was afraid you may have left for your secret meeting without me."

"You're late," I say.

Irritation flashes across his face. "Giselle cornered me in the stables on my way out."

"It must be very tiresome to have such an attractive woman fawning over you. Of course—it's nothing you're not used to, right?" My words have bite to them, but I attempt to soften them with a wry smile.

The prince gives me a knowing smirk and steps forward. "Jealous, Princess?"

"No," I lie.

Not believing me, he shrugs one shoulder, that irritating look still on his face.

"Were you expecting to go into battle?" I ask, changing the subject.

Irving has a sword at his side, and he wears a bow and full quiver on his back.

Patting the sword, he says, "It's good to be prepared."

"You shouldn't need them tonight."

"If you weren't being so cryptic about the whole thing..."

I turn from him, worried this is a bad idea. What

was I thinking?

Barowalt strides into the hall, followed by a smug-looking Milly. I raise my eyebrows at her, silently asking if Barowalt gave in.

Biting her lip, holding back a bright smile, she nods.

First Irving and now Milly. Barowalt looks agitated, and I can tell he's already doubting the wisdom of his decision.

"We need to leave," my brother says as he steps through the front.

Irving, Milly, and I follow. The knights are waiting for us, and they already have my horse saddled. Barowalt calls for someone to prepare Milly's mare, and Keven rushes to the stable.

No one questions Barowalt's decision to bring Milly. Like they always are on these nights, our elite are nervous, edgy. I, too, am having trouble staying still, and my muscles ache with impatience.

The full moon crests the horizon, alerting us the time is near.

"Nervous?" Barowalt asks from my side as we ride from the villa.

"Eager." I roll my shoulders.

Now that Milly has secured a place in our group, she looks wary, unsure what it is she's riding into. Irving, too, is quiet.

We ride through Ptarma's lush countryside, through vineyards and patches of forest where heat-hardy evergreens grow. The moon continues to rise, reminding us to hurry. Asher leads us, more familiar with the path than we are.

After almost an hour of riding, we turn onto an overgrown trail. The valley we emerge into isn't hidden, and there's nothing particularly unique about it other than it's the most uninhabited area of Ptarma. We descend the winding cliff path, but the clearing is empty.

My eyes scan the trees near the edges of the meadow, and I grow anxious.

Finally, there's a flash of white in the brush. As it always does, my breath catches when I see them, but this time, my joy is tempered with relief.

The creatures glisten in the moonlight, whiter than the ivory cliffs, more spectacular than the ribbons of lights that color the sky on cold nights in the far north.

Just in front of me, on the rocky trail, Irving tenses. He stares at the creatures, disbelief evident in the forward angle of his head and the tilt of his shoulders as he leans forward to get a better look.

Behind me, Milly gasps.

When the trail widens, I ride ahead. Asher pulls his horse to a halt, allowing me to pass. He dismounts and offers his hand, taking my horse when I'm to the ground.

I step forward, hesitant. I don't know this blessing well, and I'm not sure they'll remember me.

Cautious, a female steps forward, her mane flowing behind her in an invisible breeze. She stretches her neck up and gently rests her muzzle over my shoulder.

Very few people having seen the creature, and most picture a white horse. This creature—this unicorn— is sleek, petite, and graceful as a deer. Her ears are large and her mane is silk. Where a star often marks a horse, a horn grows from her forehead and glistens like mother-of-pearl.

There's something terrifying about them, something painfully humbling, as if you've stumbled onto a creature so beautiful, human eyes were never meant to see them.

The mare is cool to the touch and smells like sun-warmed wildflowers. I close my eyes, stroking her mane. Like a cat, she leans toward me, sweet and gentle.

With my hand still on her coat, images float in my mind, like daydreams but in disconcerting detail. Some are hers, some are mine. She shows me a memory of my father bringing Mother here for the first time, and then several times after that with Barowalt and eventually with me as well. I see the joy on my mother's face the day I was born, father's laughter when Barowalt and I were learning to spar when we were tiny...the way they hugged me the morning of that fateful day.

By the time the unicorn is finished, tears roll down my cheeks, and my shoulders quake.

She nudges me, not understanding my pain.

Unable to help myself, I cling to her, lying against her smooth, sweet-smelling coat.

Another memory assaults me, this one causing me to gasp. Her brilliant luster dulls. The fear radiating from her is physically painful, and I grit my teeth, fighting it. The blessing's sudden loss plays through my mind—the night a shadow stole amongst their numbers, leaving a multitude lifeless, gone—as empty of magic as albino deer...their beautiful, sweet gift lost to a vapid void of darkness.

Behind her, the others of her kind darken, reliving the memory with her.

Because we are linked, several of the knights gasp, feeling the pain as it were their own. Milly and Irving look about us, shocked, their mouths agape with confusion.

Barowalt clenches his eyes shut. He grasps the hilt of his sword, and his muscles tremble.

Then, slowly, the pain subsides.

I gasp a breath and turn to Barowalt. "What was

it?"

Shaken, he shakes his head. "I don't know."

My mind travels back to the rumors of the dragon in southern Ptarma. Grace said there were reports of a shadow. Now more than ever, I'm convinced the incidents are related.

"I'm sorry," I whisper, stroking her nose.

She nuzzles into my palm, and slowly her brilliance returns.

"It was if they had no warning," Rogert murmurs.

The hair on the back of my neck stands on end. The unicorns are flighty, skittish, rarely seen and even more rarely hunted. The Order has done everything in our power to make the magical species nearly a myth. Very few believe they actually exist.

What is it we're dealing with?

"We must find a safe place for you until we can discover what's done this," I whisper to her.

Though she doesn't understand my words, she looks up at me with dark brown, trusting eyes.

Asher steps forward, and the unicorn shies away, nervous even though she can scent the unicorn magic clinging to him.

"My family owns land to the north of the island, not far from here," he says. "It borders the sea, the pasture hidden by cliffs. We can take them there—keep them safe."

"You wish to round them up, corral them like horses?"

There's no animosity in my voice, but Asher winces. "I only wish to keep them safe."

"Barowalt?" I ask.

My brother steps forward. "I visited Asher's land the day before yesterday. It's secluded and easy to protect. Once we've relocated the blessing, half the Order will stay to guard them. The others will track down the darkness that attacked."

I don't want to lead them from their valley—this is their home, where they've lived for centuries. The Ptarmish blessing is the largest group of unicorns in Elden. It's familiar here; it's what they know.

It's also not safe.

"All right," I finally say. "Now that whatever it is knows they're here, I'm surprised it hasn't returned."

"They've been more reclusive than usual," Asher says. "I tried to get them to show themselves several times after the attack—but they wouldn't come out."

My stomach knots. This is our fault. My fault.

Next to me, Asher looks pale. As horrible as I feel, he feels worse.

I glance over my shoulder, scanning my knights, trying to decide who should stay with the blessing and who will return to hunt for the shadow creature.

Milly catches my eye. She's pale, appropriately

awed. Irving, however, looks as if he thinks we've somehow played a trick on him, like he can't—and refuses—to believe his eyes.

Curious, the unicorns push forward, sensing their magic on the knights. A brave young mare carefully makes her way toward Milly. Gently, the unicorn nuzzles Milly's hand. Barowalt watches the silent exchange between the two, his eyes intent.

Whether he's admitted to himself yet, it's obvious to me. He's just as in love with Milly as she is with him. He wouldn't have brought her if he wasn't.

Milly blinks several times, overcome. When she strokes the mare's mane, the unicorn rubs against her hand. My friend grins, elated and almost near tears.

My attention, however, is on Irving. His eyebrows are narrowed, and he gives the mare who stood with me a suspicious look as she comes closer. She studies him, wondering why he's not touched with magic like we are. He hesitantly strokes her nose. She tosses her head back, disliking being pet like a donkey.

Frowning, Irving pulls his hand back.

"We must hurry if we're going to move the blessing before dawn," Barowalt says from my side.

"If they'll follow us."

Barowalt crosses his arms. "They must."

Slowly, I approach the unicorn who is now staring at Irving with a reproachful look on her face. She sees me, tosses her mane, and trots my way.

I lay my hand and her coat. "Come."

Her magic tremors between us as she stretches it out. It swirls around us both, and understanding lights her dark eyes. I take two tentative steps back, testing the link, and she follows, fully trusting me to keep her from harm.

My stomach twists, and I scan the sky for danger. That innocent trust is a heavy burden.

I pass through the rest of the blessing, touching their coats, asking them to follow me. They wait, willing to follow. I gulp, terrified that leading them from their valley is a bad idea.

Barowalt gives me a reassuring nod, and I mount my horse. With Keven and Asher at my side and Barowalt and the remaining others at the rear, I lead the unicorns up the cliff and away from the shattered safety of their valley.

***

We lead the last unicorn onto Asher's land just as the first of the sun's rays lights the horizon. A half-hour ride took six hours while leading twenty-seven flighty, skittish unicorns. Even with the link, they darted this way and that, spooking at the slightest noise. It was like herding rabbits.

My nerves are frazzled, and my eyes ache for sleep.

SHARI L. TAPSCOTT

Nearby, Hallgrave calmly attempts to convince a young male to enter the pasture gate, but the unicorn tosses his head and prances backward, refusing.

"Audette," the knight calls. He's as weary as I am, and no one bothers with titles or formalities now. "I need you."

I step up to the unicorn and stroke him, trying to calm him. His eyes are huge, and he's terrified of being closed in.

"It's all right," I say, hoping to strengthen the link.

Slowly, I back through the gate while speaking soothing nonsense to the beautiful creature. Though nervous, he follows.

With a reassuring thud, the pasture gate closes. The unicorns have gathered near the base of the cliffs, and the young male darts off to join them.

Barowalt rubs his forehead and calls Asher over. "The manor is empty, correct?"

Asher nods. "I sent the staff away on holiday as soon as I knew you were coming. There's not so much as a gardener left."

"And the horses in the stables?" I ask.

"They've been removed as well."

Gathering the unicorns in the stable is a worst-case scenario in the event of an attack, but if we tried to pen them with common horses, I'm sure the vain unicorns would rather die.

88

What I'm about to ask of them is bad enough.

I approach the nervous blessing. They shift and paw, uncomfortable with leaving their valley and even more uncomfortable with being fenced in.

"You are safe here," I reassure them, hoping they'll understand. "But I need you to disguise yourselves."

They blink at me.

Fighting a yawn, and working to hide my frustration, I step forward to touch the closest. "I need you to hide."

In my mind, I imagine the unicorns, one by one, miraging into horses.

The unicorn I'm touching shakes her head, horrified. But I run my fingers through her mane. "It will keep you safe."

One by one, understanding spreads through the group. They look indignant, but slowly, the blessing of unicorns becomes an unremarkable herd of various-colored horses.

I sigh. At least to those who aren't looking for them, they are hidden.

The last thing we need is locals starting rumors of a unicorn farm on the northern region of the kingdom.

Exhausted, I turn away. Just as I begin to walk back to our group, I'm nudged in the back of the head. I turn, almost startled to see a very plain brown mare staring back at me. Now taller than I am, she playfully sets her muzzle on my head.

An image wisps into my mind of the horses running in the sunshine, grazing on the grass.

I wrap my arms around her neck. "Yes, it's safe."

Fluid and graceful, they trot into the light as the sun rises over the horizon. Finally content, they glisten in the morning's first rays, and I bite the side of my cheek, worried there's no way to disguise them completely.

CHAPTER EIGHT

The first thing I notice when I wake is the sunlight streaming through the window. Birds sing from the trees, not caring a bit that I didn't crawl into bed until after sunrise. Next to me, Milly's still asleep. I slip from the bed, careful not to wake her. She's crabby on the best of mornings.

Asher's estate is lovely but small, and Milly and I are sharing a chamber while we're here. It makes me nostalgic for the times I would visit her family's land for week-long stretches when we were young. We stayed up most of the night then, too. But instead of giggling into the wee hours of the morning and crashing onto a nest of blankets, we herded unicorns across the countryside.

Our younger selves would have been delighted at

the prospect. My older self didn't care for it.

I have a throbbing headache, my shoulders ache, and all I want is a cup of plain hot tea and one of the brackenberry scones that the kitchen maids make back home. I'll settle for the tea.

After winding through the estate, I eventually find the dining hall. It's an intimate room with a table large enough for twelve at most. Keven, Garran, and Hallgrave are already seated.

Keven looks up as I walk into the room, and he smiles. His light hair is tied back, and he looks just as handsome as usual. I, on the other hand, look like death.

"I didn't expect you up so soon," Barowalt says, worrying over me like I'm a delicate flower.

"We have things to do." I sit next to Keven, who smiles in greeting. "Moving the blessing here is only a temporary solution. We must find the beast that attacked them, and soon."

"Why hasn't it attacked again?" Hallgrave asks.

I shake my head. I've been wondering the same thing.

Barowalt joins us at the table, and I wonder if it's come to anyone else's attention that there's an absence of food.

My brother rests his elbows on the table and steeples them under his chin. "We're either dealing with poachers...or there's a darker force at work."

The thought is sobering. Though we obviously don't want poachers to hunt the unicorns, something or someone hoping to kill off the species altogether is worse.

Irving appears at the door, looking refreshed after his few hours of sleep. Apparently, he found time to shave, and though his clothes are as dirt-worn as ours, he managed to beat some of the dust from them.

I glance down at my gown, which was white yesterday. Now it's splotched with mud, trail dust, and horse hair. There's nothing I can do about it. When we left yesterday evening, I hadn't planned on leading a mass unicorn migration.

The prince takes the open seat on my other side and nods to me in greeting. He wears an easy smile, blissfully ignorant to the difficulty of the task in front of us. After a moment, he narrows his eyes at the empty table. "Breakfast seems to be missing."

Barowalt glances at him. "Asher sent the servants and maids away, remember?"

Irving raises his eyebrows and nods, an incredulous look on his face. "Ah—yes. To protect your unicorn fugitives from detection."

Collectively, Keven, Hallgrave, Garran, and I all suck in a silent breath. I turn my eyes on Barowalt, wondering how he will react. Asher steps into the room in time to hear the last of Irving's flippant remark, and he pauses by the door.

Irving, who doesn't realize he's treading on thin ice, laughs. "So this is what the noble, mighty Order of Lingard does...you play nursemaid to a herd of fancy horses."

For one heartbeat, there is perfect, agonizing silence. And then, after the abrupt clattering of chairs and an indignant and surprised holler, Barowalt pins Irving against the wall. My brother has his hand wrapped around the prince's neck. I gape at the pair, horrified.

Apparently, it was Barowalt who should have stayed in bed longer.

Irving, who's either incredibly brave or simply an idiot, begins to laugh as soon as he recovers from his shock. He holds his hands up in surrender. "Rather attached to the glowing beasts, aren't you?"

The veins in Barowalt's neck bulge, but Irving stays calm, waiting for Barowalt to release him, smart enough to know he mustn't engage physically. Irving may have proved himself with a sword, but there are very few who could match Barowalt in a fist fight.

As we watch, curious how it will play out, Milly steps into the room. The moment she sees the two men, she scoffs. "I have not had nearly enough rest for this. Barowalt, pretend you're mature enough to rule an entire kingdom and sit down so we may have a blood-free breakfast." She narrows her eyes. "If you still feel the need to kill each other after you've eaten something, then by all means—but do it outside where some poor maid won't have to clean up after you."

My pretty but rumpled friend chooses the seat next to Rogert and primly folds her hands in her lap. Then, with a fair amount of disdain and confusion, she says, "Where's breakfast?"

Barowalt breathes deep and makes a show of removing his hand from Irving's throat. Irving, after flashing a smug look at Barowalt just to further irritate him, reclaims his spot next to me.

By this time, the rest of our knights have joined us. Now that the excitement is over, we all stare at the empty table as if we can make food magically appear by sheer will alone.

"We'll have to fend for ourselves for a few days," Barowalt says, his voice cool and slightly distant. "Who knows how to cook?"

We turn baffled eyes on him.

"For crying out loud!" Milly shoves herself away from the table. "We all know why you bring me along. Milly, do this...Milly, do that...Milly, make breakfast!"

She leaves in a huff, her words trailing off until they are too faint to hear.

Barowalt raises an eyebrow at me. "Milly knows

how to cook?"

"Not that I'm aware of."

The men cringe. Who knows what she'll come up with?

"Why don't you go help her?" Barowalt says.

I bristle. "Why? Because I'm a girl, I should automatically be sent to the kitchen?"

"Fine." Losing his patience, my brother shoves away from the table. "I'll go."

As Barowalt strides after Milly, a heavy hush falls over the table. And then Rogert snorts, unable to hold back his laughter. That starts the rest of us, and we double over, too tired and hungry to care. Even solemn, practical Keven chuckles next to me.

After the moment has passed, Rogert turns his attention to me, a smile still on his face. "Have you decided who will stay with the blessing and who will hunt the beast?"

All eyes turn to me. No one wants to linger here on guard duty—they want to be proactive, hunt the creature. But some must stay. I study the men, assessing their strengths and weaknesses. If I were to choose now, I would leave Keven, Asher, Hallgrave, Percis, and our youngest knight, eighteen-year-old Ren. Not because they aren't up to the task of hunting, but because I trust them the most.

They wouldn't pout about being left behind as

Rogert and Rafe would, and they are better at defensive action.

At the same time, Asher knows the land, and he may be better suited for hunting the creature down. Hallgrave and Barowalt are close, and I don't see my brother leaving him behind. And Kevin is the best under crisis—which would serve us well in either place.

My head still hurts, and I've had too little sleep to think it over now.

"Barowalt will decide," I say.

No one questions me, but they were eager to know what their appointments would be, and now I've disappointed them.

And there's the small matter of what to do with Irving.

From the corner of my eye, I glance at the prince. Despite his carefree attitude earlier, he looks pensive. Withdrawn.

He catches me looking at him, and he smiles, the dark thoughts gone.

"Where would you like to be?" I ask him.

His smile dims, and I know whatever he's thinking of saying won't please me.

Steeling myself, I ask, "Well?"

He shakes his head, pretending it's nothing. "We'll speak of it later."

He doesn't want to be in the Order, likely doesn't

think our task is an important one. But he also doesn't know the balance. And why would he? It's a secret the Order has worked hard to hide. If people knew...our mission would be much more difficult.

The men's conversation shifts to the new drachite armor coming out of Errinton, and Irving jumps into the conversation, apparently knowing the new king and queen fairly well.

"I have a set, actually," Irving says.

Rogert leans forward, eager. "Is it true it's stronger than dragon steel?"

Irving nods, his face lighting up. "And flexible— it's the most amazing thing."

I listen without much to add to the conversation. I prefer leather armor—it's easier for me to move in. Since, as Barowalt is so fond of reminding me, my greatest asset is my agility, I don't wear anything to get in the way.

"Is it lighter?" Keven asks, putting his dislike for Irving aside for the time being.

The prince shakes his head. "No, it's still fairly heavy."

They continue on, and my mind wanders back to the shadow I saw in the unicorn's memory. I let out a slow breath, thinking. What creature moves as a shadow? Is there such a dragon?

Or perhaps the mare's memory was flawed in

her terror? Would she have forgotten specific details in self-preservation?

Eventually, Milly and Barowalt return. She doesn't look anywhere near as irritable as she was earlier, and her cheeks flush pink. I meet her eyes, and a quick smile flashes across her face. Then, schooling her expression to look serene, she quickly looks away.

I glance at Barowalt and raise an eyebrow. He gives me a look that plainly tells me to mind my own business, and I grin, hoping to get a rise out of him.

It works. He frowns as if he's above such trivial emotions such as embarrassment and turns away.

Milly deposits a bowl of apples on the table along with a plate of hard cheese. "Eat up."

"That's it?" Rogert's chestnut eyebrows knit. He looks at her with hope. "Did you forget something in the kitchen?"

She shrugs, unconcerned. "Sorry."

Grateful for anything at this point, I choose an apple and slice sections of it off with my knife. It's smaller than the apples at home, and it's as tangy as it is sweet. Not expecting it, my mouth puckers, and my eyes begin to water.

Milly sees me and laughs. "They're good once you get past the first bite."

Barowalt's eyes move to Milly, and he actually grins. "And when you eat them with the last two pastries in the cupboard."

Protests ring out, but Barowalt and Milly only smile. Groaning the loudest, Rogert throws an apple at Barowalt's head.

Barowalt catches it, chuckling under his breath. "That's what you get when you all choose to stay here, waiting to be served like a bunch of pampered princesses."

I hold my hand up. "I am a pampered princess."

Milly grins. "And you're the only one who's forgiven."

After our meager breakfast, we sit back and wait for Barowalt to decide who's stationed where.

He crosses his arms, thinking. "Audette, I'd prefer you to stay here with the blessing, but Camilla is such a busybody, she'll notice you're missing and want to know where you've gone."

Having come to the same conclusion, I nod in agreement.

"Hallgrave," he continues, "You'll return with us."

I figured as much.

"Asher, you'll stay here. Percis...yes, you'll stay here as well."

The brown-haired knight nods. He may be disappointed, but it doesn't show on his face. When he catches me studying him, he gives me a reassuring smile.

My brother drums his fingers on the table. "Garran, here. Rogert, with us. Keven...also with us. How many is that?"

"You have three here," I answer.

Barowalt turns to Asher, putting him in charge. "How many men do you wish?"

"Four should be plenty," the dark-haired knight answers.

My brother turns his attention on Ren. The young knight winces, already knowing what's coming.

"You'll stay as well."

Ren's face falls, but he nods, eager to please.

Rogert sits back, smug. I meet his eyes, flashing him a chastising look, but he only winks. I purse my lips, trying to hold back a smile, but it doesn't work well.

When I turn back to Barowalt, I find Irving studying me. He raises his eyebrows, but I only tilt my jaw a little higher and try to ignore him.

It's not easy. Though he's a respectable distance away, he almost seems too close. Without extending my arm, I could place my hand on his shoulder. If he were to drape his hand between us under the table, I could easily slide mine in his without anyone being the wiser.

If I turned just slightly, angled my legs toward him, our knees would—

"Audette? What are your thoughts?" Barowalt asks.

I look up sharply. Fortunately, only part of me was daydreaming. "I believe the attack on the blessing and the dragon rumors in southern Ptarma are connected."

Barowalt gives me a look. "You think it was a dragon?"

"No." I slice another piece of apple, knowing the commotion my comment will cause. "I think it was a wizard."

It's not like they weren't thinking it themselves.

The men shift, uncomfortable, and transfer their eyes to my brother.

"We can't know that for sure," he says.

"It's a shadow, Barowalt." I lean forward. "What creature siphons the magical essence from a being and leaves the body for scavengers? What poacher leaves the horn?"

There's only one creature I know of that steals magic, and they're as human as we are.

Rogert, serious now that the conversation has shifted, rests on his elbows. "If it is a wizard, we have to question the motives. Did he kill a few, hoping for a surge in his magic..."

"Or is it the beginning of a larger plot?" I continue for him. "Is he—or they—attempting to exterminate the unicorns all together?"

Irving glances about the table, confused.

Barowalt, noticing, turns to the prince, his face twisted in an almost-sneer. "These 'fancy horses' we play nursemaid to? Their magic keeps the balance—it locks the dark sources in the depths where they belong. You want darkness to devour Elden? You rid the world of unicorns."

CHAPTER NINE

I aim at the target and slowly release a held breath. My arrow hits the bullseye, nearly dead center.

"That's impressive," Irving says from behind me. "Can you do it again?"

Though I heard someone approaching, I still jump at his voice.

The practice targets are toward the back of our family's villa, practically hidden in the gardens. It's doubtful Irving stumbled on me by accident. He must have been looking.

A warm breeze blows through the trees, and the sun beats down, warm on my bare shoulders. Much to Milly's dismay, I've again donned my practice garb—a sleeveless form-fitting tunic and trousers. My hair is pulled back in a simple braid I wrapped myself, and

I've secured it in a twist, out of the way. I wasn't ex-pecting to meet anyone this morning.

Glancing at him, I nock another arrow and send it flying. It slides in place next to the first.

Irving smiles, apparently impressed. His hair is slightly damp, like he's just bathed, and he wears a tai-lored tunic that fits well on his nicely-muscled shoul-ders. His sword is missing; only a knife sheath rests at his hip.

"Perhaps you could show me a thing or two." He steps closer than he should, smelling nicer than he has any right to—like citrus and ocean.

"If I remember correctly," I say, stepping away. "I've seen you with a bow. I have a feeling you wouldn't carry a weapon you don't know how to use."

He cocks his head, a ghost of a smile playing at his lips. "But not with your level of finesse. You stand differently. Perhaps that's why."

Laughing, I say, "I don't stand differently...how do you stand?"

Pretending he has a bow in his hands, he takes his stance. He faces the target, his body angled straight toward it.

"You can't possibly shoot like that," I say. "There's no way."

"I do," Irving argues. "Give me your bow, and I'll show you."

I study a patch of low-growing, yellow flowers nearby. "It's not the right size for you."

He extends his palm and motions for me to hand it over. As I do, I make the mistake of looking him right in the eyes. His expression is warm, like it was the first day we met. He always seems to be smiling with some secret joke.

In the most awkward stance I've ever seen, with his arms twisted to the side, Irving shoots. The arrow flies to the target and embeds itself in the circle just outside the bullseye—which is remarkable for the first time with a foreign bow, let alone with the ridiculous way he's trained himself to stand.

He looks at me over his shoulder. "Tell me what you'd do differently."

"Well, first," I say, tilting my head as I examine him. "You need to turn so your side is facing the target."

Shifting a little, he says, "like this?"

He's still standing all wrong—it's absurd.

"How has no one teased you for this?"

Irving shrugs. "I hit the target, didn't I?"

I hold my hands parallel to each other in an attempt to demonstrate, and then I tilt them. "Turn more."

Irving's expression is blank. "Show me."

Feeling like I'm walking into a trap, I step up to

him. After clenching and then unclenching my fists, I place my hands at his sides. His tunic is soft, and under it, his muscles are lean and strong. Purposely looking at his chest and not his face, I angle him.

"Then what?" he murmurs.

Finally, I meet his gaze and give him a wry smile. "Then you shoot the bow."

Now I'm positive he's playing with me.

"How exactly do you hold it when you're at this angle?" With a hand on my shoulder, he turns me so my back is to his chest. With his arms around me, he holds the bow in front of us, locking me in place.

My heart races. A pleasant tingling sensation starts in my chest and travels all the way to my toes. Playing nonchalant, I glance over my shoulder. "You don't actually believe I'm falling for this, do you?"

He widens his eyes, feigning innocence. "Falling for what?"

I shake my head and turn toward the target. "You can shoot any time now."

Laughing under his breath, he draws the bow. I'm forced to step back, pressing myself flush against his chest, and I close my eyes.

Control yourself.

The arrow hits dead center, pushing mine aside.

"You're a talented instructor," he whispers near my ear.

I shiver and then grimace because I know he felt it. "And you're a horrible flirt."

He laughs low and nudges the back of my jaw with his chin. "I believe I'm a very capable flirt."

I duck out of his arms and stride to the target, yanking the arrows free. "It's an art you've practiced."

He follows me, taking it in stride that I walked away. "You're going to keep holding that against me, aren't you?"

Just so I'll have something to focus on, I shoot again. This time, my arrow misses the center, hitting the circle outside.

"I didn't say I was holding it against you," I say. "It's simply a fact."

He crosses his arms, almost smiling. It's a disconcerting look, and when I shoot again, my arrow lands in the farthest ring. I frown, lowering my bow.

"Why haven't you asked me about the Order?"

Startled, I turn toward him. It's true that we returned some time ago, and I haven't mentioned it yet. I'm not sure how I feel about him joining us, but at the same time, I'm not sure how I feel about him declining either.

I wish Barowalt had never put me in this position.

"Your brother offered me a place," he continues.

Setting my bow aside, I say, "Even after the 'fancy horse' remark?"

He chuckles, not looking the slightest bit re-morseful. "Even after that."

"And what was your answer?" Without meaning to, I hold my breath.

Irving steps closer, his eyes on mine. His voice soft, he says, "I declined."

"Very well." I look away.

"I won't swear my allegiance to a magical crea-ture." He turns me so I have no choice but to face him. "But I'll swear it to you."

My muscles weaken, but I shake my head. "Don't tease about something like that."

His hand strays to my cheek, and he brushes back a loose strand of hair. I freeze under his touch, uncom-fortable by how strongly his nearness affects me. It's simply an attraction, not based on true feelings, but it's undeniably potent.

"I meant what I said, Audette. I'm going to prove myself, whether you let me kneel before you now or not."

"That's all good and fine, but I have a wizard to track down. If you're not with us, I don't have time for you right now."

His thumb brushes my jaw, and his eyes soften. "I didn't say I wasn't going to help you. I said I wasn't joining the Order."

"Explain."

"I'm not going anywhere. If this is where you'll be, this is where I'll be as well."

"And you'll help?"

He nods, and his hand drifts from my face. His fingers brush over the back of my neck, and the skin, bare with my hair up, tingles at his touch.

"You're selling yourself out as a knight for hire?" I say, attempting to keep the moment light. "Isn't that below your station?"

Irving leans forward, smelling of countryside and soap. "Not when you're my prize." As he says the words, his breath brushes against my lips.

"I'm no man's prize," I murmur, but, despite the words, I give in.

Rising to my toes, I wrap my arms around his neck. Expecting Irving will need no further invitation, I close my eyes, my body humming with anticipation. He presses a quick kiss to the tip of my nose.

And nothing more.

My eyes fly open, and I find his face alight with mischief.

"I'm glad we had this talk," he says, pulling away. "Now I have things to attend to back at the castle."

"I take it back." I gape at him, and heat rises to my cheeks. "You're not very good at this at all."

In one smooth move, his arm circles my back, and he yanks me roughly against him. My hands fly to his shoulders, and I suck in a surprised breath.

"You're forgetting the most important rule in this game," he says, his voice purposely rough and low with the intent to drive me mad.

Trying not to stare at his lips, I ask, "And what's that?"

Just as abruptly as he pulled me to him, he steps away, grinning. "Always leave them wanting more."

With an exaggerated bow and another wink, he strides off, leaving me breathless, flustered, and more than a little irritated.

CHAPTER TEN

"I'm going to speak with Grace today," I say over a proper breakfast of tea and scones.

Barowalt looks up from his meal. "Javid's wife?"

"Edlund has looked into the dragon attacks, and I was hoping to glean more information from her since I believe it's related. She said he sent a band of knights to look into the reports."

Keven looks up. "I'll go with you, speak with the knights, see if there's anything that seemed too trivial to mention."

Barowalt chooses another sausage from the platter. "I'm not worried about Grace as much, but be subtle when speaking with the king's men. Rumors spread quickly through the knights' hall."

"I'll go with him," Rogert says. "I'd like to make

use of a proper practice yard."

The men of the Order have been restless since we returned. All are eager for something to fight, but Rogert is especially so. He spent yesterday prowling the courtyard, sparring with whoever was available, readying himself for a battle.

The first step will take patience. We still don't know what we're up against.

When we first returned from Asher's estate, I spent hours in the library, scouring the shelves for information on both wizards and magical creatures. I found nothing. Most of our family's books are on literature and art. And since I wasn't looking for a guide on the craft of topiary dragon sculpting, I had no luck.

"That's fine," I say, "but I'll likely be most of the afternoon. Grace said the castle's library is fairly large, and I'd like to do some research while I'm there."

"What about you Hallgrave? Rafe?" Barowalt asks.

"I'd rather stay here," Rafe says, a somewhat embarrassed smile on his face.

Pleasantly stuffed, I push my plate aside. "Who are you avoiding?"

The handsome knight grins, looking particularly guilty. "One of the queen's ladies' maids."

I roll my eyes, but I can't quite hide my smile. "You're all incorrigible." Then I glance at Hallgrave and Keven. "Except you two, of course."

SHARI L. TAPSCOTT

"Stuffy and Boring" —Rogert nods to Keven and then Hallgrave in turn— "Wouldn't know how to have a good time if it fell from the sky and struck them on the heads."

"I've had my share of good times," Hallgrave says, his voice cryptic. "I simply know how to hold my tongue about it."

This starts a round of banter between the knights and Barowalt, and I only shake my head, pretending to ignore them. They can brag in front of me, but if I were to tell them of the few stolen kisses I've had, there would be blood on my hands.

Barowalt's in the middle of a funny story about a noble's daughter from Lenrook when Milly walks into the room. He trails off, clears his throat, and turns his full attention to his plate.

She narrows her eyes at him, obviously having heard part of his tale on her way through the hall. The knights and I exchange looks, and I bite my cheeks so I won't laugh at how awkward the moment is between them.

"Will you come with us to the castle?" I ask her, hoping to ease the tension. "I'm going to visit their library. I was hoping Grace might show us around."

"That sounds thrilling," Milly says, but it's obvious that she thinks it will be anything but.

"You don't have to come if you don't want to. Do

114

whatever you like." I motion out the window. "It's a lovely day. You could paint."

Milly scrunches her mouth to the side, thinking. Finally, she says, "I'll go with you, maybe sketch in the castle gardens for a bit." She glances briefly at Barowalt and then smirks at Rogert. "Or maybe I'll sketch the knights in the practice yard."

Rogert, knowing she's only trying to get under Barowalt's skin, grins, leering at Milly in the nicest of ways.

Barowalt watches the exchange, unimpressed. "Actually, Milly, I was hoping you might accompany me today. I'm riding to the valley to see if I can find any clues to the attack in the light of day."

Milly, all four knights, and I turn our attention to Barowalt, surprised. He shifts, looking uncomfortable.

"Well?" Barowalt says, his voice gruff.

"Yes." Milly's answer is too quick, and now she shrugs. "I suppose. If you want me to."

She's trying to hold back a smile, hoping she doesn't look too eager, but it shines in her eyes.

"Very well." Barowalt stands. "I'll saddle our horses. Meet me in the stable when you're finished with your breakfast."

The moment he leaves the hall, she grins, looking triumphant.

Rogert rolls his eyes. "And I thought you were

finally falling for me."

She pats the knight's arm, sympathetic. "I hope you won't take it too hard."

I laugh as she stuffs a scone in her mouth and rushes upstairs to her chambers to prepare herself.

"I'm ready whenever you're finished," I tell Keven and Rogert.

They finish their breakfast, and we're at the castle within an hour.

"Audette," Grace says when she greets me. "What a pleasant surprise."

The duchess carries a sketchpad under her arm, and there's a smudge of charcoal on her cheek.

"Do you sketch?" I ask, nodding to the book.

"I keep a nature journal." She taps the leather cover. "My sketches aren't as polished as Javid's, but I enjoy it nonetheless." Grace leads me through the halls. "Would you like tea? Are you hungry?"

"I've just eaten. Actually, I was hoping you'd take me on a tour of the library. Perhaps help me with a little historical research?"

Looking giddy at the prospect, Grace hurries down the hall. "I would love to. Besides Javid, I've found very few people here who are interested in history or the sciences."

I laugh in agreement. "My family's library ended up being filled with literature and books on art."

"Nothing wrong with that, of course," Grace says as she leads me up a grand flight of stairs. "But I believe it's better to have a more rounded education."

She may be slightly more passionate on the subject than I am, but with that enthusiasm, I'm sure we'll find what I'm looking for if it's there to be found. We reach the library, and I step through the doors, feeling hopeful. Though not large by some standards, the room is twice the size of our villa's.

Grace sets her sketchbook and charcoals on a nearby table that's overflowing with books and papers. She glances at me, embarrassed. "I've been meaning to clean it off. I'm afraid I've become lax when it comes to the organization of study materials since I married Javid."

She stacks the loose papers, nudges a few books into a group, and then turns, obviously not overly concerned about the mess.

"Are you looking for something in particular?" She leads me to a wall shelf so tall, a sliding ladder has been built into it so a person can reach the top. She climbs the ladder and pushes herself down the row. "Are you still researching dragons?"

I can't help but shake my head at the juxtaposition that is Grace. She's as poised and proper as her name would imply, but she moves through the shelves and books with the knowledge of a fussy old master librarian. She's pretty, in a quiet way, rather than shockingly beautiful like Giselle is, but she smiles with her whole face, and that makes her even lovelier.

"Perhaps." I chew my lip, wondering how much to share. "But maybe something more along the lines of wizards conjuring something about the size of a dragon...something like a shadow."

"That's rather specific." Grace, still perched on the ladder, looks over her shoulder. "If you're worried about the dragon sightings down south, I don't think you need to be concerned."

"No, it's not just that. There's something else."

Grace studies me for a moment and glances about the library as if reassuring herself we're alone. With bright, curious, eyes, she stage-whispers, "This is going to sound ridiculous, but does this have something to do with the Order of Lingard?"

I'm dumbfounded—positively knock-me-over-with-a-feather, gobsmacked. My mouth opens, but no words come out. I don't even know what I was planning to say.

Once I recover, I ask, "How do you know about the Order?"

She climbs down the ladder, tosses her long almost-blond braid over her shoulder, and smiles like a child who just discovered she gets the last slice of cake. "When I was younger—trapped in the largest library in Elden but eager to see more of the world, I studied the other kingdoms. I read anything and everything I could get my hands on. Books, scrolls, maps...anything."

"But there shouldn't be..." I set my hands on my hips, my finger tapping in a sporadic rhythm against my gown. "Where did you hear of the Order? And what do you know?"

"I don't remember, to tell you the truth." She gives me an apologetic smile. "And I don't know much, only that the Order was founded to protect magical beings. Honestly, I didn't believe its existence until your unusually handsome, valiant knights came striding into the castle when you arrived. It triggered the memory, and I couldn't help but wonder...and then you start asking about dragons..."

She grins, almost beside herself with glee that one of her childhood fairy tales has come true.

I could tell her the whole thing is a myth, but I don't want to, and I have a feeling Grace could be very helpful in figuring out what it is we're dealing with.

Just like she did moments ago, I glance about the room. Then, quietly, I say, "Unicorns. Not all magical beings—just them."

"Unicorns?" Grace's smile is tempered with a wary expression as if she's not quite sure if I'm teasing her or not.

You can't deny the existence of dragons—they burned down half of Elden in the Dragon Wars not ten years ago. Fairies, though rarely seen, are numerous, as are griffins and gimlies. Mermaids, pixies, kelpies, phoenixes...all are creatures people know well, even if they've never seen one in person.

But unicorns?

They don't actually exist outside tapestries, or, if they did, they died off hundreds of years ago. Everyone knows that.

Everyone except for the small order of knights from Brookraven—and apparently whoever wrote the book Grace stumbled onto when she was a child.

I nod. "Unicorns."

She looks like she wants to believe me, but she just can't. "Have you seen one?"

"They're beautiful beyond description—the first time you lay eyes on them, you almost forget to breathe. They're sleek and gentle and majestic...but they have the mental capacity of a baby bird."

Grace blinks at that and then laughs.

"There's never been a magical creature so ill-equipped to defend itself," I continue. "Like rabbits, they're extremely good at hiding, but that's about the extent of it."

"But if they're magical..." Grace narrows her eyes, thinking. I'm still not sure if she believes me, but she seems happy to ponder the idea of it, even if it's only hypothetical. "Can't they use the magic for protection?"

I shake my head. "It can be used to fortify others, but they can't seem to use it to protect themselves."

Her eyes sharpen. "What do you mean 'fortify?'"

"There's a reason our knights are as large and strong as they are—they grew up around unicorn magic."

"So it's true," she whispers.

"It's true." My smile drops away as I glance at wall after wall of books. I'll never find anything on my own. "And I think you can help us."

CHAPTER ELEVEN

With half a dozen heavy, dusty volumes in my arms, I step into the castle's courtyard. Deep in conversation, Grace and I discuss what we've learned in our studies so far...which, sadly, isn't much. Grace suggested we look up information on unicorns first—find natural predators, facts on how dark wizards use unicorn magic, and so on—and go from there. Most of what we found seems like it's based more on fancy and myths, but it's worth going through.

The sky is dusky. I stayed far longer than I meant to. Milly is likely at the villa, impatiently waiting for me to return so she can tell me about her day with Barowalt—as long as my brother didn't do something foolish and mess it all up. But even then, Milly will be waiting to give me an earful.

As Grace talks, I glance around the courtyard. I'm looking for Irving, though I wouldn't admit it to a soul. He's here, somewhere. After our almost-kiss, I didn't feel the need to invite him to take a room in the villa, an idea I had been toying with on the way back from Asher's estate. Let him stay here in Aunt Camilla's hall.

Still, I wouldn't mind seeing him. Even if it's just to snub him—especially to snub him. It would serve him right.

"I'll see if I can find anything at all that seems like it might be similar to the reports in the so-called dragon attacks," Grace says.

I shake my head. "The more I think about it, the more I wonder if it is completely unrelated. The two attacks were a month ago. You're probably right—it was likely thieves robbing from farmers with wild imaginations."

"Not two." Grace stops. "There was a third. We learned of it yesterday. I assumed you'd heard."

"When was the attack?"

"The day before you arrived, in Bracken."

Shifting the books in my arms, I say, "Was it the same? Dark shadow? Loss of livestock?"

She nods.

"It doesn't make sense, though. If the blessing was attacked by a wizard, and I'm almost positive that it was, why would he waste his time terrorizing villages?"

I muse out loud. "Why bother?"

Grace shakes her head, and then she pauses. "Let's go there tomorrow."

"Go there?"

"Yes, let's go to Bracken, see what we can find out. We'll stay the night in Constelita—it's not far from there, and it has the largest library in Ptarma." She grows animated. "Javid was just saying he wanted to go down for a few days, and there's a master scholar there who I would love to speak with about the attacks. Bring your brother and some of your knights along. No one will think it's anything more than a holiday."

Since we have no other leads, I nod. "All right. I'll talk to Barowalt and see what he thinks."

To the right of the courtyard, where the practice yard is located, a loud cheer rings through the warm evening.

I motion toward the ruckus. "I need to collect my men."

The practice yard is lit with a combination of torches and burning urns, and the area is bright despite the darkening sky. At least thirty knights have gathered around the center, watching a match.

When Grace sees who's fighting, she makes a scoffing noise in the back of her throat.

Giselle faces off against Rogert, a sword in her hand. She wears armor, but not only is it the most worthless design I've ever seen, but the most scandalous. The ornate steel breastplate barely covers her chest but it manages to push it to normally unattainable heights. Her midriff is bare. A length of chain mail hangs from her hips, and it falls just low enough it covers the most critical areas. Her legs are fully visible except for the swath of gauzy, translucent skirt that falls to her ankles.

I cross my arms and watch the shameful display with disgust. "I know when I fight, I like to display the areas of my anatomy that are most vulnerable."

Grace snorts, a most unladylike sound. "Apparently she had the armor custom-made in Waldren—I know because she's told us. On several occasions. According to her, it's all the rage right now."

Rogert ducks an attack, grinning. She lunges, and—the idiot—he purposely puts himself in the way. He stumbles and falls, but it's painfully obvious to me he's let her win.

Grace and I exchange goodbyes, and I shoulder through the crowd, ignoring several surprised proclamations of "Oh, Princess, good evening" and "Your Highness, you don't want to get too close…" until I find Keven. My golden knight stands nearby, his arms crossed, a somewhat disgusted look on his face. It makes me like him all the more.

"I see Rogert's making a spectacle of himself," I

say.

Keven looks down and gives me a wry smile. "He held out for several rounds, but, eventually, he couldn't help himself. He scampered out there like an eager puppy."

I wrinkle my nose. "Is she any good?"

Obviously, she's not against our knights, but that's to be expected.

"She's clever with the art of distraction," Keven answers. "It's working in her favor."

Rogert stands and pretends to limp away, hamming it up for the crowd. Giselle laughs. With her hands on her hips and her legs spread in a strong pose, she scans the crowd. "Who's next?"

Across from us, the crowd shifts. Curious to see what's causing the commotion, Irving wanders to the inner circle. Then, looking wary as soon as he spots Giselle, he immediately turns away. He's not fast enough, though.

As he retreats, Giselle turns. "Prince Irving!"

He freezes, and his shoulders go tense.

"Oh, come now," she coos. "A strong, capable man like you isn't afraid to fight me." She swirls her sword's point in the dirt as she says it, playing innocent and coy.

Trapped, Irving turns and dons a fake smile. "I don't spar with ladies."

She saunters toward him, her hips swaying. "That's not what I've heard."

And that's all it takes for the once-dormant, jealous beast to rear its head yet again. I clench my hands around the books in my arms.

Giselle trails the tip of her sword down Irving's chest, playful. He looks irritated, not in the mood, but the crowd already cheers him on.

"Hold these." I shove my armful of books against Keven's chest.

With a free hand, Keven pulls me back. "Oh no you don't."

I turn back, glaring. "You don't think I can beat her?"

My knight leans close, nearly whispering in my ear. "One, you're in a gown. Two, you don't have your sword. Three, the knights of the Ptarmish court don't need to know that the princess of Brookraven fights with the ease of an assassin."

He's right.

I cross my arms, letting this play out as it will. Irving continues to shake his head, refusing in his good-natured way. And then the knights begin to boo him. He glances around, visibly wavering.

Without asking for permission, I yank a sword from the sheath belonging to the man on my right and stride into the circle, ignoring Keven's hissed demands

SHARI L. TAPSCOTT

ordering me to stay put.

"I'll fight you, Giselle." I swing the sword back and forth. "It looks like fun. How hard can it be?"

Giselle turns slowly and laughs. "Oh, Princess, you don't want to fight me."

"I do." I nod as that anger in my chest grows. "I really do."

Irving's eyes transfer to me, and he begins to shake his head, asking me to back down.

"All right." Giselle laughs and nods to the blade in my hand. "Be careful not to hurt yourself with that."

The princess prepares herself and nods me forward. I circle her, sinking into my familiar stance.

She narrows her eyes. "Watched your knights a few times, have you?"

"A few times."

She lunges, but I avoid her, keeping my movements purposely slow and unpracticed. She swings again, and I block her—something I don't dare try against our knights. Far stronger than Giselle is, I push her back, and she stumbles to regain her balance. Her eyes widen with surprise but then narrow in determination.

No longer playing nice, she attacks, her sword much too high.

"That's not a smart move," I say as I evade her. "If we were in an actual battle, I could easily stab your

128

unprotected stomach."

She growls, and I circle behind her. Unlike with Rogert, I won't go as far as to kick her in the back of the knees. For once, I'm in a fight against a fair opponent. Well, fair-sized.

Without distraction working in her favor, she takes sloppy, poorly planned attacks. I continue to block her, letting her tire herself out. After a few minutes, she begins to pant. Sweat glistens on her forehead.

Just as I'm about to knock her to the ground and call it an evening, I glance at Irving. He watches us, his mouth open in shock, clearly impressed. Our eyes meet, and something passes between us, something smoldering.

With my attention on the prince, Giselle again attacks. As I'm ducking out of the way, half-distracted but not terribly concerned about it, the princess grasps a handful of my hair and yanks down.

Shrieking in pain and shock, I fall to my knees in front of her. Around us, the crowd groans and laughs. As Giselle gloats over her victory, she makes the mistake of letting go of my hair.

Livid, not caring if the world knows I've trained since I was old enough to walk, I thrust my head as hard as I can into her stomach and send her backward. As she falls, I twist the sword from her grasp. Circling low and leaping to my feet—which is no easy task with my skirts tangling around my legs—I step over her and hold the point of the sword at her rapidly rising and falling chest.

The courtyard goes silent. I glance at Keven. His face is hard, and I know I'm about to get a lecture, but when I glance Rogert's way, he grins and silently claps his hands.

Giselle blinks at me. I remove the sword and offer my hand, smiling brightly like this was a fun, friendly match—one where the princess didn't pull my hair and I didn't knock her on her scantily clad hind-end.

Once Giselle's on her feet, she brushes herself off. "You're good, Princess."

Feeling dozens of eyes on me, I shrug, trying to look nonchalant. "You too."

Since I'm on display anyway, I might as well make an exit to remember. I stride back to the knight I borrowed the sword from and toss the blade to him. "Thanks."

He catches it at the hilt, a smile spreading across his face. Knowing Keven and Rogert will follow, I stride through the parting crowd, not bothering to look back.

Once I'm to the stables and momentarily alone, I let out a low groan and rub my scalp. Having your hair pulled hurts.

"That was the single most attractive thing I've

seen in my life."

I jump and then turn toward Irving, giving him a wry smile. He must have slipped away right after I finished the match, and now he's leaning against a beam, smirking.

Remembering the look we shared during the match, I grow warm. "You've never seen a girl use a sword?"

With that smile fixed on his face, he pushes away from the beam and strides toward me. He steps too close, infringing on more than a little of my personal space. Teasing, he says, "Yes, but I've never had two physically fight over me before."

Laughing, now feeling foolish, I shove him away. "Don't flatter yourself. I just wanted to wipe that smug look off Giselle's face."

Hoping he'll follow—but trying to appear as if I'm not hoping he'll follow, I stride down the aisles, looking for my horse.

"And you succeeded, darling." Irving steps in front of me, blocking my path. "Now make my evening and tell me you have a set of armor just like hers. The match would have been far more interesting if you'd worn some."

Rolling my eyes, I push past him. "You're a pig."

He catches me by the arm and swings me to his chest. "You know I'm teasing." He tilts his head and scrunches his nose. "Mostly."

Not moving away, but pretending to ignore him, I brush dirt from my sleeve.

The prince's hands find my waist, and he draws me closer. I sink into him but drop my hands to my sides, hoping that not touching him will drive him mad.

"Where were you all day?" he asks.

A mare whinnies and sticks her muzzle over her stall door.

Irving somehow frowns and smiles at her at the same time. "Do you mind?" he says to the horse. "A little privacy?"

Laughing, I say, "I was with Grace in the library."

"All day? I didn't know you were so scholarly." He rubs circles at my side with his thumb, and it's very distracting. "I rather missed you sending barbed compliments at me all day."

"If Barowalt agrees, we're going to Bracken tomorrow to investigate the latest attack, and then we'll stay at an inn in Constelita."

He trails a finger up my spine, making me shiver. "Is that an invitation?"

"Of course not." Giving in, I set my fingertips on his chest. "But if you, for some reason, decide to take a sightseeing tour to southern Ptarma tomorrow and we happen to bump into each other...I wouldn't mind that much."

He makes a low sound in the back of his throat, and my knees soften. He leans forward, almost brushing his lips over the corner of my mouth, toying with me again.

I tilt my head to look up at him. "My knights were right on my heels."

"A shame," he murmurs. "I was hoping to finish what we started yesterday. Perhaps we'll hide from them? Find a dark corner? I'm sure the horses wouldn't mind."

"So romantic."

"I could be." His voice drops the playful tone, and he looks at me with such intensity, the butterflies in my stomach riot. "I'll be whatever you want."

My heart hammers, and I'm stabbed with fear, remembering again what Milly said about love.

Ignoring the way he's looking at me, ignoring the way he makes me feel, I stand on my toes and press a fast kiss to his nose.

"I'm glad we had this talk." Like a coward, I twist out of his arms. "But now I have things to attend to."

He gives me a knowing smile, seeing my retreat for what it is. "Until tomorrow."

I glance over my shoulder, running off to who-knows-where. "If you happen to go south, and if we happen to bump into you."

Leaning against a stable door, his eyes locked on mine, he says, "You will."

***

I meet Keven and Rogert on my way out of the stable.

Immediately, Rogert pulls me into an embrace. "The classic backward head-butt." His face is buried in my hair, and his voice is muffled. "I couldn't be prouder."

A smile tugs at my lips, but I try to tone it down before I turn to Keven.

"Thank you for holding the books," I say to the blond knight after I step away from Rogert.

Ever the gentleman, Keven doesn't shove them back into my arms. "And now you know why Barowalt insists you pin your hair up when you fight."

"You don't." I gently tug a strand of his blond locks.

Cracking a smile, he says, "Men don't usually resort to pulling each other's hair."

Rogert nods, solemn. "Girls are vicious."

"Do you think Barowalt will be too upset with me?" I ask.

"No," Keven says, and then a rare grin lights his face. "But he would have been if you hadn't won."

***

When we arrive back at the villa, Milly is waiting, just as I suspected she would be. She corners me the moment I walk through the front. "Audette! We had the most amazing—" She stops, aghast. "What happened to you?"

My gown is filthy, covered in dirt from when I fell to the ground. I frown at it. "The Princess de Bellany and I had a duel."

Milly blinks at me, perplexed. "I'm sorry?"

I motion for her to follow me to my chambers. "Apparently Kent has yet to return from his hunting trip, and Giselle was bored. She was fighting with the knights, and I challenged her."

With a hand over her eyes in an attempt to block the image out, Milly groans. "In front of how many people?"

A maid passes us in the halls, and I stop her. "Would you have a bath brought up for me?"

"Of course, Your Highness." She curtsies and hurries off.

I turn back to Milly. "Most of Edlund's knights."

"Audette!" Horrified, Milly sinks onto a settee in my room as soon as we walk through the doors.

As I wait for my bath to be brought up, I peer at my reflection in the mirror. Tilting my head, I gently lift my hair to examine the tender spot on my skull.

"What are you doing?" Milly demands.

"Giselle nearly ripped half of my hair from my head."

Milly gasps. "Is it all still there?"

"Yes." I frown. "It seems to be."

Not too much later, there's a knock at the door. I usher the servants in. One by one, they pour steaming water into the metal tub behind the folding room separator. Once they're gone, I strip out of my gown and sink into the almost scalding water.

I sigh loud enough that Milly hears me.

"Better?" she calls from the other side of the partition, her voice edgy and prim.

"Much." I lie back and listen to a night bird singing from the ledge of my balcony. "You never know, Milly. You mock me now, but someday, I just might save your life."

"More like you'll be the death of me."

I grin and decide it's time to change the subject. "We're going on a holiday tomorrow."

"We are?" Though I can't see her, I can tell by her voice that her face lights up. "Where are we going?"

Now that I've sat in the tub for a few moments, the water is only pleasantly hot. I browse through oils a maid left on the small table next to me, lifting the bottle stoppers and sniffing each of them. The orange is nice, but the lavender is overwhelming. I pause after smelling a citrus and baymint blend and eventually pour a little into the tub. When mixed with the heat of the water, the oils infuse the air. I breathe them in and sink down a little more, letting the water rise to my chin.

"Constelita," I say.

I leave out the part where we'll check into Bracken to see if we can find clues on the shadowed dragon creature.

Milly will find that out soon enough.

"Have we been there before?" she asks.

"I have." I swirl my hand at the surface of the water. "But it was years ago, before your parents allowed you to travel with us for extended lengths of time."

Milly's been my lady-in-waiting for over five years now, but even before that, we were nearly inseparable anyway. Though the title has fallen out of popularity in many of the kingdoms, our family still favors a princess choosing one good friend to keep close as a companion once she turns fifteen. And a friend is what Milly is—not a lady's maid, not a servant. Her family ranks high in Brookraven's nobility. Her father sits with my uncle right now, governing the kingdom in Barowalt's absence. It's a huge honor to be chosen, and someday the title alone could land her a very prestigious marriage.

If she doesn't end up marrying my brother and becoming queen, that is.

"How was your afternoon with Barowalt?" I ask.

Milly launches into a story, one filled with longing

glances and brushed hands, and I close my eyes, content to listen without adding much. Milly's stories are more narrative than conversational.

When the water is too cold to linger any longer, I shoo Milly out of the room and crawl into bed. With memories of the conversation with Irving repeating over and over in my head, I find sleep.

CHAPTER TWELVE

A storm comes with the morning. The weather is cool and drizzly, not unpleasant but a vast difference from the sunshine we've grown accustomed to.

"It will rain on and off for months now." Grace peers out the window of the carriage, and then she sits back, looking sullen.

Javid takes his wife's hand and teases, "If you grow too tired of it, we'll sail to Waldren for the winter."

Grace gives him an indulgent smile. "No matter how charming you think you are, there's no captain you'll convince to sail in the winter season."

"We were able to find someone to sail us," I say, her words making me nervous.

"Some will risk it in late autumn, but next week marks the beginning of winter." She shakes her head.

SHARI L. TAPSCOTT

"The ships in the harbor won't sail again until spring. With the squalls at sea this time of year, it's too dangerous."

I glance at Barowalt, who's seated next to Javid. He, too, looks pensive, but when our eyes meet, he subtly shakes his head, telling me not to worry about it.

Milly, who sits beside me, smiles. "I quite like the idea of being trapped on the island."

Rafe, the sixth member of our party, smiles back at her, obviously agreeing with the statement. Barowalt chose the handsome brown-haired knight to accompany us this morning, leaving Hallgrave to scour the countryside for more clues about the attack. Keven is in charge at the villa with Rogert acting as his second. Glad to be doing something productive, Rafe was happy to join us.

Keven, on the other hand, wasn't so happy, even though he was left in charge. Knowing him as I do, he believes being left behind is a punishment for letting me fight with Giselle yesterday—knowing Barowalt, it might be.

My brother wasn't impressed, more because the rumors of my prowess are sure to spread like wildfire.

I don't see what the problem is, however. What's so wrong with a princess who can fight? My cousin Pippa is renowned for her skill with a bow. What's the difference?

140

The soft rain continues to patter on the roof of the carriage, stopping only once we grow near Bracken. I step from the carriage, grateful the storm let up for the time being. Above us, gray clouds continue to churn, reminding me the rain could begin again at any moment.

The village is rural and small. Farms lie on the outskirts. In the center, where we are now, there's an assortment of quaint buildings. A stable stands next to a smithy, and there's a tiny inn and tavern, a sundry, and butcher's shop.

I assume from the animal pens and vegetable patches that the rest are houses.

A few children play outside, and a couple chats under a covered doorway, but most of the villagers seem to have gone inside to stay dry. I don't blame them. The dirt streets have turned to mud, and it squelches under my boots. Thankfully, I wore a dark copper gown today.

"Where do we begin?" I ask.

"The tavern," Javid immediately answers. My cousin wears an eternal grin, but it grows even brighter now. "If you're looking for gossip—no matter where you find yourself—you always start at the tavern."

Javid's taller than willowy Grace, but not by much. Instead of offering his wife his arm, he takes her hand and leads her toward the building. The gesture is so

141

sweet, so genuine, it causes a dull ache in my chest.

Milly strategically places herself next to Barowalt and then feigns surprise when he offers to escort her. I shake my head at her, but she only smiles over her shoulder.

Rafe steps next to me and extends his elbow. "Your Highness?"

Smiling at the knight, I slip my hand through his arm. For as long as I can remember, Rafe's been around, training for the Order, but I don't know him as well as Keven or even Rogert since Barowalt doesn't usually send him as a guard when I go places. He's pleasant, though, even if he's a little too aware of how good-looking he is. As all the knights do, he towers over me, the epitome of strength and masculinity.

When we walk into the tavern, more than a few people stop and stare. Still early, there aren't many patrons in the establishment, but there are more than there would be if it weren't a gloomy, damp day.

A barmaid pauses in her task, almost spilling ale over the old man she's in the middle of serving. A couple of farmers glance over as well. Javid smiles at them all and leads us to a table. Bracken's too small a village to have much allure to him, and I doubt he's set foot in this particular tavern before, but he moves as if it's his favorite haunt.

Soon, the locals go back to their conversations

and food, casting only occasional glances our way instead of gaping outright.

Chilled, I request tea, and Milly orders heated cider. Javid and Grace ask for a hot black drink made from dried brown beans from Waldren that I've never heard of. Barowalt and Rafe end up ordering it as well.

I take a sip of Barowalt's when it arrives but wrinkle my nose in disgust. "It's bitter."

Javid breathes in the steam rising from the cup, looking near blissful. "It's divine."

Grace nods in agreement with Javid and sips hers. "It grows on you."

Barowalt catches a barmaid after she finishes her sweep of the room. Looking almost beside herself with joy, the girl hurries over the moment Barowalt lifts his hand to get her attention.

Next to me, Milly takes a sip of her cider, doing her best to ignore the barmaid.

"We're passing through," Barowalt says, "and we've heard rumors of a dragon in this area. Is there any truth to this?"

The girl's eyes shift about the room, and she leans in close. "Yes, my lord. Old Farmer Brig lost eight pigs a few days ago."

Barowalt nods, encouraging her to continue. "Did anyone see anything?"

She shrugs, helpless. "Brig said he saw a huge,

dark creature...but it was late." She glances around again and lowers her voice. "And he'd had several drinks that night."

"Is this the first time something like this has happened around here?" Javid asks, leaning forward to join the conversation.

The girl nods. "Yes. We've never even seen any of the wolves that live in the forests of the north."

"Where does the farmer live?" Javid asks.

"If you look toward the right when you leave the tavern, his cottage is the one at the top of the hill."

A customer hollers for her from across the room.

"Thank you," Barowalt says, dismissing her.

She bobs a curtsy, flashes him a shy smile, and rushes off.

"I suppose we're going to speak with the farmer?" Milly asks, unimpressed with both our mission and the tiny village.

Barowalt takes his first drink from the cup in front of him. He wrinkles his nose at the dark beverage, gives it a suspicious look, and then drains the rest of it.

I cringe. How is he able to stomach it?

As soon as he sets the cup down, my brother rises, ready to leave even though we've just arrived.

After taking a few hasty sips of my tea, I rise as well. It's begun to rain again. Milly groans as we leave the dry safety of the tavern and flips her cloak's hood over her hair.

The farmer's cottage is too close to bother with saddling the horses, but too far to walk in the rain. Apparently not noticing the muck and puddles, Barowalt strides up the hill. Milly frowns. Her pretty hazel eyes flash with irritation, but she scurries off after him.

Grace and Javid don't seem to notice the rain at all. Once we're free of the village, they stop at a small cow pond and begin to speak animatedly about some creature or plant or whatever it is the scholarly types find fascinating.

By the time we reach the cottage, the bottom of my skirt and my boots are filthy. Small bits of grass and weeds cling to the saturated fabric. Hopefully there will be a good laundry service in Constelita.

After leaving the cow pond behind, Grace and Javid catch up to us just as Barowalt knocks on the door. We wait several moments, but there's no answer. Looking put out, Barowalt knocks again.

This time, after a few minutes, an elderly farmer answers the door. Looking like he hasn't used a comb in ages, his disheveled hair lies this way and that, sticking straight up in some places. The tunic he wears is wrinkled and smudged—I'm not sure if he's changed it in days, and he reeks of alcohol.

The farmer's red-rimmed eyes travel over us, his expression wary and guarded. Instead of offering a greeting, he simply stands there, waiting for us to divulge what we're doing on his doorstep.

"Sir," Barowalt says, slipping into the pleasant persona he rarely wears. "We're investigating the livestock attacks, and we've heard of the tragedy that recently befell your farm."

The man's eyes flicker over us, his brow wrinkling with distrust. "The king already sent a band of knights to question me."

Grace pulls a journal and charcoal from the folds of her cloak. Looking terribly official, she steps forward. "And we're here to follow up."

"Is that right?" Anger flashes over the man's face. "Even after the leader of the band kindly informed me that I likely left the gate open and my pigs were not eaten but ran off themselves? That it wasn't a beast I saw, but the clouded clarity of a drunken stupor?"

I'm not certain he isn't drunk right now, in all honesty.

Grace makes sympathetic noises. "We're here because we do believe you. I know the entire ordeal has been trying for you—"

"It was the stuff of nightmares." The man opens the door wider and holds out a quivering hand for us to study. "I've had the shakes ever since."

I'm still holding onto my drunk theory.

"Well, of course you have," Grace says, her

expression genuine and concerned. "Perhaps, if it wouldn't be too taxing for you, you could tell us, in your own words, what happened?"

The man, again, looks at our large group with distrust.

"If it's all right with you," Barowalt says, "we'll take a look around out here."

Liking that better, the man nods and only Javid and Grace go inside the cottage. Barowalt, Milly, Rafe, and I walk around a lush herb garden toward the animal pens in the back. A few cows graze at one end of a fenced pasture, and a small herd of sheep stay at the other. Behind a gate that stands carelessly ajar, the pigpens are empty.

Barowalt and Rafe stride into the enclosure, not sparing a thought for their fine boots. Together, they stare at the ground, thinking.

I don't see anything. The mud looks wallowed in, and the empty trough is crusted with the remains of several-day-old slop. Wrinkling my nose, I turn away. From what I can tell, there's no blood, no obvious signs of a struggle.

Personally, I can see why the knights would think the man imagined the whole ordeal. Except he's not the only one. Could news from the other villages have already spread to Bracken? Was the farmer hoping for attention—could he have purposely let his pigs loose?

And if so, why? Eight pigs is a hefty loss for a few brief moments of infamy.

When I turn to Milly to ask her what her thoughts are, I find her examining her cloak's embroidered hem, which is now smeared with mud. She's looking particularly put out.

The rain continues to fall, not in great torrents, but in a soft, persistent drizzle. The clouds have lowered, and they churn in the village below the hill, soft white wisps twining around buildings. There's something beautiful about it. Except for the patter of the rain, it's perfectly quiet, serene.

Movement catches my eye on the road. An older woman makes her way toward the cottage. Her cloak is made of brown cloth, and it's dark from the rain. Her skirt and blouse are cut in a simple peasant style, but they were obviously made with care.

When she notices us standing near the pig pens, she frowns and hurries forward.

"Good day," she calls when she gets close enough. Despite her pleasant words, she doesn't look overly happy to see us. "We've already been questioned if that's what you're here for."

Barowalt explains our business, keeping his expression as friendly as it was earlier.

Her shoulders sag when she sees no malice in our faces, and she glances at the cottage, worried. "He

148

hasn't been the same in the last few days—I've barely been able to pull him from bed."

"Are you his wife?" Milly asks the clean, respectable woman, incredulous.

The woman nods, pursing her lips at my friend. "He's a good man, a hard worker. Whatever it was that he saw—it caused this bout of melancholy." She motions to the house. "You might not believe him, but I tell you—he saw something that night."

"Where were you?" I ask, hoping to keep my voice kind.

"I'm the midwife," she answers. "I was helping with a complicated birth." She lowers her voice. "The attack happened just before I arrived home."

A chill runs through me at the thought of this woman walking back from the village as the creature—dragon, wizard, whatever it may be—was roaming about.

Javid, Grace, and the farmer step out of the front door. The man's eyes are wild, and as he speaks, he waves his hands back and forth.

Worry shadows the woman's face. She turns to us, lowering her voice. "He's a respected man in the village, but no one believes him. Please don't make the same mistake. Whatever it is—it's still out there somewhere."

CHAPTER THIRTEEN

More rain welcomes us to Constelita, the large port city not far from Bracken. The streets are bustling despite the weather, and we make our way through them slowly. Several peddlers set up booths in the main square, and people huddle under canvas canopies, sorting through vegetables and wares. The city is the trade hub of the massive island kingdom, and even today, in the beginning of the winter season, it's bustling. It takes forever to reach our destination.

The Ocean Ruby Inn is one of the largest I've seen since arriving in Ptarma. Towering over the streets, it's an impressive four-story building made from the familiar white Ptarmish stone. Wrought-iron balconies decorate the exterior, and trailing vines boasting brightly-colored flowers twist through the railings.

Our carriage stops in front of the covered entrance, allowing us to exit in the safety of the shelter. Javid gives instructions to the driver, and then the men escort us through the entryway. We exchange pleasantries with the armored guards as we pass, which they return before they again face forward, stoic and solemn.

The inn's exterior is nothing compared to the main foyer. A fountain bubbles in the middle of the room, and red and orange koi swim amongst the aquatic flowers. Above us, a glass skylight lets in light, though it's dim today due to the clouds. A massive stone fireplace covers an entire wall, but, even with the inclement weather, it's still too warm for a fire. Instead, the innkeepers have placed hundreds of candles on various-sized stands inside the fireplace. Their flames flicker, cheerful and warm.

Patrons lounge on settees and upholstered chairs, and maids scurry over the marbled floors, serving drinks and tending to requests.

At my side, Rafe whistles low. "Quite the inn."

Grace nods, her eyes lighting up. "It's a favorite of ours."

"We try to come to Constelita at least once a season," Javid adds, "to visit the library and sketch the marine life on the coast."

Milly says something, but I don't pay her any

attention.

There, lounging on the settee closest to the fountain, is Irving. His eyes are on me, and a small smile spreads over his face when our gazes meet.

Even though I knew he'd find us, my stomach still flutters.

"Fancy meeting you here," he calls as soon as the others in my party notice him. He rises and meets us.

Barowalt flashes me a look. His temporarily elevated opinion of Irving plummeted when the prince refused the invitation to join the Order.

"Irving," Javid says, his voice pleasantly surprised. "What brings you here?"

"How can you come to Ptarma and not visit Constelita?" Irving says, but his eyes flicker to mine, revealing his true motivation.

"Yes, how?" Barowalt says, his voice dry and unamused.

"Are you staying here as well?" Irving asks.

"We were—" Barowalt starts, but Milly jabs him in the side with her elbow.

"We are. What a pleasant surprise," she says and then turns to me. "Audette, weren't you just saying you were hoping to stretch your legs? I'm sure Irving would be happy to escort you while we secure rooms."

"I don't mind escorting the princess," Rafe begins, but he pauses when Milly shoots him a look of death.

"But...I should stay here for now...?"

She nods, approving, and turns back to Irving with her brows raised with expectation.

"Of course," Irving says, stepping to my side. "I'd be happy to."

Barowalt shakes his head, irritated, and makes his way toward the counter along the back. The others follow, and laughter shines in Grace and Javid's eyes as they pass.

"How was Bracken?" Irving asks when the others are out of earshot.

I accept his offered arm, and we dawdle through the foyer hall before we slip through a back door to the gardens. "We didn't find anything in the way of clues, and the farmer was too drunk to take much of what he said as truth."

"Do you think he's lying?" Irving asks.

After thinking about his question for a moment, I say, "No, but his report was of little help. Like the others, he claimed all he saw was a shadow creature."

"Shadows don't eat pigs."

I nod. "But perhaps the shadow was a distraction while something of flesh and blood spirited the creatures away?"

"Are you still thinking it may be a wizard?"

"It's what I'm leaning toward."

"What would a wizard want with livestock?" Irving

asks, and then he leans close. "And how would obtaining pigs help him exterminate Elden's unicorn population?"

I shake my head, frustrated. "They don't seem related, do they?"

"Maybe they're not."

And that is a possibility I'm going to have to consider. Just because the two events took place at the same time, doesn't necessarily mean they're linked. It could simply be a coincidence.

But I doubt it.

The rain has let up, and the moisture in the air is now a low-lying mist. We walk through the gardens, and it feels as if we've been transported to a kingdom in the clouds. The air is damp and cool, and the bright colors have lost their vibrancy in the expanse of gray.

"What are your plans for the evening?" Irving asks after several silent moments.

It begins to drizzle again, and I pull my hood up. "Grace is eager to visit the library. I'm assuming we'll be there until late."

We stop in front of a tall marble statue. Despite the rain, other couples stroll the garden. A man and woman, a little older than us, smile as they, too, pause by the statue.

"How do you like this weather?" the man asks us, shaking his head.

The woman beside him frowns at the sky. "I'm afraid they'll cancel the Ships' Return Festival."

Irving shifts closer. "We're not from around here. When is the festival?"

"It begins tonight," the man says. "Well, it was supposed to. Every year the Marquis of Cravet imports fireworks and sets them off over the harbor. There's a tournament the following day—jousting, archery, hand-to-hand. The usual."

"And during the tournament, there are wine tastings and baked goods competitions." The woman smiles. "In the evening, they roast dozens of boars."

Irving's interest is peaked. "Who can compete in the events?"

"Anyone who wants to. It's open to all." Friendly, the man takes my hand and bows. "I'm Lord Murry of Rewn." He straightens and motions to the woman next to him. "And this is my wife, Lamilla."

I curtsy, and, careful to keep my title to myself, say, "Audette."

Next to me, Irving nods. "Irving."

When he says his name, they both narrow their eyes slightly, probably placing him. The prince only smiles, not offering more.

"It's a shame the rains moved in before the festival," Murry says. "It usually starts later in the season."

Irving glances at the sky. "There are still a few

hours before dark. Perhaps it will clear out?"

Murry and Lamilla glance at the clouds, obviously not convinced.

After a few more minutes, we say our goodbyes and go inside to join the others. They aren't in the foyer hall, so they must have gone to the rooms.

"Go with me to the festival tonight," Irving says, pulling me from my quest to find my party.

"But I'm supposed to—"

Irving steps closer. "Let the others go. Take the night off."

I think about it—I really do, but my conscience gets the best of me. "I can't."

His smile dims just a little, but he nods, not surprised.

"But tomorrow night, I'm all yours," I continue. "If you want me."

His expression grows mischievous. "Oh, I want you. But tomorrow there won't be fireworks."

He's a little too close for a public room. Since I'm on the edge of not caring, I step away and walk to the closest window to stop myself from doing something I'll regret. The rain has started again, and water runs down the pane. "They'll likely postpone it anyway. Come with us instead."

"I'm not sure your brother is speaking to me at the moment."

"He'll be fine. He's simply not used to being told no."

Irving smiles and leans his back against the window. I can feel him studying me as I watch the drenched flowers sway in a light breeze.

"Will you come with us?" I finally ask.

He nods. "I will."

Several hours later, with the never-ending rain pattering on the carriage, the seven of us make our way to Ptarma's largest library. Barowalt isn't thrilled that Irving's joined us, but, so far, he's kept his opinions to himself.

The library is a grand structure, and it seems half of Constelita's population has sought it out, looking for entertainment since the festival's postponement. Grace and Javid hurry off, greeting stuffy-looking scholars as they go. The usuals are easy to spot. Many wear spectacles, and most of the masters are in long robes. They hunch over their work, oblivious to the downpour outside. But their most distinguishing mark is their utter and complete disgust with the riffraff who have invaded their territory.

But it's easy to see why so many people have chosen to spend their evening here. The entryway is built in an impressive solarium style with a domed glass roof. In the center of the room, a massive relief sculpture of the known world stretches over a shallow pool of water. A fountain system pushes water from the mountains, down the streams, and into rivers where it flows into the oceans and spills off the unknown edges. Several people crowd around the map, marveling at the work of art.

The area is dotted with more sculptures and an innumerable number of the flowering plants that Ptarma is so renowned for. Even a golden eldentimber tree, native to Elden alone, grows in the corner.

Those who are not studying the art or admiring the flora lounge on settees, conversing.

There are eight pairs of double-doors constructed of heavy wood to protect the precious books and scrolls within from the direct overhead daytime light and moisture in the grand entry hall. Placards above each announce the library's different locations—Hall of Natural Science, Hall of History, Hall of Astronomy, and so on.

After Javid and Grace have finished with their greetings, they lead our group through the doors leading to the Hall of Animals and Other Species. There aren't nearly as many people here, and the atmosphere is hushed.

"What are we looking for?" Irving's stage whisper causes two scholars near the entrance to turn scowls on our party.

I give the pair a friendly, apologetic smile, and

then turn on Irving and whisper, "Be quiet!"

Though he gives me a sheepish smile, he looks like he's about to laugh. "Sorry." He lowers his voice. "But what are we looking for?"

Grace has stopped by an aisle, and she's running her finger along the spines of a row of books, murmuring the titles as she goes. She pulls a book out, offers it to me without taking her eyes off the shelf, and continues her search.

I take the book from her and peer at the title: *Unicorns: Magical Creature or Myth?* She hands me two more: *History of the Magical Species,* and *Dragons, Griffins, and Other Magical Predators.*

Irving peers at the covers and relieves me of one. "Oh, nice. Pictures."

He grins before he settles into a nearby chair and begins to browse through the book. Barowalt almost rolls his eyes, not amused by Irving's particular brand of humor, but Grace and Javid exchange a look and bite back laughs.

Soon we all have a book, and we disperse throughout the room, finding places to sit. I browse through my book but find nothing to help us.

Irving leans over. "Take a look at this."

On the page, there's an artist's rendition of an enormous shadowed beast. I yank the book from him to take a closer look. A man stands at the bottom of the page, controlling the creature.

"Often confused for magical predators, conjured beings can wreak as much havoc," I read, "but instead of feeding off flesh, their magic feeds from fear." I look up. "Our creature is conjured."

Irving leans over. "This beast wouldn't need live-stock."

I look up, my eyes shining. "The wizard is drawing from the terror it's spreading. The livestock is simply the conduit."

Feeling like we're finally on the right track, I call the others over.

"So it's a wizard," Grace says. "And he's building strength so he can finish off the blessing."

A sick feeling settles in my stomach, and I look at Barowalt. "What do we do?"

Barowalt crosses his arms. "We find him."

CHAPTER FOURTEEN

Constelita rejoices today because yesterday's storm has moved out. The Marquis announced the festival will continue as planned and moved the fireworks to this evening. Near the piers, the city is alive with excitement.

Grace, however, has missed most of it, because she's barricaded herself in the library, scouring musty tomes for more information on conjured creatures.

"I'm hoping to find a pattern," she says when I come to visit her before Irving and I wander to the festival grounds. "If there were a way we could predict where the beast will attack next, we can act first."

"Have you found anything?" I ask.

Sunlight streams through the large windows, and the library is much brighter than it was last night by firelight. With the storm long gone, there are fewer patrons milling about today, and the scholars seem happy to have their building back.

"Yes, actually." She nudges a book aside and stands. "But not from these."

She motions for me to follow her, and we end up in the Hall of Geography. She chooses a map and spreads it on a desk. "The beast struck Balt first. Then Marble and, lastly, Bracken."

"All right?"

"Balt has a tiny population, only a few farms clustered together. Marble is a little bigger, and Bracken is bigger still."

"So each village is progressively larger in population."

"That's right." She trails her finger from village to village. Following the same road, she stops at the next village and looks up expectantly.

"You think he's going to attack Coralridge next."

"I'm almost positive."

It's the village just outside of Constelita, the next largest besides this one.

"When?"

She shrugs. "I have no idea. The attacks haven't been spaced evenly apart. It could be next week...it could be tonight."

"I need to tell Barowalt."

She nods. "I'll see what else I can find."

***

"Rafe and I will go," Barowalt says. "You will stay here with Milly."

"What?" I demand. "Why?"

"Because I don't need you in the middle of it."

I know there's no use arguing with him, but as he saddles his horse, ready to take after the man who's threatening my blessing without me, I can't help it. "What's the point of all my training if you leave me here every time there's danger?"

Barowalt turns, his expression saying he won't be swayed. "The training is only a precaution should you ever find yourself in trouble."

"Fine."

He sighs, obviously wishing he didn't have to deal with me at the moment. "We're only going on Grace's hunch anyway. There's a chance we won't find anything."

Crossing my arms, I only stare at him.

Barowalt takes my shoulders and makes me meet his eyes. "You wanted to go to the festival. Go. Have a good time."

I finally nod, still not liking being left behind. "Be careful."

He and Rafe both scoff, and Barowalt says, "I'm not worried about some scrawny, pale wizard."

163

Unbidden, a smile tugs at the edge of my mouth. "Of course you're not."

My brother lets go of my shoulders. "You be careful."

"I'll be with Irving."

"That's what I meant."

Before he turns to mount his horse, I stop him. "Why did you want him to join the Order if you trust him so little?"

Barowalt looks pensive. "I thought if he belonged to something, believed in something, maybe he would prove himself."

Since I don't have a response for that, Barowalt only nods. With one last goodbye, he and Rafe ride out of the stable.

***

"What do you say I enter the archery competition?" Irving watches, eager, as men set targets in a field.

"I think you'd embarrass yourself."

He turns to me with a wry tilt of his head and a barely-there smile. "I love the confidence you have in me, darling. Very flattering."

I poke him in the side. "You don't need flattered—you need humbled."

He laughs and wraps his arm around my shoulders, drawing me close as we wander through the crowds. "You're afraid I'll embarrass you with my unique and very effective stance."

I don't believe he truly shoots like that. It's too ridiculous, even for him.

"Fine," I say. "Enter if you feel you must. I'll try not to laugh when you run from the event with your tail tucked between your legs."

He raises a brow with perfect disdain and marches toward a man collecting entries. After a moment, he jogs back. "I have to retrieve my bow from the inn. Find yourself somewhere to sit where you'll have a good view of my win."

"Front row," I promise.

With a wink that does things to my stomach that it shouldn't, Irving runs off, excusing himself as he jostles people passing by. Shaking my head and letting myself smile now that he's gone, I find a spot in the wooden stands. As people fill in around me, I realize it's the first time in years I've been alone without a guard. It's odd to be by myself with no one watching over my shoulder. Freeing, in a way. All these people have no idea who I am—and they don't care. I'm just a girl, enjoying the Ship's Return Festival, waiting to cheer her favorite competitor on.

Irving doesn't return until the event is just about to begin. He jogs up, not even out of breath, and joins the other competitors. Many are villagers, some farm boys from the outskirts, and the rest are a smattering of various nobles. In the festival spirit, they all inter-mingle.

Constelita's master archer steps forward and an-nounces the first event, a simple long distance shoot. The men are called up in sets of three, and each faces their own target. When it's Irving's turn, he finds me in the stands and grins. I nod at the targets, reminding him to pay attention.

The men take their stances, and Irving, looking like a fool, takes his awkward pose. There are titters in the crowd, and I only shake my head. Each of the men makes the shot, and all, including Irving, hit the bull's-eye. As they move away to let another round of men take their places, Irving waves to the crowd, flashing his knee-weakening smile.

Around me, several of the same women who just laughed now sigh, instantly smitten with the blond-haired competitor.

After another fifteen men take their turns, the winners progress to the next round. Each time, Irving moves on. This last shot, however, is much longer. I hold my breath as he shoots, waiting for him to miss.

He hits it dead center.

It's impossible. He shouldn't be able to shoot like that.

The men around him laugh, as surprised as I am that he's progressed this far.

"The next round," the master archer calls out. "Will test your speed. For each turn, I will toss three apples into the air. Whoever hits the most apples, wins. If there's a tie, we will have a shoot-off."

This time, Irving glances over his shoulder and gives me another mischievous smile as he nocks his arrow. After several men go, many only hitting one apple and most missing all, Irving takes his place.

The master archer tosses an apple high in the air, away from the crowd.

This time, much to my delight and the spectators', Irving doesn't bother with his ridiculous stance. He stands to the side, facing forward, looking more than competent. His arrow hits the first apple, and the master archer throws another. With admirable precision and skill, he shoots all three apples from the sky.

The crowd roars, laughing, glad for the ridiculous entertainment.

The master archer strides to the end of the field and collects the apples. Holding them in the air, he declares, "We have a winner!"

Practically bouncing in my seat, both because Irving won and also because I was right, I cheer with the rest of the crowd.

A boy comes forward, offering Irving the hefty pouch of gold. Graciously, he accepts it, but he turns to the master archer. "I am allowed to exchange my prize?"

The man looks confused.

Irving turns toward the stands. "What do you say I share the gold with you?"

The crowd cheers. People wave their hands and others whistle.

"I'll toss it to you, but you have to do something for me."

I watch with narrowed eyes, wondering what he's up to.

Irving turns his dazzling smile on me. "You have to convince the girl with wheat-blond hair, the one looking lovely in the sapphire gown, to give me a victory kiss."

CHAPTER FIFTEEN

Every muscle in my body goes weak, and my cheeks flame. All eyes turn to me, and the crowd is relentless in their applause and coaxing. Feeling foolish, I cross my arms and shake my head.

The crowd laughs and boos and continues to cry for me to meet Irving on the field.

"Come on, Audette." Irving swings his winner's purse back and forth. "I'd love to share my winnings with these good people."

My feet act of their own accord, and I march down the stands just to pause several feet from Irving.

"You're an idiot," I say, but only loud enough he'll hear me. "Well, hurry up."

He laughs at that and waves me forward. "No— you have to come to me."

I step forward with the cheers of the crowd at my back. "I'm only doing this for their benefit."

Irving's expression turns solemn. "Of course."

For a moment, feeling ornery, I think of kissing his cheek in the traditional victory kiss manner, but I don't think he'll let me get away with that. Standing on my tiptoes, I brush a kiss over his lips. The contact is brief but jarring. My chest warms, and the butterflies in my stomach riot. Flustered, I pull back.

"Oh no, you don't." He grins and catches me around the waist.

Before I realize his intent, he cups the back of my neck, and our lips meet again. The moment takes me by surprise, and my defenses drop. He coaxes me for more, and, too startled to use common sense, I give in. The kiss is urgent, careless, a little wild. I twist his tunic in my hands, drawing him closer.

The sounds fade, and there's only Irving. My hands stray to his shoulders. His tunic is warm from the sun, and the smells of grass and Ptarmish wildflowers surround us. Finally, after several more moments than is appropriate for an audience of this magnitude, Irving groans low and pulls back.

We blink at each other, both of us out of breath and slightly dazed. The crowd is in a frenzy, and when I glance their way, my face flames brighter than it already was.

Irving smirks, his eyes alight with triumph. But under the carefree expression, he looks vaguely disconcerted. Like maybe our kiss affected him as much as it did me.

Irritated with both him and my lack of control, I glare at Irving. "That was more than a victory kiss."

He raises an eyebrow. "It's all right. I forgive you."

Knowing if I fail to hold back the smile playing on my lips, he'll be more incorrigible than he already is, I turn away. He must take a moment to toss the coins to the crowd because the chaos increases.

Several moments later, Irving catches up to me, looking like a cat who fell in a bucket of cream.

I keep my eyes toward the busy street but motion behind us. "That was kind of you."

He shrugs. "I don't need it."

For once, he sounds humble. I glance at him, curious what I'll find on his face, but there's nothing there, nothing gloating or prideful. He gave the villagers the gold because he wanted to, because it was more entertaining for him to share with them than keep it.

"What?" He gives me a nervous look.

"It's possible that under that cocky exterior—deep, deep down—you may be rather likable."

Instantly, his expression flashes back to smug. "Of course I am. I've been trying to tell you this—and it's 'lovable' not 'likable.'" He grins. "And charming…

handsome...charismatic..."

In the most non-romantic way possible, I press my hand over his lips. "You should stop while you're ahead."

Laughing, he pulls my hand away. In an overly subtle move that's truly not subtle at all, Irving keeps my hand in his. We stay this way, palms linked, as we continue through the festival.

Just as the sky is growing dusky, we turn toward the pier, where we'll have a good view of tonight's fireworks. As the day grows late, the streets become even more crowded.

Irving stops to look at something in an artisan's booth. After several minutes, I tug his hand.

"Come on, Irving. We'll never find a good spot if—" I stop abruptly because my eyes land on a man and woman laughing in the shadows of the booth.

The man's hands rest at the woman's hips, and she laughs as he trails kisses down her neck. It's a tawdry display, and I would look away if I wasn't so surprised. It's my cousin Kent. Giselle's husband.

As if feeling eyes on him, Kent suddenly pauses, his lips hovering over the woman's shoulder. I quickly look away and give Irving another tug.

"Audette," Irving says. "Look at the scrollwork on this blade."

I glance at Kent again, hoping he hasn't noticed

172

us yet.

Unfortunately, my cousin's eyes are on me, and he looks both guilty and slightly ill. Irving follows my gaze, and then he lets out a low whistle.

Frowning, Kent sets his hand on the woman's back, and, without a word of greeting, ushers her across the street.

"Well," Irving says several moments after they've disappeared. "That was awkward."

I nod, my stomach still unsettled. Unable to help myself, I glance at Irving. If I were to marry him, would that be my future? Would I be sitting, bored and lonely, in the castle, while Irving entertains himself with other women?

"Are you all right?" Irving asks after he buys the dagger he was admiring from the local merchant.

Though I'm not sure if I am, I nod.

He offers the dagger to me. "See if it will fit in your boot. It's a little long, but I think it will."

I stare at the swirled etching on the blade. "You bought it for me?"

Irving gives me a funny look, but his eyes are bright. "It's a little too pretty for me, don't you think?"

Smiling, I pull the functional but plain dagger from the pocket in my boot and hand it to him. I slide the new blade in, and I'm pleased to see it fits well. "Thank you."

"You are very welcome." With that, he takes my hand again, and we continue toward the pier.

***

I've never seen fireworks before, but I've heard of them. Making them is an art rooted in science, but to me, they're magic. Sailors bring them with shipments from the southern kingdoms, but their secrets are guarded. No one in Elden has been able to reproduce them.

The western horizon glows purple, and stars dot the inky night sky. The crowd grows restless, eager for the show to begin. Irving stands with me, his right shoulder just behind my left, and though he hasn't mentioned it, his posture tells me he's protecting me from the press of the crowds.

I turn my head to look at him. "Have you seen fireworks before?"

"Once," he answers. "At a festival in Triblue."

"What do they look like?"

He shakes his head, and a warm smile tips his lips. "Almost indescribable."

I stand on my tiptoes, trying to see over the crowd, hoping to catch a glimpse of the men preparing the display on an island not far from the shore. The night has grown too dark to make them out.

With another question on my lips, I turn back to Irving. Before I can utter the words, I'm cut off by

174

a shrill shriek far to the left. I whip around, thinking the show must be starting, but there's nothing. The cry is followed by another, but it's not joyful as I first thought.

It's terrified.

The audience begins to shift. From the left, the crowd scatters and flees. More shouts fill the air, and people near us begin to run. A man strikes my shoulder as he pushes through the crowd.

"Audette," Irving yells from not far away.

There are too many people now. They jostle me and push me farther from Irving in their haste. We're too far away from the original din for the people to know why they're running, but run they do.

"I'm here," I call back, pushing through the crowd toward Irving's voice.

More screams fill the night, and, like a skittish sheep, my heart quickens its pace, warning me there's danger—warning me to flee. I fight the instinct back although my fingers involuntarily search for the sword that's tucked safely in my room at the inn.

Why did I wear this ridiculous gown? What was I thinking?

Movement catches my attention from the corner of my eye. There's something large in the distance toward the east. I freeze in place, fighting to stand firm in the sea of shifting bodies. Whatever I saw is gone.

Wait.

There's something—

Someone grabs my elbow, and I scream. Twirling swiftly, I yank my elbow away and make to attack. Irving jumps out of the way just as I'm about to drive my palm into his nose.

I jerk my hand back, and he latches onto my arm, ensuring we won't be separated again.

"I saw something," I yell over the chaos.

Irving nods. "I saw it too."

"Could you make it out?"

He only shakes his head. "It looked like…"

"A shadow."

Silent understanding passes between us.

"We have to get to the inn," I say. "I need my sword."

"You can't fight this thing alone," Irving argues.

A woman fights through the crowd, elbowing me in the back. I grunt and fall against Irving's chest. With his eyes on the eastern streets, he wraps his arms around me, keeping me close to protect me from the frantic villagers.

"I won't be alone." I meet his eyes. "I'll have you."

After several moments, he nods. "Let's hurry, before it disappears again."

The streets are thick with terror. If the creature is truly feeding on fear, then there's a feast lying at its feet.

"Dragon!" a man screams near us as he runs through the streets. "The dragon is attacking!"

With Irving's hand clenched over mine, we push our way toward the Ocean Ruby. The inn's not far from here, and luckily it's to the west, away from the creature's path. In the jumble of people, it takes double the time to reach the entryway.

People flee the building. Some pull hastily packed trunks, many with clothing tumbling out the sides. Others, likely those from the mainland who lived through the savage dragon attacks during the Dragon Wars, leave their belongings behind.

The stables are a madhouse of horses and carriages, and no one can get through. Horses shy and jerk at their reins, men scream at each other, and two near the tavern down the road have come to blows.

Nearby, a small child of five or six, likely separated from her parents, presses herself against the inn's exterior. Her dark hair is a mess. Tears stream down her face, and she gasps for breath, terrified.

Frantic, I look for her parents, but no one claims her. I hesitate only for a minute, looking over my shoulder to the east. I don't have time to stop. I must find the beast, and, more importantly, the wizard who's conjured it. But we can't leave her standing here, alone...

It's Irving who makes up my mind. Immediately, without thought, he kneels before her. She eyes him, her body quivering with fright.

"Hello, darling." He says the words like it's the middle of a warm summer day and we've chanced upon her in a garden. "Where are your parents?"

She only hiccups and begins to cry harder.

As he tries to coax an answer out of her, I gasp. A shadow moves, not far from us now, near the pier where we stood only minutes ago.

"It's coming this way." I dash into the building and call over my shoulder, "I'll be right back."

I race against the flow of people, pushing into the halls instead of out. I look for Grace, Javid, and Milly, though I'm sure they're still in the library, safe across the city. I fumble with my room key, cursing myself for being cautious and keeping it locked. When the door finally swings open, I almost fall flat on my face. There's no time to change, so I only grab the blade, not bothering with its sheath.

Sword in hand, I burst from the building. Irving's convinced the girl to move away from the wall. He holds her hand, murmuring reassuring words, but his attention is toward the pier.

When I'm close enough he can whisper so the girl won't overhear him, he says, "It moves like a living beast, but the only glimpses I catch are shadows."

The crowd is still thick, a raging anthill of scurrying insects, but the mass has thinned to nothing toward the pier.

"From what I can tell, it looks like it's tracking something," Irving says.

An involuntary shudder passes through me. "Have you seen a man lingering nearby?"

"No." Irving shakes his head. "But we don't know the tether required. It's possible he's on the other side of Constelita."

That would require a brand of dark magic so strong, I refuse to consider it.

We move farther down, putting distance between us and the creature. The little girl's sobs have quieted to tiny, pitiful gasps.

"If the wizard's not even here," I say. "How do we kill the beast?"

Irving glances at the girl, looking torn. "Stay with her, get her away from here. I'll face it."

I shake my head. "I won't send you alone. It was practically a suicide mission when we spoke of taking it on just the two of us."

As we speak, we peer around a building, watching the beast circle a spot on the pier.

"Audette." Irving's voice sounds funny. "Where exactly were we standing?"

Just as soon as the words are out of his mouth,

the creature freezes. Slowly, it turns our way. It's too dark to make out its shape, much less see its eyes, but my blood runs cold. It's locked onto us, but whether by sight or smell or some other sense, I don't know.

When we first arrived, Queen Clara told me to follow my gut intuition.

"Run." I say the word quietly at first, testing it. Then I bolt. "We need to run!"

Without the slightest hesitation, Irving scoops the girl into his arms, and we race through the thinning crowd. I don't know how, but I can feel it behind us, closing in on us.

We run for what seems like ages, darting through side-streets and racing past the last of the villagers who have yet to find safety.

When it seems we may have finally escaped it, we pause in a darkened alley, gasping for breath. Irving sets the child on her feet, and she sinks to the ground. He stretches his arms, tired from running halfway across Constelita while carrying the girl.

"I think we may have lost it," I dare whisper.

From farther down, shining like a beacon in the night, a lone torch flickers at the back entrance of a small shop. The alley is eerie, too quiet. I'm not sure how long we've been running—thirty minutes, hours. I have no idea. My legs tremble, both from our flight through the streets and also from the fear coursing through my veins.

"I don't think so," Irving says. "It may be catching its breath as well."

Which makes me wonder: why would a conjured creature need to rest? Is the wizard tethered to it, running through the streets behind it? Is he too tired to hold the magic?

After one more deep breath, Irving kneels down and grins at the child we've basically kidnapped. "Do you think you can sit on my shoulders this time?"

I chance a peek around a corner, looking down the street to see if the creature lurks farther down. "Is that safe? Won't she fall?"

"She'll hold on," he says, and then he looks back at the girl. "Won't you, darling?"

In response, her bottom lip begins to quiver, and she falls against him, sobbing into his tunic.

Murmuring soothing words, he picks her up, clutching her against his chest. "This works too."

Poor Irving. Though he's strong, his arms must be ready to give out.

We continue through the city, this time walking at a brisk pace. We travel for hours, winding through the alleys, never daring to stay in one place too long. The inns and taverns have bolted their doors, and we're locked in the streets like vagabonds.

Several times, we stop to allow Irving to rest his

arms. I carry the girl for a while, though I can't manage it for very long. Every once in a while, my senses sharpen, and I can practically feel the creature searching for us.

We pause again to catch our breath in a public garden. In the trees, birds have begun their morning songs. My eyes ache, and every muscle in my body screams for sleep. The child has fallen asleep in Irving's arms, and he carefully sets her on the ground. He sinks next to her, taking a precious moment to rest.

I collapse next to them, more exhausted than I've ever been in my life. If the birds feel it's safe enough to sing, surely the creature has given up the trail. Morning approaches. Already the eastern horizon has lightened to lavender.

Closing my eyes, I murmur, "Just for a moment."

"Only a moment," Irving agrees, already sounding half-asleep.

***

I jerk awake, but I don't dare move. The birds are silent. Even with my eyes closed, I sense something watching me from the nearby shadows, a predator ready to attack. I draw in a careful breath, fighting the panic that's freezing me in place. Slowly, I inch my hand to the hilt of my sword.

From beside me, Irving and the girl's soft breathing stays peaceful and even. How can't they feel it?

That horrifying sensation of being watched?

Just as I'm preparing to leap up and fight whatever it is that has found us, a pain like I've never known envelopes me. My vision blurs, and I cry out. The sensation surrounds me, blinding me with a white-hot, searing fire that robs me of my breath and leaves me writhing on the ground. I clutch my arms around myself, unable to escape the unfathomable pain.

As suddenly as it came on, the sensation ebbs. My screams turn to whimpers, and I curl into myself. When I finally peel my eyes open, I find the little girl at my back, huddled next to me, whether for her own comfort or mine, I don't know.

Above us, Irving stands, his eyes behind us and his bow drawn. He shoots an arrow into the night. When it meets its target, a chilling yip fills the air—the sound of a flesh and blood creature in pain.

"It's retreating," Irving says, his gaze still intent.

I begin to shiver, and my muscles tremble in violent waves. Suddenly, I'm chilled, colder than I've been in my life. When I try to talk, only a pathetic, strangled mew comes out.

More terrified of losing control of my own body than the memory of the pain, I clench my eyes shut.

"Audette?" Irving kneels next to me and then pulls me onto his lap. "It's gone." His words are reassuring, but his voice is shaken, worried.

I try to force myself to speak, but again, it seems it's an impossible task.

He strokes my hair. "Audette?"

"Is she all right?" A tiny voice asks.

"Of course," he answers, but his voice is falsely bright.

Irving rubs my arms, trying to warm me in an attempt to stop the violent shivering.

"I'm cold," I'm finally able to croak out.

Relieved, Irving clutches me closer. "I know. We'll get you back to the inn and find you a physician."

Without bothering to ask if I can walk—which I can't—he somehow scoops me into his arms. I can feel his muscles tremble. He's exhausted after carrying the girl most of the night, but I'm too far gone to care. I curl toward his chest, grateful for his warmth. Unable to keep my eyes open any longer, I let sleep take me.

CHAPTER SIXTEEN

When I wake, I find the little girl leaning over me, staring at me. With her dark brown eyes solemn, she leans back and looks over her shoulder. "She's awake."
Instantly, Milly rises from the chair not far from the bed. "Well, give her some air."

I sit up, feeling vaguely off. "What's wrong with me?"

Thankfully, the words come out with ease. That, if nothing else, is a relief.

"Nothing." Milly sits on the edge of the bed, and her features soften. "The physician said other than being unconscious when Irving brought you in, you're in perfect health."

After glancing at the small girl, half-wondering why she's still here, I lower my voice. "But what did the beast do to me?"

Milly shrugs. "They think you had a bad scare. That's all."

That's not all. The memory of the pain comes flooding back, and I rub my temples at the thought. I'm not a delicate princess who faints at the thought of things that go bump in the night. That thing did something to me. Whether it was the beast or the wizard who attacked me, I don't know.

But I intend to find out.

Milly frowns and runs her eyes over me. She stretches out a hand like she means to touch my hair. "You look..."

"What?"

"Nothing." Pulling her hand back, she shakes her head. "Just tired."

I toss my covers aside and stand, half expecting to feel light-headed. I don't. I feel...fine. Vaguely off perhaps, but perfectly normal.

And that in itself is odd.

"Where's Irving?" I ask.

The stone floor is cool on my bare feet. I cross the room and pull back the drapes. Below me, Constelita is alive with people going about their day. It's as if last night's events didn't even take place. How can things return to normal so quickly?

"Barowalt's returned," Milly answers. "Irving's

speaking with him."

I watch a boy fight with a donkey in the street and then glance at the girl, who's come to stand next to me. She's a slender thing, but probably older than I originally thought.

"What's your name?" I ask her.

Her lips twitch as she, too, watches the boy and the donkey, but she doesn't quite smile. "Letta."

"And how old are you, Letta?"

The girl turns, and her very serious eyes meet mine. "I'm seven, but the woman at the orphanage said I'm small for my age."

Milly meets my eyes over the girl's head and gives me a pained shrug.

Well, this is inconvenient.

"They'll probably be missing you," I say, hoping to sound kind. "How did you find yourself in the street?"

She turns back to the window, avoiding my gaze. "I ran away."

I'm not very good with children. I don't know what to do with them, how to talk to them. Instead of answering, I only nod and then step behind the partition to dress.

Without a word, Milly tosses underthings and a gown over the top. Once I'm dressed, Milly cinches the laces.

I suck in a strangled breath. "I think you enjoy

SHARI L. TAPSCOTT

this too much."

She laughs under her breath and gives the laces another merciless yank. "How are you feeling? Do you think you can go downstairs for a meal, or would you prefer to stay in the room?"

Glancing over my shoulder, I say, "I'll go down. I feel fine." I pause. "Mostly."

She narrows her eyes. "Mostly?"

Frustrated, I face forward again. "I feel...off. I don't know how to explain it."

"Do you hurt anywhere?" Like an old woman, she fusses over me and checks my forehead for a fever. "Are you achy? Perhaps dehydrated? Have you had enough liquids?"

I bat her hand away, laughing. "No." I shake my head, irritated I don't have words for it. "Never mind."

She purses her lips, studying my face as if she can figure out what's wrong just by looking at me. After several moments, her expression softens. "Barowalt wanted to be informed the moment you woke up. If he finds out you've already been up and talking for ten minutes now, and he wasn't informed, he'll be beside himself."

"I'll tell him," Letta says, her voice still fairly un-emotional.

I turn to her. "Do you think you should go down-stairs by yourself?"

188

The girl gives me a funny look and quietly closes the door behind her.

Turning to Milly, I say, "Why hasn't someone taken her back to the orphanage?"

Milly frowns. "She doesn't want to go."

I hold up my hands. "I don't understand what that has to do with anything."

A smile twitches at Milly's lips, and she finally laughs. "No one wants to be the villain who takes her back."

"None of the men in my Order can work up the courage to take one small girl back the orphanage where she lives? We certainly can't take her in." I rub my temples. "She's not a pet. She's a child."

Milly steps forward, giving me that look. The look that she knows will guilt me into doing something I don't think is wise. "Her parents died at sea." She waits for the words to sink in, making me remember my own loss, then she lowers her voice. "They were pirates. No one will ever adopt her."

Feeling both an ache at the memory of my parents and the slightest twinge of guilt, I step back. "It's not our business. We're already the sole defenders of unicorns of all things, surely you don't expect our mission to extend to orphans as well?"

"Of course not. But perhaps she could stay with us a few days?" She glances away, looking hopeful.

"Maybe I could buy her some dresses? Plump her up a bit? Get her a doll?"

"You're already attached!"

I have a bad feeling the rest of them are as well. What on earth do they expect to do with this little girl?

***

I find Barowalt interrogating a long-haired gypsy tied to a chair. Rafe stands beside him, looking menacing. "You're still telling me you had nothing to do with the attack?"

The man sneers. "I tell fortunes. The kind of magic required to conjure that size of beast is astronomical. It doesn't exist in the depths of all of Constelita."

The drapes are drawn, and the room is eerily dark for mid-day.

"Then what is this beast?" Barowalt asks.

"How should I know?"

Barowalt leans down, his eyes hard. "I'm sorry. I was under the impression you could 'see the future,' fortune teller."

The man tilts his head back and lets out a loud laugh. His long, dark hair falls down the back of the chair. "Even if I wanted to tell you—which I don't—I couldn't draw dark magic around you, oh brave and valiant unicorn knight."

I suck in a startled breath, and Barowalt and the man turn to me.

"Audette," my brother says, his face washing with relief.

My brother strides over and crushes me against him. When he finally pushes me away, he keeps his hands on my arms and studies me. He frowns. "Are you all right?"

I nod. "I'm fine."

He doesn't look convinced. "You're sure?"

"Yes!" I exclaim. "Why does everyone keep asking me like I don't know myself?"

"Of course. I'm sorry." Barowalt glances around the darkened room. "I was worried, is all."

I hear the truth of his words. If I'd died last night, he'd be alone. As stoic as he is, he needs me. Just as I need him.

Suddenly, tears blur my vision. The thought of losing Barowalt is too much.

Softer this time, I say, "I promise. I am fully recovered."

The gypsy snarls something at Rafe, but the knight doesn't respond.

"Who is this man?" I whisper.

"A con artist we found in Coralridge. We think he might be connected to the incident, so we brought him back to interrogate him."

A soft chuckle behind us makes my hair stand on end. When I pull away from Barowalt, I find the gypsy smirking at me.

"You're in trouble, king," he says.

"Why is that?" Barowalt demands, his voice hard and unforgiving.

The man closes his eyes, still smiling, and rests his head on the back of the chair. "I think I'll let you figure that one out on your own."

Without mercy, Barowalt motions Rafe forward. As if the man and chair were children's toys, Rafe picks up the wooden leg and dangles the man upside down. Feet flailing, the gypsy yelps.

"Again, I'll ask you, why am I in trouble?" Barowalt asks.

Somewhat recovered from the shock, the gypsy says, his voice tight, "Your sister's been marked."

"What does that mean?"

"She's trackable."

I tense even though I know better than to listen to a gypsy's words. They're notorious liars. This man will say whatever he thinks will save his neck.

Barowalt jerks his head, and Rafe tips the chair right side up.

"So there is a wizard involved."

Though his arms are still pinned by the rope, the man attempts to roll his shoulders. "I didn't say that."

Barowalt motions for Rafe to jerk the chair up again, but the gypsy yells, "I don't know!"

My brother turns to me, his face grim. "This won't be pleasant. Why don't you go for a walk in the gardens?"

Wrinkling my nose, I turn from the room.

***

Letta stares at me as I pick at my food. I try to work up an appetite, though I'm not hungry. I glance at her, notice her watching, and give her an awkward smile.

She only stares back.

"You look funny," she finally says.

Silence descends over the table. Barowalt, who's sitting at my side, pauses midway through his recount of the interrogation.

Across from me, Rafe, Grace, and Javid look uncomfortable, and Milly stiffens.

Irving, who hasn't said a word since he arrived for the evening meal but keeps shooting me silent looks, runs his gaze over my face, frowning.

And now they're all staring at me.

Grace finally sets aside her napkin and sighs. "She's right."

"Excuse me?" I demand.

Self-conscious, I pat my braid.

Apparently no one wants to speak first.

"Your hair is darker, and your eyes are too," Letta says, obviously not uncomfortable like the rest. "And you're pale, and you look cold."

I wait for someone to laugh and dismiss the sentiment as the whimsy of a child. No one does.

Turning to my brother, I say, "Barowalt?"

His brow wrinkles. "I thought it was the candlelight earlier. Your hair is darker, isn't it?"

Deciding they've all lost their minds, I pull my braid over my shoulder. My once platinum hair, identical to Mother's, is almost brown. I drop the braid like it's a snake.

"Why...what...how could that happen?" My pulse jumps and I turn to Grace. "What would do that?"

She bites her lip. "I don't know."

Irving clears his throat. "Are you familiar with the Princess of Lauramore?"

All eyes turn to the prince, and Barowalt says, "She's our cousin, though a somewhat distant one."

"Her hair is red like wine," Irving says. "But it fades to gold at the ends. It's the strangest thing you've ever seen."

I give him a look, telling him to get to the point.

"It was fairy magic," Irving explains.

Clasping my hands, trying to keep my temper in check, I lean forward. "Are you telling me that you think that the thing chasing us through the streets... was a fairy?"

"No." He laughs at my irritation, flashing me a smile that would make me swoon a little if I wasn't so disturbed. "But whatever it was, it was flesh and blood—I hit it with an arrow, and it fled." He waits a beat, making sure he has our attention. "It wasn't conjured."

We're silent as we mull the statement over.

"You think it's a magical beast?" Grace asks.

"A dragon couldn't..." I motion to my hair. "I mean, that's not how their magic works..."

Intrigued, Grace leans forward. "But what if it were something else altogether?"

A large part of me doesn't want to believe that a beast that size and that powerful is real. It seemed much less deadly when it was the work of a wizard.

"We must consider the possibility," Barowalt says, though he looks skeptical, "but for now, I think it's best we return to the estate."

Though it isn't obvious, the table's attention subtly shifts to the girl.

Her eyes dart between us, and her face falls. "Does that mean you're taking me back to the orphanage?"

CHAPTER SEVENTEEN

Letta looks out the carriage window, her eyes as bright as I've ever seen them. For some reason unbeknownst to me, we brought the girl with us. Before we left, Irving rode to the orphanage to gather her things. He came back empty-handed. Her only belonging was the dress she was wearing when we found her.

Now Letta has three dresses, two new pairs of boots, a lightweight cape, and seven guardians that have no idea how to parent her.

Grace and Javid take us to the villa, say their goodbyes to us and Letta, and then continue on to the castle. After they leave, Letta stands in the courtyard, marveling at the estate with her hands clasped over the wooden doll Milly bought her before we left Constelita.

Maids and menservants scurry about, gathering our things. At first, many do double takes when they see me, and then they send curious glances my way, which I choose to ignore. Since last night, my hair has darkened further from light brown to the color of dark ale.

I lock the door when I reach my quarters and immediately go to the mirror. My reflection startles me. With a tentative hand, I undo my braid and run my fingers through my hair. There are streaks of pale blond, areas not touched by magic, and they mingle with the dark strands, twisting in the braid-crinkled waves.

As Letta said, my eyes are a shade darker too, though the change isn't as noticeable as my hair.

The color is odd on me, different. Though I was partial to my blond hair, the reason for my melancholy is not caused by vanity. It's that I no longer resemble my mother. It used to be that if I'd look in the mirror and turn a certain way, I could see her in my reflection. Remember her.

My hand freezes as the light catches my ring. With my stomach feeling as if it's dropped to the floor, I yank my hand from my hair and examine the stone.

The light blue aquamarine, the jewel Mother wore every day because she said it reminded her of the Ptarmish sea, is as black as night.

Safe in my room, alone from pitying eyes, I allow my emotions to flow to the surface. I close my eyes and wrap my hands in my hair. Hot tears run down my cheeks. I know I'm wallowing; I know crying won't do any good, but I can't seem to stop myself.

Suddenly, I look up. In the reflection, my darkened, tear-stained eyes look determined. Hopeful.

The unicorns can fix it.

With that fortifying thought tucked in my heart, I again braid my hair and turn my back on the mirror.

***

If Aunt Camilla finds me in her hall in the wee hours of the morning, knocking on Irving's door, I'll never hear the end of it.

It was simple enough to slip past the knights in the halls. Though they might have been curious about my presence, they only nodded respectfully when I passed. Aunt Camilla would be more than curious.

Nervous, I wait for Irving to answer. What if he didn't even hear the knock? He's probably one of those people who could sleep peacefully through the castle's warning bells.

That would be my luck.

Just when I'm about to give up, I knock one more time.

I hold my breath and watch a nearby torch flicker. The firelight sends flame-shaped shadows dancing on the stone wall. After several more minutes of waiting, my shoulders sag. I turn, disappointed and feeling foolish. As I do, footsteps echo on the other side of the door, and I look back over my shoulder.

Irving opens the door, looking groggy and sleep-rumpled. Light stubble shadows his jaw, and he wears a wrinkled tunic and trousers that appear as if they were hastily pulled on.

"Audette?" Not believing his eyes, he blinks several times.

Glancing down the hall to ensure we're alone, I push him into his chambers and close the door behind us. "I have a favor to ask of you."

"There are only a few things that a nightly visit brings to mind," he says cheekily. "But you must know I'm a gentleman and wouldn't consider it."

"Of course you wouldn't," I answer, my voice dry. "But that is most certainly not why I'm here."

He didn't bother to light a candle before he answered the door, and his room is perfectly dark. A knot tightens in my stomach, and I begin to doubt the wisdom of my decision to come here. If we are caught, this will look very bad indeed.

If you hadn't run away from your wedding, you'd be here right now and no one would say a thing about it.

Heat stains my cheeks, and I'm now grateful for the blackness.

"I want you to ride with me to Asher's lands."

"Tonight?"

My eyes grow accustomed to the dark, and I can just see Irving run a hand through his hair as he stretches his shoulders.

The reason for the visit makes me feel weak. Not only do I want the unicorns to fix my hair, but I want them to share memories of my mother. I don't exactly know why, but I feel as if I lost a piece of her.

Instead of explaining, I simply say, "Please?"

After contemplating it for a moment and holding back a yawn, he finally nods. "All right. I was just thinking I hadn't gone on a moonlit ride for far too long."

"You were not," I say, my voice soft. "You were fast asleep."

He takes a step closer, and though we don't touch, I can feel him in the dark.

"Maybe I was dreaming of you," he whispers. The words are voiced playfully, but his tone is too soft to have a teasing effect. Instead, the words sound like a line from a sonnet.

A warm sensation spreads from my chest to my stomach, and common sense tells me we need to leave now or I'll do something I regret. Something like leap into his arms and let him comfort me with his pretty words and empty kisses.

Because I feel the need to move closer, I step

back. "You might want to bring a cloak. Another storm has moved in, and it's rather cool."

We slip from Aunt Camilla's hall without incident, this time weaving through empty, unlit corridors to avoid the guards. Near the entrance, the two men I passed earlier are playing a game of dice. They're relaxed, laughing as they share stories.

Irving and I peer around a corner, watching them.

"I'll distract them, and you slip out," Irving says. "I'll meet you in the stables."

He sounds almost gleeful, happy for the game. The feeling is catching. I glance at him and, unable to stop myself, grin at the intrigue.

His face softens, and out of nowhere, he cups my cheek with his hand. Slowly, his fingers slide into my hair, and he examines the darkened strands. He doesn't say anything, and I ache to ask him what he's thinking.

Before I dare, he wags his eyebrows and grins. "Be ready to slip out."

"I already am," I promise.

He strides around the corner as if it's completely normal to take a stroll through the castle in the middle of the night. I don't dare peek for fear the guards will notice me, so I stand with my back to the wall, listening.

"Evening," Irving says, his voice cheerful and

bright.

The guards sound startled at first, but then they're just as friendly as he is. They speak for several minutes, and Irving manages to lead them a few paces down the hall. When their voices grow slightly fainter, I poke my head around the corner. The men are only ten paces from their table, but they face down the hall to where Irving is motioning.

Silent as possible, I dart into the night and race to the stables. Biting my lip to keep from laughing out loud, I slip past a groom who fell asleep on his watch.

In several moments, Irving joins me.

"Did they see me?" I ask.

He shakes his head, his eyes bright. "They don't have the slightest idea that I slipped into the night with the loveliest girl in Ptarma."

I roll my eyes, but I warm at the flattery.

The prince laughs and turns to saddle his horse. I watch him for several moments, feeling disconcerted, and then I ready my mare.

In less than fifteen minutes, we ride down the road. My mind churns with the gypsy's words. If he's right, if the beast marked me, I could be leading trouble straight to the blessing. But Irving injured the creature badly enough it fled. Tonight, it will likely be in its lair, nursing its wounds.

And I need the unicorns, need their gentle

reassurance and their memories.

Storm clouds roll in, and there's no moon to light our way. The path is dark and the road unfamiliar. We travel at a much slower pace than I would like. At this rate, we won't be back before sunrise.

Barowalt will be livid if he wakes and finds me gone.

But if I do make it in time, no one will know the lengths I traveled to restore my appearance. No one but Irving, and for some reason, I trust him with this.

"Asher likely has someone guarding the blessing," Irving says when we finally draw near enough to make out the ocean in the distance.

"My men will keep our visit to themselves." I wrinkle my nose. "All would except Rogert, but, luckily, he's not here."

Irving glances over. "Why are we traveling in the dark of night to visit your unicorns?"

I nibble my lip for several moments before I decide to answer.

Keeping my eyes on the road, I hold up a strand of hair. "They'll be able to fix this."

"Are you that worried about it?" He stops, and I slow my horse as well.

"Yes, I suppose I am." I pause and then admit something I haven't even put into words before now, something that makes me grow cold. "I feel tainted.

Like I've been touched by darkness, and some of it lingers. Like some part of me, something important and good, is gone."

Irving looks worried, and he nudges his horse closer. "You said you felt fine."

"And I do," I assure him. "I'm not sick or tired, in pain or weary. I can't describe it. I just know something is off."

"And they can fix it?"

I nod. "Whatever this thing is I'm missing, I feel it most when I'm with them."

He squeezes my hand. "Then let's hurry."

***

To some extent, luck is with me tonight. We find Asher on guard.

"Audette?" he calls, recognizing me at once in the dark.

I ride forward, grateful to hear his calm, steady voice. Irving helps me from my horse, and I go to the knight.

"Something's happened," I explain, feeling more at ease talking to Asher than my brother.

His expression grows wary as if he's preparing himself for bad news. He glances at Irving, probably wondering if the prince is the cause of it. I motion the knight inside the stable where the torch light glows.

Taking a deep breath, I lower my hood.

One of the calmest, most unshakable of my knights sucks in a startled breath. "What happened?"

I don't quite expect that much of a reaction, and, feeling off-kilter, I glance at Irving. Immediately, he steps forward and explains.

Asher rubs a hand over his face, distressed by the news. "Perhaps we should bring the blessing into the safety of the stables after all."

"I think it would be best." I twist my ring. "But I'd like to visit them now."

I don't say 'alone.' The two men sense it.

Asher nods. Irving glances at the night, probably not wanting me to go out on my own with the beast's attack so fresh in our memories. I give him a reassuring smile and slip through the doorway.

Nocturnal by nature, the unicorns-disguised-as-horses graze. When I enter the pasture gate, they look up. Recognizing me, one of them trots forward, eager.

I hold my hand out, needing their comfort more than anything. But just as the mare's almost to me, she stops and shakes her head. So distressed, she sheds her camouflage. The sudden light of her coat glows dimly, and she begins to back away.

"It's me," I whisper.

They remembered me the other night. Why not now?

I step forward gingerly. If I can just lay a hand on her coat, we'll connect.

When I step forward, she darts several paces back. Her nostrils flare, and the whites of her eyes grow large. She's terrified.

Of me.

Panic strikes, fast and sharp. Suddenly, my breath goes shallow, and I stumble back, my thoughts churning.

"Audette?" Asher calls from the fence.

"They don't know me." I turn around, clutching a hand to my chest, trying to will my heart to slow its rapid beating. "Worse...they think I'm a predator."

And it's true. In their fear, the entire blessing has winked back to normal, and the dainty creatures cower together at the base of the cliff.

Asher's eyes go wide, and he watches the unicorns in disbelief.

Irving doesn't bother asking Asher to move from the gate. He leaps over the fence. With an arm wrapped around my waist, he draws me from the pasture.

Hope shatters at my feet, and my confusion mingles with fear. They can't fix me. They don't even know who I am.

What's happened to me?

***

Irving knocks softly on the door frame of the room I

shared with Milly not long ago. It's not closed, but he waits until I bid him enter. With the draperies pulled back and the windows open to the day, I watch the unicorns graze in the pasture. Asher once again convinced them to disguise themselves as horses. Tonight, before dusk, he'll bring them into the safety of the stable.

"I've been a part of them my entire life," I say, not bothering to turn toward the door. "Was introduced as a baby."

The prince must take my words as an invitation. He comes into the room and rests his hand on my shoulder. He doesn't say anything, doesn't offer words of comfort.

I'm not sure what he would say.

Absently, he pulls a lock of my hair through his fingers. "You're still you. You know that, right?"

I turn, feeling listless, and meet his eyes.

He wraps the strand around his palm. "You're not defined by your hair or the color of your eyes."

"Have you seen the way the knights look at me since we've returned? Their shocked expressions that they quickly attempt to hide? No one's even asked, but I know they're whispering questions to Barowalt when I'm out of earshot."

After watching me for several moments, not bothering to disagree, he says, "Asher sent your brother a message this morning, letting him know you're here and you're safe."

"What good am I to the Order if the blessing is terrified of me?"

"We don't know that this is permanent. It's possible the creature's magic will fade with time."

I nod, but I'm not convinced.

Irving's lips quirk in a lopsided half-smile. "But even if it does, you make a lovely brunette."

Almost smiling, I shove him away.

"No, I'm serious." He laughs and steps back. "Now you're dark and mysterious—especially with that brooding, pensive look you've had going the last few days. It's very alluring."

There's just something about him. He's ridiculous and flippant...and something more. Even with as low as I feel now, he makes me warm. Just being with him makes things better.

He makes me happy.

"Why are you scowling at me like that?" Irving tilts his head to the side, studying me.

I shake my head. I won't tell him how he's growing on me. It's the last thing he needs to know. If he senses that my affections are beginning to shift toward him, he might stop trying. And, as sad as it might be, I would be devastated.

Smiling, I hold up a length of my hair, trying not to wince at the dark color. "This doesn't mean anything, does it? It's not symbolic. I haven't changed, have I? It's just exterior."

Slowly, his eyes warm. "Exactly."

I motion to the room. "Sulking in here won't find the creature."

He crosses his arms, smiling. "It won't."

Glancing out the window, feeling a keen ache when I look at the unicorns, I say, "And whether they know me or not, whether they fear me or not, I vowed to protect them." I look back, determined. "And it's a vow I intend to keep."

There's something in his eyes, something I can't quite place. It tugs at my heart, makes my breath quicken. I turn from him. Unfortunately, I come face-to-face with the mirror. Instantly, I look away.

"No," Irving says, his voice quiet as he comes up behind me. "Don't let it frighten you, don't be ashamed. Look at your reflection."

He runs his hands up and down my arms. Bracing myself, I look back up. The first thing I notice, oddly enough, is Irving. Our eyes meet in the reflection, and, smiling, he rests his chin on my shoulder.

It's comfortable, standing with him, pretending we belong together.

Longing to belong with him. Longing for him to look at me that way forever.

Slowly, drawing strength from him, I turn my

eyes to myself. I inhale, hating that my own reflection looks so foreign.

"Look at how beautiful you are," he whispers as he, again, runs his hand through my hair.

"I used to look like my mother," I say quietly.

Irving lets his hand drop, and then, surprising me, wraps his arms around my middle, clasping his hands at my waist. My back is pressed against his chest, and his chin still rests on my shoulder. It's more than a friendly gesture, sweet but alarmingly intimate.

"I remember her," he says, his voice quiet next to my ear. "She'd visit my mother now and then."

Tears prick my eyes, and I try to blink them back.

"I can't recall what she looked like, exactly." His jaw brushes my neck. "But she had the brightest laugh. That I remember."

I turn to meet his eyes.

"Because that's what was important," he continues. "She was bright and vibrant and she made people happy. Beauty fades, hair turns gray. Some people are lost before their time. But in the end, we don't remember them for how they looked. We remember how they made us feel." He holds me tighter. "And I still feel the same way about you. Blond hair, brown hair, gray hair—it doesn't matter. To me, you're simply Audette, and nothing will ever change that."

I give him a watery nod. For the first time since

my parents died, I don't bother to hold back my tears until I'm behind closed doors, don't allow myself to feel guilty for shedding them.

And once I'm finished, I feel better. I still ache for them, still miss them, but a weight has been lifted.

"Thank you," I say, wiping away the last of my tears with the palm of my hand. I turn and wrap my arms around him, hugging him the same way I would Barowalt or one of my knights, pressing my face against his tunic. "I'm afraid you're right—you're irritatingly likable."

"Lovable," he corrects, his voice muffled in my hair. "I'm not sure why you keep getting that wrong."

CHAPTER EIGHTEEN

"How dreadful the whole ordeal has been for you!" Giselle declares, her eyes intent on Irving as he tells King Edlund the account of our night running through the streets in Constelita.

"Well," Irving says dryly. "I believe it was worse for Audette."

"Of course." Her eyes flash to me, and she looks less than sympathetic. "You poor little thing. I'm afraid your complexion isn't suited for dark hair."

I force myself to smile.

"Kent, you and Aldus were down south," Edlund says, turning to his nephew. "Did you see anything? Run into any trouble?"

Immediately, the prince's eyes flick to mine, but I look away, uncomfortable.

"No, Uncle," Kent answers.

Aldus's full attention is on a pretty noble's daughter, but he looks over and shakes his head as well. We never saw Aldus. Was my cousin there, willing to cover for Kent? Or does he even know?

Giselle strokes her husband's arm, but her eyes are on Irving. She catches me watching, and she smiles. It's not a vicious look exactly, but there's certainly a challenge there.

Next to me, Irving shifts, uncomfortable.

"This gypsy you questioned," the king continues. "You don't believe he was involved?"

Barowalt, who's seated at Edlund's left-hand side, shakes his head. "I don't believe so. He was too far away from the attack. But he knows something."

"What did you do with him?"

"Since I couldn't prove anything, I dropped him back in Coralridge. The guards charged him with minor magic use, and locked him up for a fortnight."

King Edlund nods. "That will buy us time should we need to question him again."

Grace, who's stayed fairly silent, looks up. "He can't go anywhere even when we release him, not during the winter."

"Good point." Queen Clara smiles at Grace, and Grace almost blushes at the attention.

Javid smiles at his wife. "Imagine the fun we'll

have tracking him down."

Giselle sighs, loud and dramatic. "I wish there were something to look forward to. With this talk of attacks, we've all become rather sullen." She looks up suddenly as if she's just had an idea. "Let's do a masquerade to lift our spirits."

Kent starts to shake his head, but Clara cuts him off. "It's not a bad idea. We usually do the mid-winter ball, but we could move it forward this year."

"And it must be a masquerade," Giselle says, her entire face lighting up. "I haven't been to one in years."

Clara looks at her husband, hopeful. "What do you say?"

Edlund thinks about it for a moment. "I suppose it won't hurt to give you all something to look forward to."

"While Clara and Giselle plan the ball," Edlund says. "We'll continue to hunt for the beast. If it's a creature, it must have a lair it beds down in at night. If we can find it, we may be able to catch it off-guard. We'll send out a search party, starting in the southern part of the kingdom."

King Edlund knows nothing of our Order, but his plans suit ours just fine. Barowalt nods, and they begin plotting their mission.

As dinner continues, I shift my food back and forth. Giselle's excited talk of her masquerade grates my nerves, as do the longing glances she keeps sending Irving. I have no appetite this evening.

***

"You're not excited about the masquerade, are you?" Irving asks from my side.

Again, he's found me in the archery yard behind our villa. This time, he doesn't try to fool me into an archery lesson. Taking his stance next to me—a strong, traditional stance—he shoots an arrow at the target, hitting the bullseye without even trying.

"I think it's ridiculous." I nock my arrow. "There's a beast wreaking destruction and havoc in southern Ptarma, and Giselle wants to throw a ball."

"Still angry Barowalt didn't let you accompany him on the search?"

I glance at him and give him a wry look. "A little."

Irving sets his bow down and leans against a near-by tree. "What are you going to wear?"

After I shoot the arrow, I turn to him. "I can't tell you—it defeats the purpose of the masquerade. The mystery."

He crosses his arms and leans back, the picture of ease and grace. "But how will I find you? And more importantly" —he wags his eyebrows— "how will I know how to plan my costume?"

"You'll have to wing it." I laugh. "But I'll tell you this, if you let it slip what costume you're going to don,

I promise Giselle will show up matching you."

"You're in an ornery mood." He shoves away from the tree and stalks forward, his eyes bright. "I like that."

Laughing, I push him back. "Go away. You're distracting me."

The clouds have rolled in. The morning was warm, like spring back home, but the rains will begin anytime. I'd like to get a little more practice in before I'm forced inside.

"I can distract you more," he promises, catching me around the waist.

I swat him away, pretending disinterest.

"Just tell me what color you're wearing," he says.

The first raindrop hits my arm, and I look up at the sky, scowling. "I'm not going to ruin the surprise. You'll just have to find me."

"Intriguing." He steps back. "Fine. I'll leave you for now."

"Where are you off to?"

"I promised a lovely lady a ride through the Ptarmish countryside." He gives me a mysterious, teasing look. "I believe we'll stop for lunch as well."

"You and Letta have a good time riding in the rain."

"And here I thought you said I was a scoundrel at heart." He shakes his head, pretending to be disappointed he didn't fool me. "You wondered, didn't you?

Just a little?"

Trying not to smile, I say, "No. Not even a little."

"Careful, Audette." He steps close, his brown eyes locked on mine and his voice lowered and sultry. "You just might be starting to trust me."

My breath hitches, but I try to hide it. "That would be foolish of me, wouldn't it?"

"No." With a raise of his eyebrows, he steps back, giving me room to catch my breath. "Have a nice afternoon."

I watch him wind through the garden, back to the villa. Once he's gone, I turn back to the target, trying not to smile.

***

The seamstress slips Milly's newly-finished gown over her head. The layers of orange, black, and white fall softly around her.

Milly holds out her arms and admires the gossamer wings. "What do you think, Audette?"

"I think you make a very lovely butterfly."

She grins as she ties her elaborate-winged black mask over her face. Once the ensemble is complete, she studies her reflection in the mirror. "Do you think Barowalt will like it?"

My brother returned with the search party early this morning. When I spoke with him, he wasn't in good spirits. They didn't find any sign of the creature—or a wizard's lair. Despite Irving's insistence that the creature is real, my brother's not ready to toss the wizard theory aside completely. At least not yet.

"I'm sure he'll love it," I say.

After Milly's outfitted in her new gown, the seamstress slips mine over my head. The dress is a simple magenta with a full skirt and a bodice so tight, the sleeveless gown has no choice but to stay in place. Sheer gold fabric wraps my neck and is secured at my throat with a brooch, and then it falls over my shoulders in a cape covered in carefully crafted flowers that match my dress.

Pleased the gowns fit us well, the seamstress excuses herself.

Though I may have been agitated that the ball was Giselle's idea, I can't deny that I'm excited for the evening—grateful, even, to attend something purely for the pleasure of it.

With no lady's maids attending us, Milly and I fuss with each other's hair.

Careful not to catch any strands, Milly ties my golden lily mask securely in place at the back of my head. "There, finished."

I examine my reflection in the mirror. Milly twisted my hair in long ropes this afternoon after I washed it and secured them up with pins. I hid in my chambers, looking ridiculous for most of the day. Now that she's taken the sections down, my usually sleek, straight hair falls to my shoulders in dark ringlets.

With my mask, I don't even recognize myself.

Milly preens in front of the mirror, turning to the side to admire her gown.

A quiet knock sounds at the door.

"Who is it?" Milly calls, obviously not wanting Barowalt to catch her in her costume.

"Letta," a small voice answers.

Milly opens the door, and the little girl comes in, sulking, and tosses herself on the chair. Her eyes run over our gowns, and her expression turns wistful. "I want to go to the ball."

"Masquerades are for adults," I tell her.

"But Lord Bryon's daughter is going," she argues.

Milly kneels in front of the girl. "And she's at least ten years older than you."

Letta only shrugs.

"How about this," Milly says. "Tomorrow night, we'll all wear our gowns, and we'll have a masquerade dinner right here. In the morning, I'll help you make the most exquisite costume."

Slowly, Letta's face brightens. "You promise?"

"I promise."

The girl looks temporarily appeased. "Will you invite Grace and Javid too?"

Milly nods.

It's nearing dark, and soon Keven and Rogert will escort us to the masquerade. Barowalt offered to take us, but Milly adamantly refused, not wanting my brother to see her before the ball. Barowalt, still irritated from coming back from the search unsuccessful, told Milly that if she preferred someone else take her, that suited him just fine.

I hope for Milly's sake he'll still attend.

Milly makes Letta promise to behave for the maids, and then the three of us sweep down the stairs, toward the entry. At the bottom, Letta spots a usually somber guard that she's become friendly with, and he bows to her and asks if she's had her dinner yet. Milly smiles as he escorts her to the kitchen.

It makes me feel bad that we've been here as long as we have, and I still don't know most of the staff. At least Letta is making friends.

"What are we going to do with the girl when we return to Brookraven?" I ask Milly once they're out of earshot.

My friend glances at me. "What do you mean?"

"I mean what will we do with her?"

"She'll come with us."

She says it like it's the most obvious answer imaginable.

Knowing I'll get nowhere with this argument tonight, I hold my tongue. If Letta's ever to find a lasting place with the nobility, a family must be found for her. She needs a mother and a father, not an eclectic group of aunt and uncle figures. We can't just toss the girl back and forth, sending her to spend time at one castle one week and then another the next.

I'm not sure why I'm the only one that seems to understand that.

Keven and Rogert wait for us at the villa's entry, and my mind shifts from Letta to the masquerade. Despite the festive occasion, both men wear light chain mail. Keven's tunic is deep yellow, and a rearing lion graces the front. Our golden knight has freed his hair for the evening. It falls to his shoulders in a blond mane, and he wears a black half-mask.

I laugh out loud when I see him. "You look perfect."

"I look ridiculous," he replies.

Rogert laughs, obviously agreeing with Keven. He wears a scarlet cape over his chain mail, and it just brushes the floor. Like Keven, he wears a simple mask. With his chestnut hair, and the shadow of stubble he's allowed to grow along his jaw for the evening, the knight looks more roguish than usual.

"You do not," Milly says to Keven and sets her hands on her hips, likely wondering why neither of them has mentioned how lovely she looks. "Your costume is very appropriate."

"I should have volunteered to stay with Asher," Keven mutters.

We take a carriage to the castle. I twist my long, golden gloves in my hands, growing oddly nervous.

Will Irving be waiting for me? Will he recognize me?

In my mind, I'm afraid I've elevated the ball to unattainable levels.

I enter the hall, and the music stops. From deep in the crowd, Irving freezes. Recognition dawns in his eyes, and our gazes lock. As if there's no one else in the room, he comes to me.

Suddenly, the music crescendos. Without a word, Irving offers me his hand. I place mine in his, and as the crowd looks on, Irving sweeps me into the first dance. The night flies by, and the two of us never leave each other's arms. When the final bell rings, signaling the evening's end, he draws me in his arms and kisses me...

Flushing, I glance around the carriage and hope no one noticed that I allowed myself to become lost in a daydream. It's a silly fantasy, one I shouldn't indulge in. Very childish.

Still...

The carriage stops, and a masked groomsman helps me and Milly down the steps. It rained earlier, but the sky has cleared. Due to the moisture in the air, the night-blooming flowers in the gardens send a heady fragrance wafting through the courtyard. It smells exotic and sumptuous, and it makes my already-quickened heartbeat thrum just a touch faster. Already, I'm being carried away by the ambiance of the evening.

More carriages line up behind us, each filled with members of Ptarmish nobility who are eager for a night to forget the growing threat that's stalking the villages in the night. Around us is a great hustle and bustle. Horses prance on the cobblestones, and the sound of their hoofbeats echoes in the night.

Two guards dressed in just-polished armor open the doors, allowing us entry into the castle's grand foyer. Music filters from the great hall. Dozens of instruments play together, and their unique songs twine into one. Giselle must have hired all the musicians in Ptarma.

With Keven escorting me and Rogert at Milly's side, we pause outside the great hall. With a flourish, another set of guards swings the doors open, revealing the party. The room is dark, lit only with hundreds, possibly thousands, of long tapered candles. Massive bouquets of Winter's Bloom roses stand just inside the entry, and a black carpet, newly brought in for the masquerade, trails down the stairs.

Already, hundreds of guests loiter about, their faces hidden behind masks. I gawk at them as they mill about the room. Like crown jewels, gowns sparkle and glow in the dim light, each one spectacular and ridiculous. Most men have forgone a costume, choosing to wear only masks, but, not to be outdone by the women, their tunics and doublets are velvet, brocade, and silk.

I scan the shadowed room, hoping to spot Irving, hoping just perhaps our eyes will meet.

Unfortunately, they do.

He stands in the corner, dressed as a mercenary knight. He wears a brown cloak with a hood and a mask of thin, tan leather. His sword gleams at his side, making him look unnervingly masculine and capable.

Just as in my daydream, he spots me immediately. Just as in my daydream, time stands still.

In fact, the only detail differing from my daydream is that Giselle is draped rather intimately in his arms.

CHAPTER NINETEEN

The dark-haired vixen looks my way, possibly wondering what's captured Irving's attention. For half a moment, her expression is confused, but then she recognizes me, and a satisfied smirk crosses her face.

Keven, sensing me tense next to him, turns toward the couple. Behind his mask, the knight's face goes hard and stays that way even after Irving none-too-gently pushes Giselle out of his arms.

Irving sends me a look, a look that tells me that I know him well enough by now not to go off of appearances alone. But there've been so many rumors about the prince. It's hard not to believe them when I find him like this.

I tighten my arm in Keven's and whisper, "Dance with me?"

"Of course."

The knight leads me into the room where couples have gathered and are twirling with the elaborate, haunting music. Keven dances well, strong and sure in his steps as he leads me. I catch several women on the edges of the room smiling behind fans, giggling with each other as they watch him.

He, however, seems oblivious to their attention. There's a hardness to his features, an underlying irritation.

"I'm all right," I say when the music shifts to something slower, something more intimate.

He turns his light blue eyes on me. "I don't like him, Audette."

Unable to hide a smile, I pat his shoulder. "You wouldn't like anyone interested in me. You're as bad as Barowalt."

Keven stares at me intently, but just when I think he's going to answer, Irving taps him on the shoulder.

We pause in our dance, and couples swirl around us.

When Keven doesn't release me, Irving smiles. "If it's all right with you, I'd like to cut in."

"It's not all right," Keven answers.

Muted irritation flashes over Irving's face, but he schools it quickly. "How about we let the princess decide?"

The image of him and Giselle flashes in my memory, obliterating the much more pleasant one I had concocted.

Not meeting his eyes, I say, "Perhaps later."

Irving steps forward, ready to argue, ready to apologize. "Audette—"

"You heard Her Highness," Keven says, his words curt. "Now please step away."

With a long, slightly exaggerated sigh, Irving takes several steps back. When my eyes flick his way, he frowns. His mouth presses into a thin line, and he looks like he wants to ignore my wishes and pull me from Keven's arms.

Part of me wishes he would.

I look away, and Keven leads us deeper into the other couples, away from Irving.

"Perhaps I should speak with him?" I say after several tense minutes.

Agitated, the knight yanks his mask's strings and draws the fabric from his face. "You deserve a better man than him."

Sighing, my shoulders fall. "But I'm afraid I like him."

Keven's jaw works, and I wait for him to form his thoughts, knowing if I push him, he won't speak at all. Finally, he says, "I think Giselle purposely stumbled into his arms."

I study my knight for several moments. "Why didn't you say that to begin with?"

"Because I don't like him." A tiny, almost smile plays at his lips. "And perhaps you look so lovely I wanted to keep you to myself this evening."

My feet still, and I freeze, wondering if there's more to his words than he's letting on.

Keven releases me and nods to the corner of the room where I, too, noticed Irving's been brooding. "Go on."

"And what will you do?" I ask.

Keven glances toward a group of girls who watch him, starry-eyed. His voice wry, he says, "I'm sure I'll find someone to keep me company."

"Keven—"

My golden knight truly smiles this time, but it's not as bright as his rare smiles usually are. "It's all right, Audette."

When I hesitate for several moments, again, he jerks his head toward Irving.

"Thank you." I squeeze his hand and push into the crowd.

I find Irving near a corner, as far from the festivities as a person can get without leaving altogether. A few unattached women flitter near him, probably hoping they'll catch his eye. To their disappointment, he doesn't even look their way. His mask lays discarded on the table near him, and he idly drums his fingers next to it. A half-finished tankard of mead sits next to him, forgotten.

Without a word, I take the seat beside him. "Not impressed with the evening, either?"

He glances at me from the corner of his eye, and a wry smirk grows on his lips. "I knew if I waited long enough, you'd finally seek me out."

Teasing, I begin to rise. "I can go—"

He catches my wrist and pulls me back. For a moment, I almost lose my footing. I catch myself before I fall right onto his lap. Smiling, I narrow my eyes, letting him know I'm onto his game. The prince raises an eyebrow, playing innocent.

"This is the part of the evening where you explain how, exactly, you and Giselle ended up in such an intimate embrace," I say.

The humor leaves his face, and it's replaced with such irritation that I don't doubt his next words are true. "She stumbled, losing her footing. Thankfully I was right there, able to catch her before she fell to the floor."

"Thankfully," I droll.

"What baffles me," Irving says. "Is where her husband has gotten himself off to again."

"He's not here?" I ask, surprised.

Surely Kent could manage to leave his mistress

for one night—just to keep up appearances with his wife if nothing else.

"I don't imagine I would have found Giselle in my arms if he were," Irving answers.

My voice dry, I say, "I'm not so sure about that."

A new song begins, this one livelier than the last.

"Do you forgive me?" Irving asks, though he already knows that I have.

"I suppose."

He motions toward the middle of the hall. "Care to dance?"

I glance at the crowd, and for some reason, despite its allure, my heart isn't into it anymore.

"I'd rather walk," I say, standing.

Gallantly, he offers his arm. "Then walk we shall."

After several minutes, we find ourselves on a darkened balcony that overlooks the garden. We're far enough from the ball that no one loiters nearby, and we have the area to ourselves.

In the dark, with the music from the masquerade filtering out the doors and the smell of the night flowers in the air, Irving releases my arm and takes my hand.

His fingers play over mine, teasing me, and, finally, he clasps my palm.

"A hired knight?" I say, addressing his costume.

Irving smiles. "I wanted you to find me since you

wouldn't tell me what you were wearing."

He leads me to the balcony's edge, and I lean against the railing. The stone is cold at my back, and the cool air is welcome after the heat of the great hall. The sky is clear tonight, a reprieve after the frequent evening storms we've been getting, and the stars are bright.

"You didn't seem to have any trouble finding me," I say.

Irving steps near, possibly a little too close, but in the dark of the night, and with no one nearby, I see no reason to object. "How couldn't I? You are the most beautiful woman here."

I shake my head, trying not to smile at his flattery. Chastising him, I say, "Pretty words, Irving."

He grins and shifts even closer. "You're the only girl I've met who seems to detest them."

"Not detest." I loosen the clasp of our hands and trail my finger over his palm. "But rather, I know how well they've been practiced."

His free hand finds my waist, and I try not to suck in a telling breath.

"Practice implies I've been perfecting them for the right time. The right girl." His voice is low. "Perhaps I've found her."

My heart stutters and then skips, but I force myself to stay levelheaded, to not let myself be carried away by his charm.

"You're doing it again," I whisper.

"I like you," he suddenly blurts out, no longer sounding as smooth as before. "More than I wanted to."

A breath catches in my chest, and I wait for him to continue.

His eyes search mine. "When I first saw you in the hall on the day of our wedding, I felt a spark—a spark I hadn't felt for far too many years, but when I hunted you down to bring you back...I didn't expect..."

"Expect what?" My voice is breathy, but I'm not sure he even notices.

Irving's hand tightens at my waist, and he looks off. Nervous.

"When you snubbed me tonight," he says. "It was as if you stabbed a knife in my heart. I was mad with jealousy." A smile flickers at his lips again, but then it's gone. "I wanted to challenge Keven to a duel right there in the middle of the hall."

Trying to keep things light though my chest is hot, I whisper, "That would have been very entertaining. I've never had two men fight over me before."

At that, a wide smile spreads across his face. He shakes his head, moving closer. "That's it—right there. On this very romantic, very private balcony, I'm about to tell you that I'm falling in love with you, and you won't even let me finish. Why do I like that so much?

Why is that so appealing?"

Feeling light and giddy, scared and hesitant all at the same time, I set my hand on the back of his neck. "Don't let me stop you."

"I want to marry you, Audette. Not because our mothers wanted it. Not because it will secure my crown. But because, now that I've gotten to know you, there's no one else I can imagine at my side."

Because I can't help myself, because I'm an idiot at times, I ask, "What about the gypsy?"

He lets out a single low laugh in the back of his throat, his expression oddly warm. "Rosie's a lovely person, and I wish her and Dristan the best." He wraps his arms around my back, pulling me flush against his chest. "But now that there's you, I am so grateful she turned me down."

I close my eyes. My heart tells me there's nothing in my life that has ever felt this right, but my brain warns me to be cautious.

"Please tell me this isn't an act. I couldn't bear it if it were. If you care about me at all, don't pledge your love if you can't swear it to me forever." I open my eyes. "I don't want to end up like Giselle, with a husband who'd rather spend his time in the arms of a mistress."

"I promise—you won't." Irving looks hurt, but his expression is thoughtful. "In my exuberance over this 'eureka' moment I've had, this conversation was perhaps premature." His thumb works at my waist. "Am I right in understanding you don't quite trust me enough yet?"

"I want to."

He nods and smiles at me so suddenly, the brilliance of it takes me off guard. "Then look at the progress I've made. A month ago, you hated me."

I laugh. "You're not upset?"

His smile turning slightly ornery, he brushes his jaw near mine. "Upset that you like me enough to let me whisk you away to this ridiculously romantic hideaway, just the two of us?"

My mouth goes dry as his lips brush near my hairline.

"Upset we're all alone, with only the stars for company?" he whispers.

His words tickle my ear, and I shiver. Gently, he unties the ribbon securing my mask. He pulls it from my face and lays it over the balcony's edge.

"I'm not upset about any of those things," he continues, his voice low and promising. "But do you know what I am upset about?"

"What?" I breathe.

He brushes my hair behind my ear and leans even closer. "I can't kiss you, because if I do, you'll continue to think I'm some roguish scoundrel."

Quieter than a whisper, I ask, "And if I were to kiss you?"

Irving angles his head so our eyes meet, and he very subtly shakes his head as he hides a smile. "Then I'm afraid I'd be forced to believe that you, darling princess, are a roguish scoundrel."

"You know," I say. "You really are a bit of an idiot."

Without giving him any warning, I stand on my toes and press my lips to his. He obviously expected more banter. For one heartbeat, I've startled him so thoroughly, he freezes. Then he comes to his senses—and rather spectacularly so. He steps into me, pushing me closer to the balcony's edge. The railing bites into the ties at my waist, but I couldn't care less.

There's only Irving and the need to get as close to him as possible. He deepens the kiss, and I let out a breathy gasp, which he answers with a groan.

His hands are in my hair, at my back, and mine trail over his chest. I should pull away, pretend that spark he spoke of didn't just roar into a fire.

But I don't want to.

"Please tell me why we've been fighting this?" Irving growls, barely breaking the kiss. "Are you sure we can't move things along a bit?"

Startled, I pull back and gasp for breath. "What do you mean?"

His eyes, which are dark with desire, brighten. He

grins, obviously liking whatever it is that he's thinking. "Marry me tonight."

I blink at him. "What?"

He clasps my arms. "We'll ride to Vallen Harbor— just us."

"It's the most ridiculous idea I've heard." I shake my head, trying to clear it. "We just decided that I don't even trust you yet. Don't you remember?"

"But you do." He nods, believing it. "You're just scared to admit it to yourself."

When I start to protest, he kisses me again, and all wisdom flees. Just when my mind is pleasantly fuzzy and warm and incapable of making a rational decision, Irving sinks to his knee in front of me.

"I pledge my love and my sword to you, Audette— my future queen," he declares, dramatic. "Marry me."

I glance toward the party, where Barowalt and my knights dance, unaware of what absurd decision I'm about to make. I can't tell them. They'll talk me out of it.

Milly, though—she'll toss the rice.

Finally, I look back at Irving. He wears a hopeful expression, one that's slightly mischievous and fully charming. Against every ounce of my better judgment, I let a foolish smile spread over my face. "All right."

CHAPTER TWENTY

I wait until Milly and Barowalt finish their dance, and then I tug her away.

"What is it?" she asks, her eyes bright like she already knows there's intrigue afoot.

Glancing around the hall, nervous someone will overhear, I whisper, "Irving and I are going to be married tonight. Will you cover for me when I disappear? I don't want Barowalt to find out until after it's done."

She gapes at me. "You're...what now?"

I roll my eyes and shift my weight to my other leg, eager to be away. "I'm marrying Irving."

"Didn't we decide we hated Irving when we found Giselle in his arms?" She sets her hands on her hips, grinning. "Weren't you dancing with Keven? When did this happen?" She raises an eyebrow and her lips turn in a smug look. "And I thought you weren't going to fall in love."

Crossing my arms, refusing to answer, I stare at her until she finally laughs.

"Fine," Milly says. "You can give me all the details later." She glances at Barowalt. "I think I can keep him distracted long enough for you to slip out."

I clasp her arms before she saunters away. "Thank you."

"You better hurry." She nods toward the entrance, where Irving said he'd wait for me. "He's been spotted by a harpy."

Sure enough, Giselle is flirting at him again. His arms are crossed and his expression is closed, but that doesn't keep her from running her hand down his arm. Relief flashes over his face when he sees me making my way toward them.

"I'm sorry, Giselle. I promised this next dance to Audette." He immediately draws me into his arms and sweeps me into the dance.

"I thought we were leaving," I say as we spin.

"We will," he promises, "the moment Giselle looks away."

That moment takes a while. From the side of the room, her eyes are locked on Irving, and she doesn't seem pleased. Finally, a woman comes to speak with her, congratulating her on the night most likely, and she turns away, smiling radiantly.

"Now's our chance," Irving whispers in my ear.

A thrill runs through me, and I nod.

"Barowalt's not watching," he continues. "Milly's flirting with your knights, and he's too busy scowling at them to notice you leaving."

I take a deep breath. "All right."

Trying to look nonchalant, I slip through the doors when the guards open them for me. I wait in the gardens, pretending I just needed some air in case someone should notice me. Several long moments later, Irving jogs down the stone entry.

When he reaches me, he catches me in his arms, pulls me into the shadows of a low-growing tree, and kisses me like he hasn't seen me in a fortnight.

"Are we really doing this?" he asks, his eyes bright.

Breathless, I nod.

"You know this is the second time we've slipped from the castle together." He raises his eyebrows. "You're a bad influence on me."

I only laugh and push away from him so I can catch my breath. If we're not careful, we'll waste the entire night here.

***

I rush into the villa. The guards posted don't question my presence, and Irving waits in the entryway. Letta, after seeing us arrive on horseback, runs down the

239

stairs. Dressed for bed, she follows me to my chambers.

"What are you doing home early?" she asks.

I glance at her. By the time Barowalt returns, he'll already know I left with Irving. I could tell her.

But she might giggle it to the maids...who might mention it to a guard...who in return may go to Barowalt and rat me out.

"Shouldn't you be in bed?" I say instead of answering.

Letta frowns. "I couldn't sleep."

"Go down to the kitchens and tell the cook you'd like a warm milk. She should still be up." I shuffle through my wardrobe, looking for a gown appropriate for my wedding day. Since we didn't have time to change when we left Primewood, I still have the light green gown I wore on the day I jilted Irving. I look over my shoulder at the girl. "That's what I do when I can't sleep."

The girl narrows her eyes. "You're not running away, are you?"

A nervous laugh bubbles out of my throat before I can stop it. "What would make you say that?"

"You're packing."

I shove the gown back in the wardrobe. "I'm not. I'm changing."

"Are you going to go back to the party?"

Her expression has turned quite serious, and I sigh and kneel in front of her. "Go to bed. I'll see you tomorrow—I promise."

She nods, not convinced. Looking lost and lonely, she stares at me.

And for one short moment, my heart winces. It's not a pleasant sensation at all, especially after trying so hard not to become attached to the tiny urchin.

Rolling my eyes, I pull her close. After several moments, I nudge her back to arm's length. "Now go downstairs, get some milk, and go to bed."

A small smile twitches at her lips, and she finally nods.

The moment she's out of the room, I dart back to my wardrobe. I can't wear the gown I deserted Irving in. It carries too many bad memories.

Instead, I take off the elaborate gold cape I wore for the masquerade and look at myself in the mirror's reflection. Without the mask and the cape, the magenta gown I'm wearing is quite lovely, even if it's far too dark to be traditional.

But what about our wedding is traditional?

I glance at my mother's now-black ring. I play with it, rolling it around my finger. It seems wrong to wear it now that it's been tarnished. I begin to slide it off, but just before it leaves my finger, I push it back. I'll exchange it as soon as Irving gives me a ring, but for now, it feels better having it there, even if it's no longer aquamarine.

After choosing a cape, I quickly make my way down to the foyer, where Irving waits. He has Letta in his arms, and when I come down the steps, she turns to scowl at me.

"You're getting married in Vallen Harbor," she accuses. "And you didn't tell me."

I give Irving a stern look, but he only shrugs. "I didn't see any harm in telling her."

My stomach squirms, but he's likely right. She's not going to tell anyone, and even if she does, the maids aren't likely to believe her.

Irving gives the girl a tight hug, and she laughs and squeals. Then he narrows his eyes, faking a stern look. "What are you doing up? It's late. You should be in bed."

She gives him an innocent look. "It is?"

I cross my arms, trying not to smile. She gives Irving one last hug, glances at me like she's still angry I didn't tell her, and disappears up the stairs.

Thirty minutes later, Irving and I ride through the darkened streets of the harbor village. Despite it being the nicest night since the rains started, there is no one about. Even the tavern is closed.

"Well, this is odd," Irving says when we come to the locked chapel.

On the Elden mainland, chapels are usually left open at all hours, and it's never difficult to call on a bishop. Perhaps it's different here.

A little spooked, I glance over my shoulder, feeling as if something is watching. "Do you think it's because of the attacks?"

"Probably." Irving nods and turns his horse around. "Let's try Kallert. It's larger. Surely we're bound to find someone there."

It takes us another hour to ride to Kallert, and I'm yawning by the time we reach it.

Though the streets are far quieter than they were the first night I visited with Milly and Keven, a great many shutters are open to the night, and music and laughter can be heard from inside many of the establishments and cottages.

"The people must be taking precautions," Irving says as we dismount near a stable.

After searching out and paying a stable hand, we venture down the streets, looking for the nearest chapel.

Like many of the other buildings, lights flicker in the open windows. When Irving tries the door, I'm relieved to find it unlocked. We walk through the building but find no one. Finally, we locate the bishop and his family sharing a late dinner in the little cottage just off the back of the chapel.

After Irving knocks, a woman with bright eyes opens the door and waves us inside.

"Are you hungry?" she asks after we introduce ourselves—omitting our titles, of course. "We have plenty to share."

Despite our protests, the family ushers us to their table. Their two boys scoot down the bench, making room for us.

"What brings you here tonight?" The bishop asks, his eyes friendly.

Irving smiles, charming them just as he does everyone he meets. "We wish to be married."

The bishop and his wife exchange a warm look, and the man pushes his empty plate back, ready to talk. "That's wonderful. And when were you thinking?"

"Tonight." Irving says it like it's nothing. Like people show up at the man's house every day requesting to be immediately wed.

The man's smile flickers, and he scratches his neck. "That's a little hasty, don't you think?"

The boys, who are too old to be children and too young to be men, look like they want to laugh, but their mother shoots them a look. They return to their plates, still smiling but silent.

Feeling the need to explain, I say, hesitant, "Our parents entered a betrothal agreement between the two of us when we were young." I pause, feeling awkward. "When our wedding was to take place, I…I mean there was…"

Irving wraps his arm around my shoulder, grinning. "She left me at the altar."

The family gapes at us, and my cheeks grow red.

"But we've worked out our differences, and here we are," he adds.

I try to smile, even though a tiny part of me wants to jab Irving in the side.

"So you've already gone through a promising ceremony?" The bishop asks.

Irving and I exchange a glance, and he says, "Not technically."

"We're from the mainland," I say, as if that will explain it.

"Ah." The bishop nods, slightly confused. "Well, I suppose if you're sure…"

A tiny seed of doubt works its way into my heart. My stomach tightens, and then I grow cold. What am I doing? Is this what my mother would have wanted? Would my father have approved?

I smile, trying to look serene.

Suddenly, and much too quickly, we're ushered into the small chapel.

Nearly frozen in place, I stand while the bishop begins the ceremony with only his family looking on. His words become muffled, and I try to focus on

Irving.

He's so handsome and carefree and kind. And, despite how I told myself I could control who I care about, I can't. Somehow, in this short time, I've come to love him.

But do I want to be married in a tiny chapel in Ptarma? And Barowalt—how hurt he will be. Mother and Father wouldn't have wanted that.

Irving meets my eyes, a smile on his lips, and takes my hand. I try to smile, but his eyes flicker.

"Stop," he says, quite suddenly.

The bishop pauses, surprised.

"I'm going to take a moment with Audette," Irving says, his voice quiet.

Suddenly, my heart leaps to my throat. He's changed his mind. Despite all he's said, he doesn't want me. This was a game to him, an amusement. I left him, and now he's leaving me.

It's fair, really.

He ushers me into the hall, and I wait for him to speak first.

"I can't go through with this." His voice is soft, but his eyes are guarded.

I can't look at him, so I only nod.

"I thought it was what I wanted, but my motivations are wrong," he continues. "You are exquisite and tempting, but I will show restraint. In fact, I need to prove it to you that I can. Perhaps I need to prove it to myself."

Finally, I turn to him, confused. "What are you talking about?"

And now he looks confused that I'm confused. "I think we should wait, be married at home. Not here, not like this."

"You still want to marry me?" I blurt out, not caring how pathetic the words make me sound.

His eyes widen, and then a smile builds on his face. "What did you think?"

Now embarrassed, I only shrug. I won't put my thoughts into words.

"Yes, I still want to marry you." He steps close, smelling of night and horse, and lowers his voice. "I meant what I said—you're the only person I want beside me. I know that. I have no doubts. But, I want to do it right, and that means waiting until we're home." He runs his hand down my bare shoulder, and I shiver. "I don't want to rush it."

"Then what was all this?" I ask, trying to sound exasperated when, truly, I'm so relieved that his reservations match my own.

He steps nearer and leans close to my ear. "At the time, all I was thinking is that we needed to be married before I sneaked you to my chambers." He catches me around the waist, grinning, and presses a quick kiss to

247

my lips. "But you'll just have to be patient, darling. I can't have you corrupting me further."

My eyes widen, I laugh, surprised. I smack his shoulder with the back of my hand, but I don't put much effort into it.

Hand in hand, we go back in the room.

The bishop and his family look up.

"We think, perhaps, we've been a little too hasty," Irving says, and he grins when the bishop gives us a look that says he agrees. "But perhaps you could still do us a favor?"

The bishop smiles, trying not to laugh. "And what would that be?"

I have no idea what Irving is going to say, but he looks down at me and smiles. "Can you do a traditional promising ceremony instead?"

"Of course," the man says, looking as if he approves.

Several moments later, I place my palm over Irving's hand. My blood thrums through my veins, and I feel tingly, but this time it's in the best way. This, more than anything I've done in the last season, feels right.

The bishop ties a simple white ribbon around our wrists. "The promise is binding."

At his words, the family politely claps, congratulating us on our engagement.

Irving grins at me, his mouth tilted in a

mischievous look. He raises our hands, which are still linked by the ribbon. "It's too bad I can't keep this on you until the wedding—then I'd know you couldn't run away."

I roll my eyes and am about to say something when a man barges into the chapel, his eyes wide. He sees us, but he's too concerned to apologize.

"Bishop Baylor," he says, "the shadow dragon has attacked Vallen Harbor."

CHAPTER TWENTY-ONE

"What were you thinking?" Barowalt demands the moment he meets us in the castle courtyard.

My brother, Keven, Rogert, Rafe, and Hallgrave are all five dressed in full armor, ready for battle. Their horses prance, nervous in the commotion the king's knights make as they prepare to take after the beast. From the murderous looks on my men's faces, I know I'm in for it.

Barowalt's agitation is marred with relief, making him all the angrier. He knows I was missing, but does he know why?

I glance at Milly, who's practically wringing her hands behind my brother.

She looks apologetic, and she nearly whispers, "Once the attack was announced, I had to tell him where you were."

Sighing, I give her a tight smile, hoping she knows I'm not upset with her.

"Well, I suppose you don't have to answer to me," Barowalt snarls, speaking to me but glaring at Irving. "I have no jurisdiction over you now."

Beside him, Keven and Rogert's faces are hard. I try to get a smile from them, but they don't waver. They look hurt. Hurt that I ran away, hurt that I didn't tell even them.

Hallgrave looks conflicted, hating that there's tension between the five of us. His eyes move from Barowalt to me, and he frowns.

"We didn't marry," Irving says, his voice clipped.

At his age, the prince obviously doesn't appreciate being chastised like a child. It's not surprising. He's the future king of a kingdom that, though small compared to Vernow or Errinton, is five times larger than Brookraven.

When another degree of relief flickers over Barowalt's face, I step forward, now irritated myself. "But we did have a bishop perform a promising ceremony."

Milly, who's face fell when Irving said we didn't get married, now lights up, her eyes sparkling. She bites back a grin, obviously not wanting Barowalt's irritation to transfer to her.

My brother lets out a slow, calming breath. "Very well."

I glance at Rogert, and he finally gives me a small grudging smile. I know he's not angry. He simply doesn't like to be left out of the loop. Keven, however, doesn't look as forgiving.

"We need to leave if we're going to track the beast," the blond knight says, not even looking at me.

Irving nods. "I'll go with you."

Keven looks like he wants to argue, but Barowalt gives Irving a curt nod. The men's attention turns to Javid, who's leading one of the parties, and I catch Irving's arm.

"Be careful," I say.

He raises an eyebrow. "I'm always careful."

Something passes between us, and I want to step into him, brush my hand over the soft hair at the nape of his neck. Kiss him like my brother and his men aren't standing an arm's length away.

As if he can tell where my thoughts have strayed, his smile turns to a smirk.

"Barowalt." I turn away from Irving before I do something I'll regret. "Let me come with you."

"Absolutely not." He doesn't even think of it.

"In the last two attacks, the beast has appeared in places I was either in or just left." I pause, waiting for my words to have an effect. "If I come...it might find me."

My brother's face goes hard. "You already put yourself in enough danger for one night."

"How were we to know the creature had moved to northern Ptarma?" I argue.

"It doesn't matter. You're not going."

Just when I'm about to argue further, Milly lays a hand on my arm. I glance at her, and she gives me a look that subtly tells me Barowalt's had enough for this evening.

"Fine." I step back. "I'll stay."

I cross my arms as I watch the men ride out of the courtyard and into the night.

***

We stay the night in Aunt Camilla's quarters, and Milly and I linger up until almost dawn, waiting for the men to return. Just after the last bell announces it's after four in the morning, the search parties return. Exhausted, and not expecting a report until morning, Milly and I find our beds and sleep well past breakfast.

It's nearly afternoon by the time we venture into the hall. I hesitate outside Irving's door, wondering if I should knock or if I should leave him be after such a taxing night.

Milly, seeing my hesitation, says, "Let him sleep for now. He'll find you soon."

Nodding, I step from the door, and we venture to

the hall to see if there is anything left of the morning meal.

"They're too fond of fish here," I whisper to Milly when I browse the platters that have been left in the hall for the late risers.

Each one is piled high with smoked fish, rolls, different types of cheeses, and an assortment of grapes. Already, several of the men who arrived home in the wee hours of the morning have come down and are dining in clusters. The atmosphere is hushed, tense, but Milly and I glean bits of information from nearby conversations.

The beast wasn't found. With the streets as desolate as Irving and I found them last night, it's not a surprise to learn the creature was unable to harm anyone or anything in the village, but, almost seemingly in anger, it destroyed a docked ship this time.

Three sailors were lost.

Milly has said little, which surprises me. I expected her to ask dozens of questions about my evening after I left with Irving, but her mind seems preoccupied.

Grace wanders into the hall when we're nearly finished. She spots us and sinks into a seat across from us. "Good morning."

The dark circles under her eyes belay that it's anything but.

"How is Javid?" I ask.

The duchess sighs. "Tired, discouraged. They didn't find any trace of the beast last night."

I nod toward a group of nearby men. "So we've heard."

She frowns, looking thoughtful. "From what the villagers said, it prowled the streets for nearly half an hour before it attacked the ship."

"It sounds like it was looking for something," Milly says.

"Me." Ice works its way into my stomach, and I feel slightly ill as I remember the gypsy's words. "It was looking for me."

Grace and Milly turn their attention to me, looking concerned.

"But why?" Grace asks.

"I don't know." Then I pause. "Or maybe I do."

Milly looks horrified, but Grace looks curious. She brushes her long, dark honey hair over her shoulder. "Well?"

"Maybe it senses them on me."

I won't say 'unicorns' in the great hall, not with so many ears nearby, but Grace nods, not needing further prompting.

In hushed tones, Grace leans forward. "Do you think this thing, whatever it is, knows about the Order?"

"It obviously hunted the blessing before it began

its tirade through Ptarma," I answer. "Perhaps it needs their strength."

"And perhaps it's getting low again," Milly says, her face growing pale.

Grace drums her fingers on the table, looking pensive. "This is ridiculous," she finally says. "All we can do is guess until we find out what we're up against."

Javid enters the hall, and several of the men call out to him. As Grace said, he looks exhausted. As I turn to greet him, my eyes settle on the couple who are quietly arguing at the table behind us.

I hadn't noticed my cousin until now.

Kent's eyes stray to mine, and I instantly yank my gaze away, feeling guilty. Like I was eavesdropping. From what I saw, Giselle looked unsettled, agitated. Kent says something else to his wife, and then he pushes away from the table and stalks out of the hall. I watch him for a moment, frowning.

Suddenly, Giselle looks my way. Her expression is icy, and I turn away first.

Despite all her bluff and bravado, the princess seems just as unsettled by the attacks as the rest of us.

***

King Edlund has called a meeting, and all the nobles who still linger at court, the few who haven't traveled home to check on the wellbeing of their families, gather in the great hall. Barowalt speaks quietly with Keven,

Rogert, and Javid, but I stay to the side. I have no information to add to the conversation.

I sense Irving a split-second before he steps up next to me.

"You slept most of the morning," I say quietly, happier to see him than I should be.

"I was up half the night."

Stepping slightly closer, brushing his arm with my shoulder, I ask, "Did you learn anything last night?"

"Only that I'm glad we didn't linger in Vallen Harbor."

He says it lightly, but there's a solemnness in his words. I shudder, remembering our night running through Constelita. I, too, am glad we left the port village for larger Kallert.

"Do you know what the meeting is about?" I ask.

Irving shakes his head. "I'm not close enough to the nobility to have been informed." He glances over. "But I did overhear something about Barowalt's gypsy friend."

The thought of him, the thought of his dark eyes boring into mine while he darkly promised I'd been marked, sends a tremor of apprehension through me.

As much as I wanted to dismiss his words at the time, it's becoming more difficult to deny there may be truth to them.

Edlund stands in front of us, and a hush falls over

the small crowd. "I'm afraid we learned little in our search last night."

The crowd murmurs their agreement.

"Which leads me to believe Barowalt and his men are right when they suggested the creature might be the work of a wizard."

There are several exclamations and surprised gasps.

Next to me, Barowalt shifts.

Irving shakes his head, ready to speak, but then it seems he changes his mind and keeps quiet.

"I've sent a party of knights to Coralridge to have the gypsy, who was arrested the day after the attack in Constelita, brought here for additional questioning."

I pull Irving to the side as the king continues to speak. "But you said it was a creature of flesh and blood."

Irving crosses his arms, and his finger twitches against his arm. "It had to have been. How else would my arrows have injured it?"

"You should tell them," I say.

Slowly, Irving nods. "I will, but let's see what this gypsy has to say as well. He might know more than he's letting on."

Again, I grow cold.

Sensing my anxiousness, Irving takes my hand, and we turn back to the conversation.

***

"What do you mean, the gypsy has escaped?" Edlund says, his voice growing loud in the small stone room.

"According to the jailer," the knight says, "he broke out the day before yesterday."

The day before the masquerade.

It's a small gathering, limited this time to family. Irving's not here and neither are our knights or Milly.

Javid paces, rubbing a hand over his face as he thinks. Grace sits quietly, not far from him, tapping a charcoal over a sketchbook. Both look like they should have taken a nap this afternoon like many of the rest of us did.

"I knew it. He's involved," Barowalt practically growls.

Knowing my brother as I do, he's probably wondering why he didn't run the gypsy through when he had the chance.

Kent sits in the corner near his father, the king's brother, silent. Though he's third in line for the throne, he almost looks bored of the political strife, like he wishes he were off on one of his hunting trips instead of here.

Giselle is oddly absent, and I can't help but wonder if it's because the pair is still fighting. Perhaps she found out about his mistress.

If that is the case, I don't blame her for being

angry.

The prince catches me looking at him, nods a greeting, and then looks back to his uncle.

There's something about him. Something I don't like.

A knock at the door draws our attention, and we turn as Giselle enters with a young, dark-haired farm girl I've never seen before.

"Forgive the interruption," the princess says. Her eyes gleam, and she's obviously proud of herself. She motions to the girl next to her. "This is Nadia. Her family runs the stables near the inn in Vallen Harbor."

Edlund nods, his expression striving for politeness although he's obviously irritated with the intrusion. "I know her family." He turns to Giselle. "But I don't know why she's here."

Nadia flushes and looks at the ground.

"She knows the whereabouts of the beast." Giselle looks particularly proud of herself, like she's the one with the information and not the girl.

The king straightens. "Well, then, please tell us."

The girl looks terrified. She's practically shaking, and she twists her apron in her fingers. Her eyes dart from the floor to Giselle. When the princess gives her a threatening look that I think is meant to be reassuring, the girl begins. "My grandfather has fallen ill, Your Majesty, and I stayed the night to care for him.

I left his cottage early in the morning, before the sun came up, so I could tend my chores before I needed to help Mother with breakfast. We'd had no news of the attack. I was passing the bluffs to the east of Vallen Harbor when my horse became skittish." She gulps and continues on, "My mare's not the flighty type, and I hurried past. That's when I heard it."

Nadia trails off, looking to Giselle for reassurance. Giselle nods her on, impatient.

"It stopped my heart cold. It sounded like the cry of a wolf—"

"And I told you there are no wolves this close to the shore," Giselle hisses, growing impatient with the girl's rambling. "Just tell them what you saw."

The girl's eyes go wide. "I saw the shadow dragon, Your Majesty. He turned to vapor in front of my very eyes...fizzled away into nothing."

Edlund leans forward. "And?"

Nadia looks back at Giselle, nods, and then turns back to the king. "In his place was a man."

CHAPTER TWENTY-TWO

Irving's words circle in my mind. He said the beast was of flesh and blood, not conjured as so many, including my brother, are now determined to believe. And how couldn't they after hearing the girl's testimony?

The girl is flooded with questions. She tries to answer them, but she's unused to this much attention, and she looks ready to pass out.

Feeling the need for air, I step from the room. I slip into a nearby alcove, a tiny nook with a soft upholstered chair by a window. On a better day, it would be the perfect place to read or sew.

I sit and stare out at the garden.

Perhaps Irving was mistaken? It was dark that night, and he was as exhausted as I was—perhaps more, for he was carrying Letta as we raced through the streets.

The doors to Edlund and Clara's private meeting rooms open, and people filter out. I watch them pass by, but they don't seem to notice me here, tucked away.

Barowalt, Javid, Aldus, and the king's brother discuss gathering another party to hunt the wizard down. They speak of leaving immediately, hoping to catch the man in his hideout before he moves on.

I bite my lip, thinking.

I'm jolted from my brooding by a hissed conversation.

"You will not go with them," a woman says. "There are plenty of volunteers. They don't need you."

A man lets out a low, mirthless laugh. "Careful, someone might think you care about my fate."

Feeling like an intruder, I peek around the corner, careful to keep hidden.

Giselle purses her lips, trying to control her temper. "Your safety is always my utmost concern. You are the most important thing in my life."

Oddly, there's true conviction in her words. She looks at her husband as if he's dear to her, precious.

It's odd, considering the predatory look that darkens her eyes when she spots Irving.

Kent shakes his head, his eyes flashing. "I thought so once. But I know you well enough now. Your lies mean nothing to me."

He turns, and she sets her hand on his arm, her face softening. "Stop, Kent—"

With a jerk of his arm, he strides off, leaving her staring after him with her hand still raised. I shouldn't watch her, shouldn't pity her, but for some reason, I can't help myself. As soon as he turns the corner, her face crumples. She looks pitiful, like a petulant child who didn't get her way, but there's true worry in her expression.

Before she sees me, I slip back into the chair and wait for her to walk down the hall.

***

The day is just dawning. Nobles and knights prepare their horses—a small legion of men all going after one man.

Even a wizard doesn't have a chance.

Still, a sinking feeling settles in my stomach.

Behind me, Irving sets a hand on my shoulder, drawing my attention. I turn and put on a smile for him.

"You'll be careful, won't you?" I try to keep the words light.

He gives me a look I'm coming to know quite intimately. It's his cocky, nothing-in-the-world-can-touch-me expression. He raises an eyebrow as his mouth twists into a lopsided smirk. "I'm not worried about a gypsy."

I step forward and trail my hand down his arm before I meet his eyes. "We both know that's not what you're walking into."

"The fortune teller escaped the day before the attack, and they have the girl's word." Irving shrugs, but his eyes shadow. "I must have been mistaken."

His chain mail is cool under my fingers. I trace the pattern of the metal rings with my finger before I finally let my hand drop. "We both know you weren't."

He grins, easy. "I can admit it when I'm wrong, Audette."

A tiny smile tips my lips. "I can admit when you're wrong as well." I lock my eyes with his. "But this time, I don't believe you were."

Like always, he thinks of brushing the solemn moment away, but then he lets the pretense drop. "Then what are we riding into?"

"I don't know," I whisper.

He wrinkles his nose and looks into the distance. "Can I ask a favor of you?"

"That depends on what it is."

His answering chuckle makes me tingle, makes me want to say something humorous just to have him laugh again.

"Give me a token." He says the words lightly, a bare smile on his lips. "Something insignificant, something you won't miss."

I think about it for a moment, and then I draw the knife from the pouch at his side. Just as I'm about to slice a small lock of hair, he stops me.

"Don't cut your hair," he says.

"I'm not overly fond of it right now anyway." I give him a wry look, and then, feeling like a maiden from a bard's tale, I cut a small section. "I won't miss it."

As I hand it to him, the dark lock shimmers to the color of wheat in the sun. I'm so startled, I drop the hair on the courtyard stones.

Irving's eyebrows knit with disbelief as he kneels to examine it. "Well, that's disconcerting."

"Why would it do that?" I demand although I know Irving doesn't know the answer any more than I do.

After several moments, he makes to pick up the fallen lock.

"Leave it," I say, my voice clipped.

Slowly, Irving stands, and his eyes return to me. He pulls my hair forward, scrutinizing the section I cut. I only took off a few inches, and since I took it from the nape of my neck, it's barely noticeable.

"It's strange, but I'd almost say it's darker than it was a few days ago," he says. Then he shakes the thought away, his forehead scrunched. "Let's not dwell on it. The whole hair as a token thing—it's a slightly creepy tradition anyway."

Despite my horror, a giggle bubbles past my lips. It feels good to laugh.

He takes a step closer, too close, and the laugh catches in my throat.

"Do you know what's not a creepy tradition?" His words tickle my lips.

"What's that?" I breathe, knowing I should back away.

There are too many men nearby, including my brother and my knights.

But I don't care.

"A kiss for luck."

I haven't allowed myself to get this close to Irving since the night we almost married. It's dangerous being this near him. I lose all judgment, all access to rational thought.

When he's this near, with his short, light hair brushing against my temples as our foreheads touch, with his dark, laughing eyes staring straight into my soul, there's nothing else.

Rising on my toes, I brush my lips against his in invitation. He must be more anxious about this outing than he lets on because he meets me with an urgency that takes my breath away. Lacing my hands together behind his neck, I melt into him. Every one of my muscles warms and relaxes until I feel as hot and

267

carefree as if I were lying in a field of wildflowers on a summer day.

That lovely feeling ebbs the moment my brother clears his throat rather loudly from behind me.

I break away from Irving, my face flaming red.

"That's quite the sendoff," Rogert says, grinning with a wicked, teasing glint in his eyes. He holds his arms out. "What about a goodbye for your favorite knight?"

Irving tenses next to me and then slides his arm around my shoulder, making a quiet statement. Barowalt flashes Rogert a warning look, and the knight lowers his arms, laughing under his breath.

Choosing to ignore Irving's proximity to me, Barowalt says, "You and Milly are not to leave the castle."

"Why can't we return to the villa?"

"All of our remaining knights are coming with me. It's safer for you here."

Not liking being told what to do, I cross my arms. "We could ride to Asher's."

Never mind that the unicorns are terrified of me.

My mind wanders to the lock of hair that changed back to the color I was born with, and I can't help but wonder what dark magic I've been infected with.

"Don't be difficult, Audette," Barowalt says.

I give in because I don't see any point in arguing

this time. What difference does it make if I'm here or there?

"Barowalt," I say as they turn to leave. "Be cautious."

He nods once, mounts his horse, and rides toward the gates. Rogert follows, but Keven glances back at me. I give him a small smile. He thinks about it for a moment, but finally, he returns it.

It's not much, but it's something.

After Keven rides off, Irving shakes his head at the knight's back. "I'm not used to such stiff competition." He flashes me a smile. "You prefer roguish princes to brooding knights, don't you?"

Yanking hard on his tunic, taking him by surprise, I pull him toward me. "Despite my better judgment, I seem to like you more than anyone."

He raises an eyebrow, obviously enjoying his current position. His eyes glide to my lips, sending a wave of heat through me. "Good."

***

Milly paces the sitting room that connect our chambers. She, too, is uneasy about the mission. Something feels ominous, something I can't quite place.

The door swings open. Expecting it to be the tea we requested, I turn, ready to chastise the maid for not knocking. But it's not a maid.

Grace's hair is disheveled, and she looks absolutely

exhausted. Letta tags in behind her, looking bored. Without a word, Grace slams an open book on the table between Milly and me.

"There," she says, her voice full of certainty.

After Milly and I exchange a glance, we look at the page.

Milly's eyes go wide, and she sits back. "What is that?"

I lean forward, my hands tingling as my breath quickens. Though I never truly saw the creature in the dark, there's a recognition deep inside me.

The illustrated beast is easily as large as a dragon, black as night, and covered with plated scales.

"Ludrako," I say, testing the word.

"L-u-drako." Letta automatically corrects, making the "u" short.

I give the girl a questioning glance, but she only stares back.

"What is it?" Milly gasps, horrified.

Like a griffin resembles a lion and an eagle, the ludrako is a wolf-dragon. His body is strongly muscled, his head canine. But his back, legs, tail, and skull are covered in armored plates. Only his underbelly is furred.

Golden eyes shine in the picture, and even in the illustration, I feel as if they're watching me.

"The ludrako is the rarest of the predatory

magical beasts," Grace reads. "*Supposedly native to northern Waldren, the creature is rarely seen, and many believe it to be a myth. Its hide is encased in dragon-like armor that is virtually impenetrable, and its sight and sense of smell are heightened. Capable of sleeping for hundreds of years, it only rises from its hibernation when it scents magic nearby.*

"*Ravenous once woken, it seeks out magical beings and feeds from their essence. After an initial glut, it's said that the ludrako will find a safe lair to restore its strength. Various cases throughout history have been recorded where humans have woken the beast to manipulate it for their own agenda. Like a dragon, it is a creature of reason and can be persuaded to attack in exchange for a steady supply of magic.*

"*Early reports state that entire blessings of unicorns have been wiped out by the beast, but considering the questionable existence of the hoofed creatures, and the little information we have on the ludrako itself, it's impossible to know whether this is a beast of fact or fancy.*

"*Either way, it's doubtful anyone in this age will ever encounter one.*"

Grace looks up, her eyes triumphant.

"Do you know what this means if it's true?" I ask no one in particular.

Milly looks pale. "We're in a lot of trouble."

"That...and the girl from the village was lying."

Grace narrows her eyes, thinking. "But why?"

I look back at the page, the illustration haunting

me. I'm wondering the same thing.

CHAPTER TWENTY-THREE

"You're strong, Princess," one of the remaining knights says as I block his attack.

Quickly darting to the side, I acknowledge his praise with an unladylike grunt.

I haven't even bothered to ask his name. He's simply part of the endless string of knights and guards that I'm venting my worry on.

The men left yesterday, and we've had no word of them since. The bluffs outside Vallen Harbor are only an hour's ride away. We should have had news. We should have had it yesterday.

King Edlund's sent scouts to see what's become of the group. Over breakfast, he mused that the wizard was gone and they're trying to track his steps.

But I fear they ran into something much larger

than they were prepared for.

We haven't been able to tell the king about the ludrako because it would elicit far too many questions. So we wait and hope, praying the men will have approached the lair with caution.

I dance to the side, narrowly missing the knight's blade.

Though my opponent is formidable, he's nothing compared to the men I'm used to training with. Still, I feel as if I'm just recovering from a bout of sickness. I feel fine, but I'm weak. My muscles don't respond as quickly as normal, or with as much speed.

As I turn, the tail of my dark braided hair catches my eye. I scowl, wondering why I'm so slow, why I'm tiring so quickly.

Eventually, after circling again for several moments, each of us studying the other for a weak spot, the knight catches me off guard. I fall, but before I crash on the hard cobblestones, he catches me around the waist.

With a hesitant smile, he rights me and takes a step back.

Sweat runs down my face, and I wipe it away with my arm. Milly, who's dutifully watching from the side, glares at me, making a face as she tries to silently remind me to mind my manners.

I make a face back and gratefully accept the water

a young page offers me.

"Where did you learn to fight like that?" the knight asks as he leans against a nearby wall. He looks as exhausted as I feel.

At least I kept him on his toes. With how off I'm feeling, I can take pride in that.

"Barowalt," I answer as I twirl the point of the sword on a stone. "And my father."

As always, there's a touch of sadness in my voice. But I'm getting better; I'm healing. Thinking of my parents no longer makes my heart feel raw. It doesn't make my throat constrict.

"I'm sure Barowalt is proud of you." After an awkward moment, he adds, "And I'm sure your father would have been as well."

He says the last words with hesitation, so I give him a small smile so he knows I'm not offended.

After I've rested for several minutes, and just as I'm about to challenge the knight to a rematch, there's a great commotion at the front gates. Trumpets sound in a warning cry, and the peasants standing about don't seem to know whether they should find shelter or run to the gates and see what the ruckus is.

Before I even see them, my heart seizes.

The men have returned, but I doubt they're bringing back good news.

I push through the crowd, determined to be at the

gates when they enter.

Milly's right at my back, and when she sees them, she lets out a muffled, agonized cry.

Barowalt's in the back of a farmer's cart that's been hitched to a knight's horse. His chest and torso are bloody, and he breathes in shuttering, labored intervals.

Terrified and shocked, I watch as they wheel my brother into the courtyard.

Milly races to him, demanding someone tell her what happened, but my eyes are frozen on Barowalt. Never in my life has he looked so mortal.

Chaos ensues around us, people yelling questions over each other, noblewomen rushing forward through the throng of peasant gawkers to find their husbands and fathers.

Suddenly jarring awake, I search madly for Irving. Only half of the group seem to have returned, and they're all suffering injuries, some nearly as grim as Barowalt's. I finally spot Irving toward the back, riding next to Javid. He looks more serious than I've ever seen him. Both the men's horses pull carts, and I realize several more of the knights' do as well.

Most are filled with the injured, but some of them are covered with thin canvas, hiding their loads from sight.

I suck in a breath as panic builds in my chest.

Now frantic, I search for my knights, my elite. I can't find any of them. They should be at Barowalt's side, helping the men who have arrived with a stretcher carry him to the court physician.

Where are they?

Irving dismounts, looking weary, and scans the crowd. Giselle reaches him before I do. She sets her hands on his arms, offering him comfort, but when he spots me running toward him, he brushes her off without apology.

I don't take the time to look at her, to see if there's a jealous glint in her eyes, but I'm sure there is.

Right now, I don't care. Let her comfort her own husband.

Almost stumbling on a loose cobblestone, I run toward Irving, not caring how it looks. He opens his arms, and I leap into him. He returns my embrace and crushes me to his chest. He smells like blood and battle, and a hard lump forms in my throat, threatening to choke me.

"Are you hurt?" I demand, my voice breaking. I pull back roughly so I may check him over.

A nasty bruise grows above his cheekbone. His tunic is torn, the chain mail is smeared with dirt, and blood shows underneath.

"Not badly." He pulls me back and buries his face in my hair.

277

"Barowalt," I say, pulling out of his arms. The relief of knowing he's safe soon fades as the fear that my brother might not see another morning claims me. "What happened?"

Irving's face goes hard as he watches the servants and guards carry more knights to the infirmary. "We found more than a wizard."

An anguished cry sounds over the rest, and we turn toward it. Several knights speak with Queen Clara, their eyes on the ground and their faces ashen. Clara turns to Edlund and grasps his tunic. Sobbing, the queen falls against him. The king looks stunned, unable to process the news he's been given.

Two carefully-wrapped bodies are taken from one of the carts and carried into the castle. Though we don't know who the men are under their shrouds, the crowd goes silent with horror. From His and Her Majesty's reactions, I have an idea.

Giselle, turning their way after hearing the heart-wrenching commotion, scans the men who have returned, likely looking for Kent. Her eyes fall on her husband, and shock mars her usually regal features. Kent is transferred to a stretcher, and the princess's eyes go wide as all the color drains from her face.

Her husband is conscious, but blood oozes from a hastily wrapped bandage around his chest. Hysterical, Giselle forgets Irving and runs to his side. Ugly sobs rack her body, and she follows him as servants carry him inside.

"What did you find?" I ask Irving, though I already know the answer.

Irving shakes his head at the memory and pulls me against him again. "A creature—a monster—I have no name for."

***

Prince Aldus is dead.

So is the king's brother, Prince Frederick. Fourteen of Ptarma's knights have also been lost.

And we lost Rafe.

Keven, Rogert, and Hallgrave were brought in unconscious, and are now in the physician's care, all suffering from the same blackness that stained my hair dark.

And Barowalt barely clings to life.

Suddenly, what's always seemed a bit like playing with swords and traveling about, pretending to protect the unicorns, has turned into something much more solemn.

I watch, almost numb, as a bishop places a circlet on Kent's head. With a quiet, serious audience of grief-stricken nobles, King Edlund officially declares his nephew to be the heir to the Ptarmish throne. Both men wear dark shadows under their eyes, their pain on display for all to see. Edlund lost a son and brother, and Kent lost his father and his dearest friend.

Kent's chest is wrapped, his face is pale and clammy, but he's on his feet. That's more than can be said for many of the men who ventured out on that fool's mission.

Quiet applause echoes off the stone walls once the ceremony ends, and, slowly, we filter out. There's quiet murmuring, but very few talk. The light Ptarmish castle has been cloaked in stifling sadness.

Giselle stands toward the back, too lost in her blubbering over losing two close members of Kent's family to stay in her seat toward the front. She dabs her eyes with a handkerchief, but I see no sign of tears.

It may be callous, but I can't help but think she simply wants people to pity her, to look at her and give her the attention she so obviously craves. Why isn't she with her husband? Kent's father and brother died the day before yesterday, and he's been thrust into a position he never expected to take.

Her eyes flick to me and then they fall to Irving's hand, which is clasped over mine.

Unable to help myself, I give her a haughty look, step closer to my betrothed, and sweep past her.

It's no secret I blame her and the foolish girl who claimed to have seen the beast change to vapor—not that the girl is a good vessel for my wrath now. Nadia's locked in the dungeons, much to her family's dismay.

After twenty-four hours, she still swears she only reported what it was she saw.

She might not know it, but the dungeons are the safest place for her. The king's son and brother are dead. There are people who scream to have the girl hanged for her false witness.

It's obvious to all now that the creature is not a conjured shadow. He's not a vapor, not a mirage, but a beast of nightmares.

One who, once again, has disappeared.

Irving's hand is warm in mine, and I cling to him like a lifeline. Silently, we walk through the halls. Irving doesn't ask where I'm going. He knows.

I knock on the physician's door, and one of the maids answers. She ushers us in, her eyes soft and downcast.

Though I didn't expect there to be, I was hoping for some drastic change in Barowalt's condition. I can tell from the girl's expression he's the same as he was this morning.

As Milly has been since Barowalt returned, she's at his side. She sits in a chair, but she's leaned over, her head resting on Barowalt's uninjured stomach, and she's fast asleep.

She looks more peaceful than she has since my brother left.

My eyes shift to my remaining knights. Hallgrave

woke yesterday, and I've sent him to Asher's estate to inform them what's taken place and warn them to be especially diligent in their care. Before the knight left, I studied him for signs of the same change I went through—darkened hair, darkened eyes—but his hair was already dark brown with his eyes matching.

I couldn't make out a difference.

The change in Keven, however, is disconcerting. Like me, he's no longer blond but brunette. Earlier, he began to stir, and now his and Rogert's cots are empty.

"Did Lord Kevin and Sir Rogert wake?" I ask Physician Benjamin.

The man, turns, looking weary. Grace told me yesterday that because he's needed for little more than stomach ailments and the occasional pain relieving tea, he is most often found in the courtyard, fussing with his roses and herbs. His skin is surprisingly tan against his graying hair, but he looks pale today.

"Yes, Your Highness," he says. "I've directed them to walk in the gardens for a short while before they return to their duties."

Despite the dour atmosphere of the infirmary, I almost smile. Only in Ptarma would a physician prescribe a walk amongst flowers.

Without thinking, I wrap my arms around him in a quick embrace. "Thank you for everything you've done."

He pats my back like the sweet grandfather he is. "I'll continue to do everything I can for your brother."

Tears sting my eyes as I step back. I blink them away and nod.

Irving stands at my shoulder, offering me quiet strength. His usual smiles are gone, replaced with soft eyes and a serious set jaw.

I miss his lightness, his wry wit, but there's something about him like this that makes my heart soften even more toward him.

Not wanting to wake Milly, I only gaze on Barowalt for a few moments before I turn for the door. As we're leaving, the king and queen enter with Kent.

Clara's eyes are red, and her nose looks raw from crying.

The kingdom may have lost their future king, but she lost a son. How Aldus's absence must weigh on her shoulders. It's a suffocating pain I'm all too familiar with. But to lose a child? I can't even imagine.

As always, when Kent sees me and Irving, he grows uncomfortable. But this time, his grief and pain outweigh his embarrassment at having been caught with a mistress.

"Though he insists he's fine," Edlund says to Benjamin. "I'd like you to take another look at Kent's injuries."

"And I told him it's healing as well as can be

expected—" Kent begins.

The king holds up a hand, cutting him off. Kent nods once and falls silent, probably too numb from the sudden loss of his father to argue with his uncle.

The physician nods and motions for the prince to sit. I squeeze Clara's hand as we turn to leave, unable to put into words how truly sorry I am for her loss.

She clutches my hand, blinking as she nods, and then turns back to her nephew.

Just as we're stepping through the door, Benjamin calls, "Prince Irving, I'd like to see how your wounds are healing as well. Can you wait for a moment?"

"I'm fine," Irving says. "You have more important things to attend to."

Benjamin looks up, a wry look on his face that tells me perhaps Irving's injuries were slightly greater than he wanted to let on.

"It will only take a moment," the physician assures him.

Feeling uncomfortable, I find a place near the wall.

I try not to look as Benjamin strips the bloodied bandage from Kent's chest, but my eyes flutter that way in morbid curiosity. I suck in a quiet gasp when I see the yellowing flesh and the raw, oozing wound.

Benjamin frowns. "Infection's setting in."

The tension in the room is palpable.

"What can we do?" Edlund asks.

The physician wraps the wound, swishes his hands in a small tub filled with an herbal solution that gives me a headache, and turns back to the king. He sighs and rubs the back of his neck. "I will continue to treat it with salves, but it's not yet responding."

Clara grows paler than she was before.

Kent clasps his aunt's hand and gives her a look of mock bravado. "I'll be fine."

She blinks back tears and turns to Benjamin. "We'll track down whatever you require. Anything. Tell us what is needed to save these men." Her voice breaks. "Ben...please...I can't lose any more family to this."

Benjamin sinks to a stool. "If I knew what poison was running through their veins...but no one can tell me what this beast is. I have no way—"

"It's a ludrako," I blurt out, glancing at my dwindling brother, usually so strong and yet so weak now. I turn back to the physician, knowing that there may be questions I can't answer. Surer this time, I say again, "The beast is a ludrako."

"How do you know?" Edlund demands. "And what in Elden's kingdoms is a ludrako?"

Suddenly exhausted, I lean against the wall. "Find Grace."

Surprisingly, Edlund only nods, and then he, Clara, and Kent step out to find the duchess.

Weary, wondering how we're going to explain why we've been researching magical beasts that devour magic, I rub my hands over my face.

"Let's take a quick look, Irving," Benjamin says after the door swings shut. "Take a seat."

Irving argues with the elderly physician, but eventually, he sits in the spot Kent just vacated. Without a word, he strips off his tunic.

I look away, but my traitorous eyes find their way back and slide over his tan, toned torso. Just as I had suspected, he's built of lean muscle.

Sensing me looking, for the first time in days, he flashes me a wicked grin.

A riot of butterflies wakes in my stomach. Blushing, I bite my lip but don't look away.

Benjamin fusses over a gash in Irving's side, but my eyes find a series of faint, odd scars that stretch across his arm, shoulder, and chest.

The physician excuses himself, off to fetch something, and we're as alone as we can be in a room of wounded men and maids.

Standing, I cross to Irving. With a tentative touch, I run my finger down the scars and breathe, "What happened to you?"

"Dragon." When he turns his head, his mouth is close to my ear, and the word sends a tremor straight to my stomach.

I set my hand on his chest, and his breath hitches softly.

Trying to hide his reaction to my closeness, he murmurs, "The physician in Lauramore lied. He said it wouldn't scar." He raises an eyebrow. "But I'm glad it did. Makes me look rather dashing, don't you think?"

"You're an idiot," I whisper, smiling.

But what I really want to tell him is that I love him.

It's a terrifying thought. When you love people, it hurts all the more when you lose them. How could I let myself fall? What would I have done if Irving had come back as wounded as Barowalt?

What would I have done if he'd died?

To care is to hurt.

As if he can tell where my thoughts have drifted, Irving wraps his hands around my waist and pulls me toward him. He grazes his jaw just under my ear, making me shiver. "No changing your mind at this point, Princess. You're stuck with me."

I'm about to climb onto his lap when Benjamin clears his throat from the doorway.

I step back and smooth a wrinkle on my skirt.

Irving, obviously delighted by my discomfort, grins at me over the physician's shoulder.

After several minutes, Benjamin has Irving's side wrapped.

"Audette?" Benjamin says as we're about to leave. "What is this beast you spoke of?"

Irving gives me a soft nod, and I take a deep breath and explain everything from the book, leaving out the part about the unicorns.

"So it's a magical species?"

"Yes."

Benjamin purses his lips, thinking. He glances at the remaining men, all suffering silently before he turns back to me. "I need the assistance of a gimly."

Where am I to find a gimly? That particular magical species looks nearly identical to humans, and they very rarely choose to make their presence known.

But they are renowned for their healing abilities.

I've begun to shake my head, to tell him it's impossible, but then I stop.

If it's a gimly we need to save Barowalt's life, then a gimly I'll find.

CHAPTER TWENTY-FOUR

"Finding a gimly is no trouble," Grace says as she browses for more information on the ludrako in the castle's library. "In fact, there's a scholar in Constelita we could ask. I'd like to go back to their library now that we know exactly what beast it is we're looking for."

Javid nods. "We'll go now."

Like Irving, Javid wasn't injured badly. He's a little bruised, a little scratched up, and he walks with a slight limp, but other than that, he fared the attack well.

"There's a gimly scholar in Constelita?" I ask, my voice incredulous.

Grace smiles. "Yes. According to her, there's more of them living amongst us than we'll ever know."

I shake my head, processing it. "Do you think she'll come?"

Javid and Grace exchange a look that seems promising, and then Grace nods.

"Thank you," I breathe, a small weight lifting off my shoulders.

If we can find the gimly in time, then surely she will be able to save Barowalt.

"I'll help you prepare the horses," Irving says to Javid, and the two men leave the library.

I watch them walk through the doorway and then turn to Grace. "How is it, do you think, they came out of the attack so unscathed?"

"Irving didn't tell you what happened?" the duchess asks, surprised.

"I haven't asked yet. Every time he thinks of it, he becomes agitated."

She places an unwanted book back on the shelf and motions for me to join her on a padded bench near a window. Once again, it's raining.

I miss the sunshine we had when we first arrived. An occasional rain is fine, but to have it storm every afternoon and most mornings...it makes me melancholy.

Grace runs her hand down her long braid. "When they arrived at the cave, your elite, heeding your warning, cautioned the group to tread carefully, but Aldus and Frederick were of a different mind. They wanted to storm the lair and take the wizard by surprise."

"They led the charge," I say.

She nods. "Kent was toward the front as well, but he somehow evaded the creature."

"And our men hung back, planning."

"But they couldn't just do nothing when they heard the slaughter, so they joined them."

I shake my head, growing angry. If Edlund and Barowalt had simply listened to Irving...

"According to Javid," Grace says, lowering her voice. "The moment your brother and knights stepped into the cave, the creature sensed them. With single-minded determinedness, first it attacked their minds, sending them to their knees, and then it lunged on Barowalt. It gave the king's remaining knights a chance to attack it. It didn't even notice when they came at it with their swords. According to Javid, they couldn't wound it."

Remembering the pain all too well, I shudder. "Only the men of the Order fell in pain?"

"Yes."

Suddenly, it all makes sense.

I stand abruptly. "It was feeding off the unicorn magic that clings to us." I grasp a lock of my hair. "And the magic it used marked us with its darkness."

That's the thing I'm missing. This odd feeling I haven't been able to place, this vague weakness that afflicts my muscles. I no longer carry their protective essence with me.

"But what does that mean?" Grace asks.

A cold feeling slithers through my stomach. "It means the Order can't fight this creature."

Her brow wrinkles. "Perhaps. Unless the ludrako has already fed off the magic. In that case, when you meet it a second time…"

Staring out the window, watching the clouds swirl in the countryside, hope blooms in my chest. He can't hurt the four of us again. Our magic has already been lost.

I look back suddenly. "Grace? If the creature set its wrath on Barowalt, how is he alive?"

"Irving saved him."

"How?"

Grace only shrugs, looking helpless.

She'd just said nothing they did wounded the beast, but Irving injured it in Constelita. And apparently again in the cave.

What is he doing differently?

***

Grace and Javid left to find the gimly, and I pace the courtyard, waiting for Hallgrave's return. If I'm right, and I think I am, the unicorns should have shied away from him just as they did me. If they did, then we'll know their magic is lost to us.

Then we'll know we can attack the ludrako.

Irving sits on a barrel, watching me with a ghost

of a wry smile on his face.

"What?" I finally demand, unable to bear his silence any longer.

"You're a vision in leather armor, with your hair braided back and your eyes fiery with determination." He grins slowly, knowing he's flustered me.

"Why didn't you tell me you saved Barowalt's life?" I ask abruptly.

Irving's eyebrows shoot up. "Who told you that?"

"Grace."

Stretching, acting nonchalant, he crosses his arms and slouches against the wall. "It was a lucky shot."

"Why is it that the one time you have no reason to play humble, you—wait. You shot it again? Like the night in the streets?"

He gives me an odd look. "Yes."

"You shot it with an arrow?"

The light shines through the trees, highlighting his hair, making him look especially heroic and noble until he ruins the image by smirking. "That's typically what you shoot something with."

"And no one else tried to shoot it?"

He looks confused, but that irritating smile still plays on his lips. "Several people attempted it. Apparently I had the lucky shot."

I shake my head. "No, that's not it."

Rising, he strides to me, cocky now. "Are you

saying you're finally willing to admit my superior archery skills? I knew you would eventually."

I raise a brow. "That's certainly not what I'm saying."

He rubs his jaw against my shoulder, distracting me. "You're sending me mixed signals, darling."

"Stop that," I say, pushing him back. "I can't think."

There something different about Irving's arrows. Something he'd said...

Practically purring, he steps toward me again, pushing me backward until I'm against the large, gnarled trunk of a tree. "I like it when you don't think."

Laughing, I try to press against his chest, but he won't budge. My heart picks up its pace, and for the millionth time, I wonder why I didn't first marry him in Primewood when I had the chance.

"You smell good," he murmurs, his lips brushing against the crook of my neck. "You're dressed like a goddess warrior, ready to take on a mythical creature of old, and yet you took the time to dab perfume oils behind your ears. I rather like that."

I tingle where his lips trail, and I'm about to close my eyes and give in when that thing that was floating just out of my reach suddenly pops into my head. "Drachite."

Startled, Irving backs up only enough to meet my eyes. "I'm sorry?"

"Your arrowheads—you told my knights they were crafted from the new alloy King Rigel of Errinton created—the same as the armor you were speaking of."

Understanding dawns on Irving's face, and he takes a swift step back, serious now. "They are."

"And you're the only one who's been able to inflict harm on the beast."

He raises an eyebrow, pretending arrogance. "I am."

"How many arrows do you have left?" I demand.

Irving wrinkles his brow, thinking. "Of my drachite arrows? Two...maybe three."

It's not enough.

"What about your armor? Could we smelt it? Craft a few swords?"

He looks like he's swallowed a toad. "You want me to smelt down my priceless, rare, very coveted set of drachite armor to make swords?"

"That's right."

Gritting his teeth, yet somehow smiling, he sucks in a slow breath. Finally, he closes the distance between us again. Against my ear, he says, "You're very lucky I like you."

***

We find Rogert in the practice yard, sparring. I scan the men for Keven. The two knights are rarely apart.

As if sensing Irving and me, a knight looks over,

and our eyes meet.

I suck in a startled breath. My golden knight, my lion, has cut his hair. It's now so short, it doesn't even brush his ears. And it's as dark as teak.

After Keven excuses himself from the crowd, he kneels before me. "Your Highness." He pauses, his face tortured. "I'm so sorry for what happened to Barowalt. I should—"

"Stop." I motion for him to rise. "I was the creature's victim as well, don't you remember? I know there was no fighting it in that moment."

He nods, but his jaw stays tight. Then he turns his attention to Irving. "Word has it you saved him. You saved all of us."

Irving wears a cautious, friendly smile. "Don't mention it."

Slowly, as if it almost pains him, Keven extends his hand.

Next to me, Irving hesitates, but then he takes it. As they shake, their smiles grow. Their new camaraderie makes my heart happy.

Not to be left out, Rogert bounds over and crushes them both in a bear hug. "They've made a truce! Get in here, Audette. It's a momentous occasion!"

Squealing, I try to get away, but Rogert is too quick. I'm smashed in between them, laughing. "Let me go! We have things to do."

Not an hour later, the three of us stand in the smithy with Edlund's personal armorsmith. Irving, who's fetched his drachite armor just as I asked him to, looks ill.

"It's not melting down." The armorsmith shakes his head. "I don't know what secret Errinton holds on it."

Irving sucks in his cheeks and looks at the ceiling. "Rigel said he had to superheat the forge with fire talc." He practically groans the words.

Trying not to laugh at his distress, I squeeze his hand, hoping to comfort him.

It's beautiful armor, dark and sleek and polished. I hate to destroy it, I really do. But the chance of us killing the ludrako with three arrows is slim to none.

"Fire talc," the armorsmith muses, rubbing his jaw and getting it sooty in the process. "I suppose I can try if someone can track some down for me."

It takes all day, but we finally find a merchant in Kallert selling the talc. We deliver it to the armorsmith the next day. To my disappointment, he tells me it will be too dangerous for me to linger.

Irving, not having the stomach to watch his precious armor melted down, excuses himself as well, trusting Rogert and Keven to oversee the process.

"It's for a good cause," I assure him as we walk into the castle.

"You're awfully bright-eyed," he says, his tone only slightly sour.

I stop to face him. "This is going to work. Once the swords are made, we will attack again, and this time, we will slay the beast."

"Why do you say that as though Barowalt will let you go?"

Tossing my hair over my shoulder, I continue to the castle. "Because I won't give him a choice."

Irving only chuckles under his breath and follows me through the entryway.

I pause by the nearest guard. "Have the Duke and Duchess Marfell returned yet?"

"Yes, Your Highness," the man says. "They arrived over an hour ago."

Not wasting any more time, I thank the man and rush through the halls to the infirmary with Irving at my heels. I knock on the door, impatient.

This time, when the maid answers the door, she wears a smile.

"Good news?" I ask her, my heart swelling.

She grins. "Wonderful news."

I walk through the door and find Kent sitting on a cot with Giselle at his side. A red-haired woman sits on a stool in front of them. She has her hand pressed to the prince's chest, and her eyes are fixed on the wound in concentration.

298

Slowly, before our eyes, the swelling goes down and the yellowed skin begins to pink. The oozing slows, and the wound starts to knit.

"There." Smiling, she opens her eyes and draws her hand away. "Now it will heal just as it should."

"Can't you heal him completely?" Giselle demands.

The gimly woman turns to her. "There are too many injured to concentrate on only one."

Giselle looks murderous. "But he is the heir to the Ptarmish throne!"

"And I have taken the infection and the poison away." She smiles at Kent. "You will be just fine."

Kent smiles and lets out a long contented sigh. "I already feel better. I'm in your debt."

His wife's eyes flash, but she keeps her mouth shut.

The gimly rises, and I look at Barowalt, hopeful.

"Who next?" she asks Edlund, who lingers in the corner.

"Please," Milly croaks, looking near tears. "Please help Barowalt."

Edlund nods, smiling. "Yes, please."

I take a seat next to my brother. Milly, who looks near death herself, clutches my hand. She's trembling, terrified it won't work.

But I know it will.

"My name is Pella," the woman says softly, smiling at Milly to reassure her. She nods to Barowalt. "And who is this?"

"Barowalt, King of Brookraven." My voice cracks when I finish, "My brother."

Pella nods and sets her hand on Barowalt.

Irving grips my shoulder as we wait.

After several moments, Barowalt's breaths soften. Soon after that, color returns to his face.

Pella shudders and gasps, but she doesn't remove her hand. Finally, with a loud exhale, she opens her eyes. To Physician Benjamin, she says, "Change his bandages and keep applying the salve to his wounds, and he'll be fine."

Milly, so overcome with relief, begins to cry. She clutches her face in her hands, sobbing.

I'm about to wrap her in my arms when Barowalt stirs. I freeze, watching my brother as he opens his eyes. Blinking, he looks around. Immediately, his gaze lands on Milly, who hasn't yet noticed through her veil of tears.

"Milly?" His voice is scratchy and rough.

She jerks her head up. Her face is already wet, but when she sees him, she cries harder.

He sits, cringing at the pain of the movement. "What happened? All I remember is the beast."

Milly sets her hand on his arm. "I didn't know if

you would..."

His gaze intensifies as if he's truly seeing her for the first time. Even though we're all here, gawking, he yanks her to his chest. Threading his fingers through her hair, he kisses her.

"Marry me," he says after several long moments. "Enough of this game."

Laughing while holding back another wave of tears, she nods. "Yes."

My own eyes begin to sting. I blink quickly and turn away to give them privacy.

"Thank you," I say to Pella. "How can I repay you?"

"There's no need. I'm happy to help." She glances about the room and then pulls me into the corner. "What is this creature?"

"A ludrako."

"I've never heard of it, but its magic is fierce." She eyes my hair. "Be wary. It's marked you and your brother. I don't know why."

"I don't understand the purpose of the dark magic."

She shakes her head and fidgets with a strand of colorful beads at her wrist. "No—the magic isn't dark. It's not inherently evil, but rather predatory. Similar to that of a dragon."

I sigh, thinking.

Pella lowers her voice further. "It can track now.

Perhaps there is someone using the beast to find those protecting the blessing." When my eyes widen, she leans close and pats my shoulder. "Don't be afraid. I'm a gimly. I can see things humans can't."

Slowly, slightly spooked, I nod.

With another twist of her bracelet, she turns away, off to help the next man in need of her services.

CHAPTER TWENTY-FIVE

"You were only able to craft five swords from a full set of armor?" I ask the armorsmith, my voice on the shrill side.

"Your Highness," he says. "We used the fire talc, but the metal reacted strangely. I'm not familiar with the alloy. You're lucky you got five."

He's brought them to the villa, where we've now returned with Barowalt. We stand in the courtyard, and birds sing from the trees.

I glance at the swords. Not only did we get five when I had hoped for ten, maybe even fifteen, but they are ugly swords at that.

Sighing with defeat, I thank the man.

Once he leaves, Irving picks up a sword and studies its rough construction. It's gnarly and pitted, and the blade is anything but straight.

"You're not going to cry, are you?" I set my hands on my hips.

"No," he says with an exaggerated wobble in his voice. "I'm fine."

When he tries to slide it in his sheath, a divot in the blade catches on the leather, hanging it up.

I press my lips together, trying not to laugh.

Since we're alone, I step forward and ease the sword into the leather sleeve. "They will serve their purpose, and I will buy you another set of Errinton's prized armor when we return home."

He cocks his head to the side. "A wedding present?"

"If that's what you'd like to call it."

Grinning, he loops his arm around my waist and tugs me closer. "I can think of something I'd rather have—"

"Honestly," Keven says as he strides out the villa's entryway, rolling his eyes.

He and Irving may have made amends, but that doesn't necessarily mean the knight likes seeing us together.

Luckily, Keven's quickly distracted by the new swords. He pokes one with his dagger as if he doesn't want to sully himself by touching it. "What are these?"

Hallgrave and Rogert soon join us, and after

several moments, Barowalt hobbles out with the assistance of a staff.

My brother tires quickly, but Benjamin said it's best if he walks for short intervals several times a day.

It's strange to see my brother so helpless, so at the mercy of those around him.

Like a worrisome mother hen, Milly follows him out.

"Where is Letta today?" I ask her.

Since we've returned, the girl has barely left Milly's side.

"She's visiting with Grace," Milly says, and she looks somewhat relieved.

As much as Milly dotes on the girl, taking care of both her and Barowalt seems to be a little more than she can handle at the moment.

Barowalt leans against a stone garden barrier and picks up one of the swords. "So you believe these will kill the beast?"

"Yes," I say, completely sure.

"As long as he doesn't get in our heads again." Rogert rubs his temples at the memory.

I turn to Hallgrave. "The unicorns were just as frightened of you as they were of me, correct?"

The knight nods. "Terrified."

Satisfied, I pick up one of the swords, testing its weight. It's slightly heavier than what I'm used to, but it will do.

"What are you doing?" Barowalt asks me, his voice too even.

"Surely you don't think you're going to fight the beast in the condition you're in?" I turn to him. "This time, whether you like it or not, I'm leading my knights."

"No." He shakes his head. "I forbid it."

I motion the men, Irving, and Milly away with my head. They don't need to be present for this.

Once they've gone into the villa, I turn back to Barowalt. "I love you. I respect you. But I've given you too much of my power when it comes to the Order."

"You can't handle this alone."

"You're right. I can't do it alone. But that doesn't mean I need you taking the reins. Barowalt, this is my duty. I don't know why the responsibility is passed to a female, but it is the way it's done. I have to do this." I pause, letting my words soak in. "And you have to let me."

His jaw is tight, and he starts to shake his head. "If something were to happen to you—"

"It would be just as devastating for you as it was for me when I saw them haul you in on that wagon, bloody and barely breathing."

"You don't understand." He looks torn, his once familiar eyes too dark. "I promised our parents before they passed that I would take care of you." His eyes are full of memories. "I promised."

Gently, I wrap my arms around his middle. "But you can't protect me from everything—especially my duty."

"I know." He sets his arm on top of my head and rests his chin on it.

The gesture used to irritate me when we were younger, but now it's comforting.

"If you're this protective of me," I say, "what in the world are you going to do when the Order falls to your future daughter?"

He growls. "I don't even want to think of it."

I laugh and pull away, giving him a mischievous smirk just to irk him. "Your and Milly's future daughter."

He tries to hide a smile but fails. "If I'm lucky, we'll only have sons."

Shaking my head, I turn back to the atrocious swords. "I'll be fine. I promise."

Barowalt shifts, hobbling next to me. He meets my eyes, his look meaningful and mildly threatening. "You had better be."

***

The only thing left to do is wait for the beast to attack again. Another month passes, and there hasn't been any sign of it.

I'm growing increasingly anxious. I want to be done with this.

The storms have let up as spring approaches, and we've had more days of sunshine. Villages around Ptarma have slowly continued their festivals, and villagers are beginning to again walk the streets at night. People are starting to speculate the beast died in the last attack.

What if it did?

What if Irving's shot was so true, he actually killed it?

But it wasn't there when we went back to scout the cave. Dead creatures, even the magical species, tend to leave bodies lying about when they die.

Half-bored, I sit with Milly, Grace, and Aunt Camilla in Queen Clara's sitting room. Since Aldus's death, the queen's been sullen, and I was surprised to receive an invitation for tea this morning.

"Where is Giselle?" Clara asks several minutes after the maids have brought in the tea. "I spoke with her earlier, and she said she'd come."

"I haven't seen her today," Grace answers.

I drum my fingers on my leg and stare out the open balcony doors, watching the pink blooms of the amberwood tree wave in the slight breeze.

"Audette," Clara says. "Would you mind checking her quarters for me?"

Startled, I look back at the queen. "You want me to go to Giselle's rooms to look for her?"

The queen smiles. "I know there's tension between the two of you. It's time you make amends."

Grace very subtly wrinkles her nose, but, being ever the lady, she keeps her mouth shut. Milly looks flat out disgusted at the thought, but she keeps her thoughts to herself as well and, instead, spreads marmalade over a scone.

It's Aunt Camilla I expect to say something, but she only offers Grace another small cake.

"All right." I stand, feeling awkward. "I suppose I can try to find her."

I'd rather walk the castle halls than sit for tea, anyway.

After stalling as much as possible, loitering about the halls and admiring the plants and art, I finally make my way toward Kent and Giselle's rooms. I knock on the door, hoping to find the chambers empty.

Unfortunately, Giselle's handmaid opens the door.

"Oh," she says, startled to see me. "What can I do for you, Your Highness?"

"Queen Clara is expecting Giselle for tea. Is she feeling well? Does she still plan on attending?"

Please say no.

The girl motions me inside. I hesitate but don't

want to be outright rude, so I follow her in.

Giselle looks up from the chair by the window, more surprised to see me than her maid was. "Audette. What can I do for you?"

I explain to her why I'm here, even though I know she overheard me speaking with her maid.

"It slipped my mind." She sets her embroidery aside as she rises. "The queen always insists on keeping the balcony doors open. Would you be a dear and fetch my wrap for me?"

Glancing to the dressing table, I raise an eyebrow.

Does she truly expect me to serve her?

The answer to that is obviously "yes" because she sends her own maid on another errand. I take a deep breath, paste a smile on my face, and walk to the dressing table.

My hand freezes inches from the wrap. There, next to the brush, sits a brightly-colored beaded bracelet.

"Oh, do you like it?" Giselle asks from behind me. She picks up the wrap herself.

I meet her eyes in the mirror above the table.

Giselle smiles and brushes her dark, full hair behind her shoulder. "I thought it was the dearest bauble, and I convinced that little gimly witch to give it to me."

Gimlies are as far from witches as unicorns are from ludrakos, but I keep my mouth shut.

Knowing she's flustered me, Giselle raises an eyebrow. "I wanted it. And I always get what I want."

Undaunted, I turn to look at her, smiling. "But you could have any bracelet you please. Why take hers?"

"For the pleasure of it." She shrugs, and both of us know she's not speaking of jewelry.

"Someday you're going to run into someone who's not keen on the idea of sharing."

Her eyebrow twitches just slightly. "I don't see how that matters. Like I said, I always get what I want."

Anger boils under my skin. "Should we be going?"

"Of course." She dabs perfumed oil on her wrists. "I'll follow you."

All the easier for her to stab a knife in my back.

**

"I know who's been manipulating the ludrako," I say to Grace in the privacy of her and Javid's quarters.

The duchess looks up, surprised. "I thought we had decided it was the gypsy."

"I think it's Giselle."

Grace widens her eyes, obviously not sure how to respond. Carefully, she says, "I understand she isn't your favorite person—"

"No," I cut her off, agitated. "That's not it."

I pace back and forth, ready to argue my point. "The beast originates from Waldren, right?"

"Audette."

"And Giselle is from Waldren."

"Yes, but—"

"And now Kent is next in line for the throne." I turn to her, sure I'm right. "The beast eliminated the two men directly in front of him—and Giselle orchestrated the whole thing, using that girl from the village. You realize, don't you, that she's going to be your next queen!"

Grace places her hands in her lap. "She's never left the castle—not once."

"So she has people working for her," I argue. "That makes more sense anyway. She wouldn't actually soil her hands." I stop pacing and turn to her. "And the attack in Constelita! It's no secret she wants Irving. To have him, she needs me out of the picture."

"If I remember correctly, Irving was with you that night. Why would she have the beast attack him?"

I shake my head, now more convinced than before. "It's her."

Grace wrinkles her brow, obviously thinking about it. "You did say it seemed as if the beast tracked you, didn't you?"

"Yes," I answer, relieved she's finally contemplating it.

Her eyes flick to mine. "Right after you saw Kent with his mistress?"

I tilt my head to the side. "I'm not sure what that

has to do with it."

I've lost her. She's in her own world.

She continues, "And Kent's been on a hunting trip every time the beast attacked..."

"Are you saying she's using her husband? They don't seem to get along well enough to plot together."

Slowly, the color drains from her face. "Now he's going to be king, and the attacks have suddenly stopped."

"Right," I say slowly. "So it's Giselle."

"No." Grace looks impatient that I'm not following her. "But it may be Kent."

CHAPTER TWENTY-SIX

Rogert lunges at Hallgrave in the courtyard. One misshapen drachite blade meets another misshapen drachite blade, and the men's shadows dance in the torchlight.

I sit on the short wall, waiting for my turn. Clouds have settled, cloaking the stars, but I don't think we'll have rain tonight.

Hallgrave finally bests Rogert, and the two take a moment to catch their breath once the match is over.

"I'm exhausted," Rogert says, breathing hard. "I've never tired this easily in my life."

Hallgrave nods, resting his palms on his knees.

I chew my lip, concerned.

We certainly are at a disadvantage. If we'd never known the unicorn's magic, we wouldn't miss it so acutely.

With another deep breath, Hallgrave rights himself. "Keven, Audette? Who's next?"

Keven looks at me in question, but I motion him on.

Just like Grace, none in the Order believe me about Giselle. They all think I'm jealous, involved too deeply to see how foolish my accusation is. Grace's theory about Kent—that they're willing to consider.

But I saw the look on his face at the ceremony that pronounced him as Edlund's heir, the misery etched into the lines of his brow. I simply can't believe he killed his own father.

Giselle, though? I believe she'd kill anyone or anything that gets in her way. She said it herself. She always gets what she wants.

Rogert flops next to me as Keven and Hallgrave circle each other. "I'm retiring after we kill this ludrako beast."

I give him a sideways look. "I find that hard to believe."

He wipes the sweat from his brow with his tunic. "This 'being like everyone else' thing—it's exhausting."

"No matter if you leave the Order or not, you'll always be missing the unicorn's magic."

"Yes, but I could be sitting fat and happy on my estate and not facing down the beast of nightmares."

I elbow him in the side. "You want to live the life of a house cat?"

"Yes, yes I do."

He smirks, and I know him well enough not to ask what he's thinking.

Rogert opens his mouth, about to tell me anyway, when the rapid sound of a horse approaching catches our attention.

Hallgrave and Rogert pause in their duel, just as surprised as we are that someone is coming calling this late, and at such a rapid pace at that. My heart nearly seizes with apprehension when I make out the rider in the night.

Irving draws his horse up to an abrupt stop, and he leaps to the ground. Urgently, he says, "Audette, I need to speak with you."

"What's happened?"

Irving glances at my men. "I can't...we need to speak alone."

My knights look at him with suspicion, wondering, as I am, what he doesn't want to say in front of them. He looks more than worried...possibly slightly guilty. Like he has something to confess, and he wants to do it before...

There's the sound of another horse, and, again, we turn toward the road.

"Audette, please," Irving pleads, true fear flashing

in his eyes.

Barowalt races into the courtyard at a much faster pace than is safe for him while he's still healing. He sees Irving, and there's murder in his gaze.

My shoulders begin to tremble.

"You have no right to be here!" Barowalt shouts, his whole body rigid with anger. "I want you off our land!"

Still injured, my brother can't swing down from his horse as gracefully as Irving did, and Rogert rushes forward to assist him.

"What happened?" I demand of Irving.

"Nothing," he insists, his eyes sincere. He grasps hold of my hands. "I swear it."

Leaning on Keven, Barowalt stalks forward, limping. He's seething, livid. I've never seen him this mad. "As we were leaving Aunt Camilla's quarters, we saw Giselle sneaking out of Irving's door."

Irving shakes his head, matching Barowalt's anger with his own. "Nothing happened!"

"She was barely dressed, Irving!" Barowalt yells.

Stunned, I take a step back. Just when I think my knees will give out, Keven takes my arm.

No, Irving couldn't have...

My stomach rolls, and I'm afraid I'm going to be sick in front of them all.

"I had nothing to do with it," Irving insists. "I don't

know how she let herself in, but the moment I found her, I told her to get out."

No one believes him.

I'm not sure I believe him.

As if sensing my trust crumbling, Irving turns toward me. Practically groveling, he takes a step in my direction, but Hallgrave blocks his path. Irving steps to the side, craning his neck around the knight. "Audette. You know me now. You know me. I didn't do this. I swear it."

"I think you should go," I whisper.

He looks as if I knocked the wind out of him. His shoulders slump; his face crumples. "Audette..."

"It's late." I turn from him. It hurts too much to look at him right now. "I can't...tomorrow. We'll figure this out tomorrow."

"Stop this. Look at me," he pleads. "Let's talk, just us. Please, you have to listen—"

Though I won't look, I can hear the scuffle between him and Hallgrave as the knight pushes Irving to his horse. If he keeps resisting, a fight is inevitable.

"Audette, I lov—"

"No!" I whip around, finally looking at him. "Even if it's true, don't say it now. Don't sully it."

He stands by his horse, holding the reins. "Tomorrow."

I nod, not quite meeting his eyes. "Go now."

Reluctant, he mounts his horse.

The sound of the fading hoofbeats nearly does me in.

Without a word, Keven escorts me into the villa and walks me to my room. When we reach the door, he asks, "Will you be all right?"

Unable to answer, I give him a bare nod. He hesitates but finally closes the door behind him. I fall on my bed, numb. A raging, void bleakness grows in the pit of my stomach until it consumes me. I finally cry.

I'm not sure how long I've been here, cradled with my blankets, when Milly lets herself in and sits next to me.

Several moments pass in silence before I finally ask, "Were you with Barowalt?"

She doesn't answer right away, but when she does, her voice is faint. "Yes."

I turn toward her, still clutching my blankets. "Did you see her?"

Her face contorts with pain. "Yes."

My shoulders shake, and I clench my eyes shut, trying to block out the image of the two of them together. Barowalt is prone to overreacting, but Milly—Milly wouldn't upset me unless it were absolutely true.

"But I didn't even have a chance to question Irving," she whispers. "The moment he and your brother saw each other, it was if it were a race to the stables to reach you first. If it weren't for Barowalt's injuries, I know they would have come to blows."

That's how Irving arrived first. He simply outran Barowalt.

"I would have raced after them, but we had Letta with us. I couldn't leave her."

I nod, suddenly too ill at the thought to speak of it further.

Hoping to signal her that I can't rehash any more of it tonight, I pull the blankets over my head. The bed shifts, and Milly lies down next to me, just like when we were little. She doesn't say anything else, but having her here, knowing she cares enough to stay with me, helps. Even if it's only very little.

I don't sleep well. Every time I close my eyes, I see Giselle in Irving's arms. Thanks to her ridiculous armor, I can regretfully imagine her scantily dressed, and it makes my nightmare vision all that much worse.

But with the morning light comes clarity.

Either I put my trust in Irving, or in his reputation. Those are my only options.

I sit up and shove the blankets aside. Milly, always a late sleeper, is stretched out on the other side of the bed and snoring softly. On any other day, I'd wake her just to tease her about it.

Not today.

I dress as quietly as possible and then slip out of

the room. Hoping to sneak out undetected by Barowalt or my knights, I slink through the halls. I turn the last corner, almost to the servant's entrance in the kitchen, and scream out loud when I find someone right in my path.

Letta steps back, just as shocked to see me as I am to see her.

Clutching my chest, I demand, "What are you doing up?"

She looks as solemn as usual, her eyes wide with fear. "I was hungry."

Taking several deep breaths, I try to smile. "Of course. I'm sorry."

Nodding, she steps out of my way, half-terrified of me.

What kind of ogre am I that I scare a small child like this?

"I'm sorry," I say again, trying to keep my voice softer this time.

She only nods.

Without another word, I exit through the door and step into the cool, sunny morning. Spring has come to Ptarma, and it's beautiful.

My mind is elsewhere, and I don't have time to dwell on the new buds in the gardens or the blooms in the fruit trees. Working quickly, I saddle my horse and ride toward the castle.

By the time I deposit my mare in the care of a groomsman, my hands are shaking.

I'm terrified to speak with Irving, but it's best to get it out of the way. If I dwell on it further, I'll go mad.

Evading all but servants and maids, I wind through the castle halls. The way to my aunt's quarters is familiar now, and I barely think about which way I'm going. I'm so lost in thought, I don't look up in time to realize Giselle is at the end of the hall I'm walking down.

Our eyes meet, and for a split-second, hers flash with triumph. Quickly, she hides the expression. "Good morning, Princess."

I try to nod and walk past her.

"It's awfully early to visit Irving, don't you think?" She pauses, thoughtful. "He had an eventful night. He might not be...decent yet."

Unable to ignore her, I whip around.

Her eyes are bright, even if her features are smoothed in innocence.

"You set him up," I say, stepping forward. "You knew Barowalt and Milly were visiting Aunt Camilla yesterday, and you timed it all just right."

I had all night to think about it, and I know I'm right. Just as I know she's the one controlling the beast.

She widens her eyes in mock innocence. "And how would I know that? You poor thing. It's amazing the lengths some people will go to protect themselves." She steps forward, hips swaying. "You just can't handle the thought of us together, can you?"

I bite my cheek to stay silent.

"Why would he want you, naive princess, when he could have me?"

"You're lying. He didn't want you. When he saw you, he told you to get out." Just as she did, I let a heavy pause settle between us. "He didn't want you."

I say it with such conviction that for one fraction of a heartbeat, her veneer cracks. She tries to cover it, but she knows she's slipped.

Her expression turns angry, but I only smile as I try to brush past her. As I do, her hand catches my shoulder, and her fingernails dig into my skin.

I gasp, more startled than hurt.

"He's a man like any other," she hisses near my ear. "He'll only hold out for so long, and then he'll fall. They all do."

Yanking my shoulder away, I glare at her. "What is your plan this time? Are you going to sic your pet ludrako on me again? It didn't work well the first time, and I promise it won't work the second."

Startled, Giselle takes several steps back. "What are you insinuating?"

"You know exactly what I'm insinuating. Don't play coy."

She's unarmed, and I am too, but my fingers itch for my sword.

Slowly, she glances down the hall, one way and then the next, and then she smiles. "I have heard you're trying to stir up rumors that I'm the one controlling the beast. But no one believes you. They think you're a jealous child."

"I don't care what they think." I turn to leave, a little leery of having her at my back. "Eventually, as it always does, the truth will reveal itself."

"Audette?" Giselle calls as soon as I think I've stunned her into silence, her voice unsettlingly sweet. "You should watch your words. I'd hate for something bad to happen to someone you care about."

I glance over my shoulder. "Is that a threat?"

She shrugs, holds my eyes for several more seconds, and then disappears around the corner.

With my heart beating madly in my chest, I hurry on to Irving's quarters. I beat on the door, not caring that it's early.

If he slept any better than I did, he deserves to be woken abruptly.

Almost immediately, he swings the door open. His eyes are guarded, but when he sees me, his whole body sags with relief. Not bothering to explain my presence, I throw myself at him, wrapping my arms around his waist.

He gasps and clutches my hair, murmuring all kinds of alibis and promises. None of it matters.

"I believe you," I say against his tunic.

Holding me tighter, he pulls me to a chair, where he sits with me perched on his lap. He clings to me like he has no intention of ever letting me go. "You do?"

"I do."

Eventually, he sits back and looks me in the eyes. "I love you—desperately, completely, with my whole heart."

Playing with the trim at the collar of his tunic, I say, "I didn't want to fall in love with you—didn't want to trust you. Didn't want to come to care for another person just to have them ripped away from me. It hurts...so much." I look up at him. "But I can't help it. I do. I love you. And I do trust you...with my whole heart."

After brushing my unruly, untended hair out of my face, he presses the softest of kisses to my lips. Needing him, needing the reassurance that we're all right, I wrap my arms around his neck and lose myself in the moment.

We linger together in the sweetest of ways, kissing, talking, planning, dreaming, for most of the morning. Irving never coaxes me for more, and though I burn with an intensity that, again, makes me wish we were already wed, I never offer it.

By early afternoon, hunger finally ousts us from Irving's quarters. Thankfully, we don't run into Giselle on the way to the kitchens.

"You know we have to speak with your brother and his knights," Irving says after he swallows the last bite of an apple and tosses the core into a bucket of kitchen scraps.

I tear an herb roll into small pieces. "They're not going to believe you."

Irving steps forward and pulls me into his arms. "You do. That's all that matters to me."

Still, by the time we reach the villa late in the afternoon, my nerves are practically vibrating.

"What is he doing here?" Barowalt demands the moment we find him hobbling the garden paths.

"Giselle set him up," I say. "I met her in the hall. She practically admitted—"

"It doesn't matter right now," Barowalt says, his voice on edge. "Have you seen Milly?"

The worry at convincing my brother of Irving's innocence shifts to something more acute, like ice in my belly.

"No. Should I have?"

"Letta asked to go on a picnic, but that was before noon."

I take a step forward. "They should have been home hours ago."

"I know." He limps forward, leaning on his staff as if he is in more pain than usual. "I've sent Keven and Rogert to look for her."

Fear grows, and, suddenly, Giselle's words fly to my mind.

Feeling ill, I find a nearby bench and sink into it. Milly's disappearance has nothing to do with Giselle. It was an empty threat spoken in a moment of anger.

Or was it? I don't have any doubt she's controlling the beast. Why would I doubt her ability to get to Milly and Letta?

"We have to find them," I say, rising, already running up the steps toward my room so I can change and fetch my sword. I quickly pull on my leather armor and braid my hair into a crown at my head.

Just as I'm coming back down, Barowalt hollers, "Audette!"

I race down the stairway, my heart leaping to my throat. I find Barowalt, Irving, and our three knights standing in the entryway. My brother looks like he's about to come undone.

Keven holds an arrow and a piece of parchment in his hands, and his expression is ashen.

"What is that?" I demand, wary.

"It was attached to the door," Keven answers. "It must have been placed there just after you and Irving arrived."

"Is it a ransom note?" I ask, my throat thick.

Keven shakes his head, his expression grim. "Not exactly."

"Well?"

"It says Milly and Letta have been taken to the ludrako's lair. If we can't locate them by morning, they will be fed to the beast."

CHAPTER TWENTY-SEVEN

"We have no idea where the ludrako's made its lair," I exclaim.

"No, but we better figure it out," Barowalt growls. "We don't have much time to find them."

Pacing, Hallgrave asks, "But how? Where do we start?"

"If we knew where to find the beast, we wouldn't have been biding our time here all winter," Rogert adds.

I glance at the sky. The clouds are on fire with the glow of the impending sunset, and the vineyards and fields beyond the gardens are gold. We only have an hour or so before dusk.

Fear grows in my chest, its icy fingers stretching through my veins, threatening to make me worthless.

329

I fight the feeling back. If we're to find Milly and Letta, I have to keep a level head.

"We have to go to Grace," I say. "She's the only one that may have found enough information on the ludrako to know where its lair might be."

Keven shakes his head. "If she knew, she would have already told us."

His newly-dark hair still makes me uncomfortable, and I don't quite meet his eyes. "If you have a better idea, by all means..."

We stand in tense silence for several moments.

"Fine," Barowalt says. "Let's ride to the castle."

I want to tell him to stay here, to be careful not to overexert himself. But I can only imagine what his wrath would be if I did.

We reach the castle in record time, but Grace isn't in her quarters, and she's not in the library. Finally, we find Javid in the practice yard.

"Where's Grace?" I demand, out of breath.

He's startled by our abrupt entrance, and he has to think for a moment. "I believe she mentioned she was going to walk to the lake this afternoon. Why? What's happened?"

Keven, Rogert, and Barowalt stay to explain the situation to Javid, but Irving and I mount our horses and ride through the castle's gate, off toward the nearby lake.

The sun is just sinking behind the horizon when we find Grace on the dusty road, sketchbook clutched under her arm, walking toward the castle, lost in her own world.

With as oblivious as she is, it's fortunate she wasn't kidnapped as well.

"Grace!" I holler, and her head jerks up.

"What's wrong?"

"I'll explain on the way back to the castle." I hold my hand out to her, offering to help her onto the back of my horse.

The duchess's eyes widen when she realizes what I mean for her to do, and she takes several steps back, shaking her head. "No, I don't particularly like horses..."

"Grace!"

Irritation flickers in her eyes, but it's quickly replaced with determination. She strides to my mare, half-terrified. After several attempts to swing herself up, she cries out in frustration. Finally, Irving hops from his own horse and holds his hands out, offering her a step up. With me yanking on her arm and Irving boosting her foot, she's finally able to find her seat.

"This better be an emergency," she hisses in my ear.

"It is." I kick my horse back the way we came and warn, "Hold on."

Like bars of iron, her arms clamp around my waist.

"Don't fall off," I call over my shoulder.

"I'm trying not to!"

I tell her of Milly and Letta's disappearance as we ride. As soon as we reach the castle, Grace half-slides, half-falls from my horse.

Javid looks shocked that I convinced her to ride, and he reaches out to steady her. It takes her several moments to find her legs, but as soon as she does, she's hollering for us to follow her to the library. Irving's at my side, and our knights and Barowalt are right behind us.

Grace practically runs through the halls, and people stop to gawk at her, surprised that the duchess is moving at a pace that is anything but dignified.

She bursts into the library and goes straight for a large, teetering stack of books and parchments on her desk. Apparently she hasn't cleared the area yet. She thumbs through them, murmuring titles and thoughts as she goes.

"Do you have any idea where the lair is?" I bite my thumbnail.

Irving, seeing my distress, pulls my hand away from my mouth and winds his fingers through mine. I lean into him, grateful he's here.

The knights finally show up behind us. Barowalt's

face is twisted with pain, and he sinks to a nearby bench as soon as he walks through the doors.

"No." Grace's eyes flicker to mine. "But I was able to find more information on the ludrako when I last visited Constelita."

Finally, she finds the book she's looking for and whips it open, flipping pages until she locates the one she's marked.

"They make their lairs in wooded, rocky areas," she summarizes as she runs her finger down the text. "They stay close to freshwater sources such as lakes, and they prefer warmer regions, so I think it's safe to say it will make its home near the coast where the elevation is lower."

I cross my arms. I'm not sure how any of this really helps.

"Now," she says, shoving the book aside. "We just need to look at a map and see how many areas fit this description."

She unrolls a map that's leaning against the desk and slaps it on a nearby table. With a charcoal stick in hand, she begins circling places on the thick parchment.

"No, not that one," Javid says, leaning next to her. "It's a lake near the coast, but it's not wooded."

Grace nods, undaunted, and crosses out the one she just circled.

Together, they go through the map. Grace's hand hovers as she searches, and then her fingers stop abruptly. She turns to Javid. "Did I circle that one?"

His brow furrows, and he examines it closer. "No. It's not even the same charcoal stick."

I shove my way in to see what they're speaking of.

A previous, hastily drawn circle marks an area just like Grace spoke of—a lake at the base of a ridge, near the forest's edge.

"How far is that?" I ask.

"Several hours," Javid says.

Grace looks up, worried. "Why would that have been circled? No one comes in here but me and you." She lowers her voice. "You don't think it's a trap, do you?"

I stare at the area, somehow knowing it's where we'll find Milly and Letta.

"I don't know," I answer. "But someone wants us there."

"What if that someone is hoping to lead us astray?" Barowalt demands.

Everyone stares at me, waiting for me to make the decision.

I rub my temples, thinking. My responsibility seems so much heavier now that Milly and Letta are involved.

"How many other options are there?" I ask Grace.

"Seven that fit the exact description from the book…probably hundreds that are similar."

That makes up my mind.

"We're going to the area that was already circled," I decide.

The men look uneasy, but they nod.

Javid yanks Grace into his arms, playing dashing, and kisses her square on the mouth. With a quick smile, he says, "I'll be late tonight. Don't wait up for me."

"I don't care how late you are," she says. "Just be sure you come back."

Irving squeezes my hand, and I turn away from the couple.

"Are you sure you don't want to stay here with Grace?" he whispers just loud enough I can hear him. "No one would think less of you."

I shake my head. "No. I've trained for this my whole life, and Milly's my dearest friend. I'm going."

He doesn't try to talk me out of it. Brushing his thumb over my knuckles, he nods.

After Javid and Grace say their goodbyes, Irving slides his drachite sword from its sheath and hands it to Javid. "You'll need a weapon that stands a chance of slaying the beast, and I'm better with my bow."

Javid's eyebrows shoot up when his eyes land on the ugly blade. He grins as he accepts it and holds it up to inspect further. "You weren't joking. This is the most hideous sword I've seen in my life."

I glance at Barowalt, wondering how he's faring. He's the only one of us without a drachite weapon. Even though Milly's in the beast's clutches, he's in no shape to fight.

"I'm coming," he says when he sees the pitying look I'm giving him.

We all begin to protest, but he holds up a hand, silencing us like the regal king he is. "I'll hang back on my horse, but I'm not going to sit here and wait."

Stubborn fool.

As if reading my mind, a wry smile flashes across his face.

Shaking my head and waving a casual goodbye to Grace, like this is just a quick trip and we'll be back by morning, I lead my men from the library and into the night.

***

Two hours after dark is possibly the worst time to infiltrate the lair of a massive, nocturnal armored wolf, but we're certainly not going to wait around until dawn.

The lake is neither small nor large but somewhere in between. Clouds shift overhead, occasionally letting the moon shine down to light our way. Most of our ride has been in the twilight hours, but now, even the western horizon is as black as pitch. Huge boulders

336

line the lake, one time fallen from the gradually slop-ing ridge to the north of us. It's almost impossible to find a route the horses can navigate.

On all other sides of the lake, the shore is thick with trees and brush.

I'm uneasy. I feel as if there are eyes on us, but I don't know if my senses are picking up on something that's truly lurking, or if I've spooked myself.

The others are tense as well, and we haven't spo-ken since we neared the lake.

Keven holds up his hand, silently getting our at-tention, and then he points to a dark area toward the side of the cliff.

He's found our cave.

Without a word, Barowalt holds back as we move forward, just as he said he would. It's probably killing him, but he knows if he were to go in with us, he'd only be a liability. Since Milly and the child are his top priority, he waits.

We dismount, leaving the horses in a grassy, weeded area near the mouth of the cave.

Keven and Rogert take position in the front, swords drawn. Javid and I follow, and Hallgrave and Irving take the rear. Stealthy as possible, we take our time moving forward, careful of rocks, stalagmites, and holes in the uneven cavern floor.

The cave smells musty, and the air is heavy. Lying

underneath the usual cavern aroma is the encouraging odor of wet dog.

Every hair on my arms stands on end, and my skin prickles as the cool, damp air seeps under my armor. Not only am I wary of finding the beast, I am half-expecting an ambush. I wish we could light torches, but that would only alert others to our presence.

We walk for what seems like hours, but at the snail's pace we're moving at, we've probably made very little progress. As we venture from the lake, the air becomes slightly drier, still damp but dustier.

My nose itches as the dog scent intensifies.

I squint in the dark. Up ahead, it almost looks as if there's a dim glow, but my eyes may be playing tricks on me. We continue to inch forward, and the light grows brighter. When we get close enough that we can see each other's silhouettes in the dark, Keven and Rogert flatten themselves to the cave wall and continue on. We all do the same, moving at a cautious but slightly quicker pace now that we can somewhat see the obstacles in front of us.

Rogert is the first to peer into the lit cavern. He creeps forward, half-crawling, half-squatting on the ground like a frog. He hides behind a boulder and peers around it. He makes a frantic motion back to us with his hand.

He's spotted them. After several moments, he

makes his way back to Keven. They have a conversation that's so quiet, I can't even hear their whispered words. Keven passes the message to Javid, who then turns to me.

"Milly's tied up off to the side," he whispers. "But there's no sign of Letta or anyone else."

"What of the creature?" I ask.

Javid shakes his head.

After several moments of hushed conversation passed along from person to person, it's decided that Keven, Rogert, and Javid will go in first and Irving and Hallgrave will linger here, ready to shoot if necessary.

We wait, but nothing happens. Eventually, Milly must have spotted them because she lets out a muffled squeal that sends hope washing over me because I now know she's alive. At the same time, I'm terrified of what they might have done to her.

With no sign of imminent danger, Hallgrave, Irving, and I rush into the cavern.

Keven's already undoing the ropes holding Milly to a tall stalactite that hangs from the ceiling, and Rogert unties a gag from around her mouth. A lone torch burns nearby, but except for us and Milly, the cavern is empty.

"Where's the beast?" Rogert asks as soon as he pulls the fabric from her mouth.

She chokes back a sob, but she puts on a brave

face. "You just missed him. I'm sure he sends his best."

"I'm so glad you're all right!" I crush her to me, so relieved she seems to be uninjured.

"They're going after the blessing." Milly urgently pushes me back. "Kidnapping me was a distraction to lead you farther from Asher's land."

I freeze, horrified.

Milly may have been scared, but now she's livid. "And Audette, you were right."

"About what?" I pull the torch from its makeshift stand and am already heading toward the passage that will take us back to the lake.

We don't have time to linger.

"It's Giselle." Milly spits the name out.

The men are obviously shocked, but now's not the time to rub it in that I was right. Later, though. Later.

"Did they take Letta with them?" I ask. "Is she all right?"

We're able to move at a much swifter pace now that we have a light.

Something about Milly's silence makes me pause. I turn back to find Milly's face is twisted, and her eyes brim with tears.

"What is it?" I ask.

Surely Giselle wouldn't have hurt the girl. She's just a child. Innocent in all of this.

Milly motions us forward, knowing we can't stop.

"She's with them."

"We'll get her back," I promise.

With a choked sob, Milly yanks my arm, making me look at her. "No. She's with them."

"She's part of it?" I breathe.

How is that possible?

"The gypsy is working with Giselle," Milly says. "She sprung him from the prison to make it look as if he were the wizard behind the whole thing. He orchestrated the mirage that the girl from Vallen Harbor witnessed. They set us up." Milly pauses. "Letta is his daughter."

She's not an orphan at all. She lied to us...so did the orphanage. How much did Giselle have to pay them to do that? And why?

"We have to keep moving," Keven says.

I nod, still stunned, and we continue on.

"Letta's been spying on us this entire time." Milly trips but rights herself before she falls face first on the rock-lined ground. "And it was Giselle who told her to ask me to take her on a picnic. She had all this planned."

The beast attacked the night I ran away to marry Irving in Vallen Harbor...after Irving told Letta where we were going. And Letta knew Barowalt and Milly were visiting Aunt Camilla the other evening when Giselle pretended to sneak from Irving's chambers.

The thought of it makes me ill.

"But why? Giselle has all she wants. She's killed off everyone in line for the throne—she's going to be the Queen of Ptarma. What does she care about the blessing now? Why not let them be? Why draw more attention to herself?"

"Payment to the beast for services rendered," Javid says darkly.

"That," Milly says, "and Giselle hates Audette. What happened between you two in the hall this morning?"

I wrinkle my nose. In retrospect, it probably wasn't wise to antagonize the woman who controls the beast that has the power to decimate the unicorns I've been charged with protecting.

"It's not important right now," I answer.

The unicorns are sitting ducks.

There haven't been any attacks in over a month. Asher's not expecting it, and why would he be? The silly things are probably out grazing right now, completely oblivious to the creature that stalks them as we speak.

"How did they find the location of the blessing?" Hallgrave asks. "We've been careful to keep that information from the girl."

"I don't know," Milly says. "But I overheard them say they were going to attack while you were all out looking for me."

"Other than the gypsy, did she have any men working with her?" Keven asks.

"Five or six guards? I'm not positive."

We reach the mouth of the cave, and Milly steps out. She jumps back when she sees the silhouetted figure of a man on horseback almost hidden in the nearby trees, but when she realizes it's Barowalt, she races toward him.

He has his bow at the ready, prepared to protect us from someone who might sneak in the cave behind us. Now he balances it on the back of his horse and climbs down from the saddle.

The moment Milly's in his arms, she begins to cry. He clings to her, holding her like his life depends on it. Tears prick my eyes. I blink them away, pretending it's just an itch.

I stride toward Barowalt. Hating to interrupt them but knowing I have no choice, I say, "The beast is going to attack the blessing."

"When?" he demands.

"Now."

He nods, solemn. "Go. I'll take Milly to the villa."

"I don't know what I'm doing," I whisper, suddenly realizing I'm in over my head.

Meeting my eyes, he says, "You're ready. I know you can do this."

Choking back my panic, I nod.
I wish I were as sure as he is.

CHAPTER TWENTY-EIGHT

It's well into the wee hours of the morning when we arrive at Asher's estate. The clouds have cleared out, and the moon shines on the sea. The only noise besides the breeze blowing over the grass is the gentle, rhythmic sound of waves lapping at the rocky shore.

There's no sign of attack. Everything is perfectly, deceptively peaceful. The pasture is empty, the unicorns tucked safely into the stables for the night.

"Do you think they had the location wrong?" Hallgrave reins his horse next to mine.

Instead of answering, I scan the area. Nothing seems out of place.

Ren spots us from his watch at the front of the stables. The young knight runs across the pasture. He looks more than a little worried to find us, galloping like dragons are on our heels, coming up the narrow road in the middle of the night.

"Wake the others," I call across the field.

Immediately, he changes his course and heads toward the estate.

Once we reach the pasture fence, we dismount. The night is so still, so calm.

I walk down the fence, stretching my legs after the long, arduous ride. Looking over my shoulder at the others, I say, "Perhaps..."

The words trail off as I see something shift in the brush just to the right of the road, something large. I squint, wondering if my eyes are playing tricks on me.

The men turn as well, following my gaze, and unsheathe their swords. Irving pulls the bow from his back, but he doesn't yet nock the arrow.

Several moments pass, slow painful heartbeats, but the dark form I saw is gone. The moonlight shines through the trees, casting speckled shadows on the brush below.

"I must be imagining—"

Suddenly the brush parts, and a creature charges from the bracken. For one moment, I'm so stunned, I can only stare. Wide-eyed, I watch the beast advance. The moonlight glints off the ludrako's sleek black scales, and his golden eyes shine.

He's beautiful in his own right, mesmerizing—a

wolf as large as a dragon, armored and sleek. Thick, black fur lines his underbelly, legs, and tail.

Suddenly I realize how it located the blessing. Using the magic it marked us with to stay behind us at a stealthy distance, it followed us from the cavern. Giselle had no idea where we'd taken the unicorns, so she tricked Milly. We led the beast here.

As he nears, his pace slows. Ears back and teeth bared, he stalks forward, padding silently through the tall grass off to the side of the road.

Slowly, so as not to draw attention to himself, Irving nocks his bow.

My knights wait, poised to attack. With a trembling hand, I, too, draw my sword.

I wait, heart in my throat, wondering if I'm about to fall to the ground again, clutching my head and screaming, like the last time I met the creature.

The ludrako stops abruptly, a snarl in his throat, and lifts his nose into the air.

"We charge on the count of three," Hallgrave says through clenched teeth. "One, two—"

Just as we prepare to rush forward and engage, the ludrako lunges, charging us.

Spurred into action, we run forward, ready to meet him, but just as we're about to collide, the wolf crouches low, and, propelled by powerful hind legs, leaps clean over us.

I gasp as he flies over my head. Expecting him to double back, I turn on my heel.

Instead, he races for the stable.

"No!" I leap over the fence and run as fast as I can toward the beast.

The men are behind me, but they're not as fast as I am. I'm going to reach the wolf first.

With single-minded determination, the beast rams into the locked doors. Terrified whinnies ring out from within. The distressed cry of a unicorn is a chilling sound, horrifying enough to bring a person to their knees.

I try to ignore it, but it seeps into my bones, almost paralyzing me with the hopeless desperation it carries.

Again and again, the creature lunges. Just before we reach him, he breaks through.

Wood splinters and flies, and the unicorns flee, racing around him. As they pass, several stumble, screaming in agony as he robs them of their magical essence.

For the first time, I'm thankful we're no longer linked.

Then an arrow flies. The drachite arrowhead pierces through the beast's scaled armor and sinks into his shoulder. The ludrako stumbles, yelping in startled pain.

More unicorns leap around the beast, a flood of white silk glistening in the moonlight. They scatter like rabbits, following each other like sheep, too terrified to think.

The beast stumbles, and then, consumed with rage, turns on us, temporarily forgetting the blessing.

Just as we're about to reach the wolf, a battle cry sounds from behind us. We turn abruptly to find Giselle's men charging us.

I duck a blade just in time, stumble to the side, and then regain my footing. I dance around the man, blocking his attacks, but I'm not as graceful as I was at one time.

Keven and Hallgrave have engaged with the beast, trying to lure him away from the rest of us. Javid and Rogert fight three men, and Irving's replaced his bow for his usual blade. He fights another guard, a man I recognize from our own estate—the guard Letta became friendly with.

My temper flares even brighter than before. How dare Giselle place spies in my home.

The anger gives me a burst of adrenaline, and I spring forward, taking the man fighting me off guard. He trips on the uneven pasture ground, and I knock his sword free. It goes flying out of his grasp, and I hold my blade to his throat.

Now what?

I've never killed anyone in my life.

The guard realizes it, too. Just as he makes to knock my sword away, Rogert bashes him unconscious with the hilt of his sword.

"You hesitated!" my knight yells.

My stomach clenches with fear and disappointment. I did. I hesitated—even after Barowalt warned me so many times not to.

I don't have time to dwell on it because Rogert is attacked from behind. My knight turns, welcoming the assault. He's been waiting for this moment since we arrived in Ptarma.

Sensing someone approaching behind me, I whirl around. The gypsy stands, grinning at me with that same smirk he wore in Constelita.

But, this time, he's not tied to a chair.

With the memory, the sadness over losing Rafe rushes back. He was there that day, very much alive. And because of this man and Giselle, he's lost.

I stalk forward, ready to meet him. As I advance, he steps back toward the shadowed cliffs.

"This doesn't end well for you and your men," he says, cryptic.

The hair on the back of my neck stands on end. Is that something he has seen? Or is he bluffing?

"Why do you run away?" I ask, continuing to stalk him through the pasture. "You're not afraid of a girl, are you?"

A terrified cluster of unicorns darts as we grow near.

From the corner of my eye, I see Keven and Hall-grave are still distracting the beast, but by now they must be growing weary.

The gypsy only smiles.

Just as I've almost backed him to the cliff, the point of a dagger meets my back, right between my shoulder blades.

"I see you wore your hair up," Giselle says, her voice taunting. "Apparently you learned it's not wise to fight while it's down."

I grit my teeth, cursing myself for not hearing her come up behind me.

"But you forgot the very important lesson that you should always keep watch behind you."

I knew she'd stab me in the back eventually. I should have seen this coming.

"Put your hands behind your head," she demands.

When I can't think of a way to maneuver from the bite of the blade, I lace my fingers and do as I'm told.

From the corner of my eye, I notice Asher and the rest of my knights charging from the estate. I want to yell at them to stop, to turn around. Since they've never confronted the ludrako, they're worthless to us.

"This should be interesting," Giselle purrs. "Let's

watch, shall we?"

Since the blade is at my back, I have no choice but to turn.

I can tell the moment the ludrako scents the knights. He stiffens and turns.

Hallgrave takes advantage of the moment and lunges. Just before he stabs the sword into the creature's chest, the beast turns on him.

I scream as the ludrako clamps his jaws around my knight and flings him to the side of the pasture. Then, knocking Keven away with the swing of his head, the beast turns toward Asher and the others.

My men fall to their knees, crying out as they clutch their heads.

The memory of the pain makes me ill. Nearby unicorns, too, scream and stumble, affected by whatever magic the wolf creature sends out.

"Why are you doing this?" I demand of Giselle. "You have what you want. You're going to be queen."

She leans close to my ear. "You have been a thorn in my side, Princess, since you arrived."

I shudder, my heart hammering in my chest as I watch the people I love suffer.

Suddenly, a small figure ducks under the pasture fence and runs into the middle of the fray.

Letta waves her hands, trying to stop the fighting as only a child would think she's capable.

Irving's eyes go wide, but he's still engaged with a guard. Keven's unconscious; Hallgrave hasn't moved. Rogert and Javid each have a man of their own. And the rest are on the ground, writhing in agony.

The beast turns on the girl.

"Letta, no!" I scream.

From my side, the almost-forgotten gypsy hollers for his daughter, and then he runs into the fray. A dark, swirling mass gathers around him, a shrieking mist that makes my veins turn to ice. Then, as if he can't hold it in the unicorns' midst, the darkness dissipates. Even unarmed, the gypsy runs toward the beast.

At the last possible moment, the ludrako turns his attention from the girl to her father.

The gypsy cries out and stumbles forward, fighting to conjure his dark magic. Showing no mercy, the beast leaps on him.

Letta's screams drown out the rest of the noise, rising above the fighting, above the blessing's terrified whinnies.

The man opposite Javid falls, and the duke grabs the girl. Though she flails, kicks, and screams, he tosses her over his shoulder and runs her toward the estate, to safety.

Giselle nudges the knife closer, and I arch away from the blade.

"I think it's time we finish this," she says, sounding

bored.

"Beast!" she cries, sliding the dagger to my throat when I try to escape. "Take her!"

The ludrako turns, and his topaz eyes lock on mine. There's comprehension there, understanding.

He leaps forward.

"Audette!" Irving yells from across the field.

I can't move. Giselle's knife digs at my throat, and I can already feel a trickle of blood running down my neck.

The sound of an arrow whooshes past me, so near my ear, that for one split moment, I wonder if I've been shot. The blade falls away as Giselle crumples to the ground behind me.

There's no time to dwell on the skill of Irving's shot because the beast is upon me. Just as I feel his hot breath on my face, I somersault forward. I yank my crude sword from its sheath as I roll, and I stab upwards, into the ludrako's soft, fur-covered belly.

It lets out a nightmarish cry, and I scramble away as it falls.

My hands are stabbed by sharp weeds as I crawl away. My hair falls from its braids, and long strands plaster themselves to my face.

Behind me, the ludrako's sharp scream turns to whimpers, and then it stumbles to the ground and falls silent.

The night goes still.

I push myself to my feet, breathing hard, and stare at the fallen beast in shock. Only the sound of the waves on the shore meets my ears.

Giselle's men are down, one dead but the others unconscious. Giselle's gone. So is the gypsy.

We've won.

Just as I'm about to sink to my knees, Irving's eyes lock on mine. He's bloody and bruised, and his armor is filthy. With a fire in his eyes, he tosses his bow aside and strides across the field. He picks up speed until he's running toward me. Then I'm rushing to him.

We crash together, and he holds me so tightly, I almost can't breathe. Then he pulls back, his face solemn and intense. "Audette, I have something to ask you."

With relieved tears in my eyes, I nod, breathless. "Anything."

Like lightning, a mischievous grin brightens his face. "How awesome was my shot?"

I'm surprised by my laughter. "I just killed the ludrako!"

He grins, not holding back. "That was pretty good too."

Just as I'm about to kiss him, I freeze.

"Hallgrave," I whisper.

Immediately we pull apart, and I run to my fallen

knight. Rogert's already at his side.

"He's breathing," Rogert says. "We need to get him into the villa."

Irving steps forward and gently scoops the knight up under his arms. Rogert takes his feet, and, together, they make their way toward the estate.

Keven's already stirring, and I kneel beside him.

"Are you all right?" I ask.

The knight blinks several times, and then he bolts upright. When he sees the fallen beast, his eyes go large. "How?"

"I didn't hesitate this time."

He lets out a slow disbelieving breath, and then his eyes fall on Asher, Ren, Percis, and Garran—all of them unconscious. "We have to get them inside."

While I'm nodding, there's a gentle bump at the back of my head.

Slowly, with hope blooming in my heart, I turn.

The small mare, the one who greeted me in the valley, nuzzles my hair. Overcome, I turn and cling to her.

She replays the memory of me slaying the ludra-ko in my mind, and with it, I feel her great relief. As the beast died, his tie with us was broken. Eyes closed, I watch in her memory as my hair shimmers from almost black to blond.

Gasping, I turn toward Keven.

In my worry, I hadn't even noticed that his hair returned to gold. I grasp the tail of my braid. Next to the unicorns' glow, it shines blond.

As I marvel at it, a wonderful warmth spreads over me. It seeps into me like sunshine, easing every muscle, relieving every ache.

For the first time since Constelita, I feel whole.

"Thank you," I whisper to her, stroking the unicorn's neck.

Slowly, the rest of the blessing presses in on me and the others. One by one, they place their horns to my knights, healing them.

The gash on Keven's head disappears, and they wake Asher and the others. A mare trots toward Irving and Rogert. Slowly, they set Hallgrave down, letting the unicorn touch the knight.

Before our eyes, the wounds knit. His eyes fly open, and he gasps a breath.

I blink back tears as the mare turns to Irving.

She studies him for several moments, and then she lays her horn on his arm. Irving goes still and closes his eyes as the magic envelops him.

The mare accepted him. Whether he likes it or not, he's truly one of us now.

From the villa entrance, Letta watches, her arms wrapped around her body. Her face is too young to be etched with that much misery.

Without thinking, I walk across the field and leap over the fence.

She flinches when she sees I'm coming for her, but I only pull her into my arms. "You were very brave. Not many would have had the courage to try to stop the fighting."

Big, fat tears roll down her cheeks. "Can they save him? Can the unicorns fix Father?"

Even they can't bring back the dead.

Biting my lip, I shake my head.

She crumples to the ground, and I take her in my arms. As I rock her, knowing there's no way to ease her pain, a young unicorn lowers his head to her shoulder.

In awe, Letta looks at him, unblinking.

Once again linked, I can feel the magic he pours into the small girl. Exhausted, she falls asleep.

It's all we can do for her right now.

Javid steps forward and takes her from my arms. I stand as he carries her into the villa.

From behind, strong arms wrap around me, hands clasping at my stomach. Irving kisses my cheek and sets his chin on my shoulder.

"If I pretend to fall asleep," I say in a teasing tone although my heart feels weary, "will you carry me into the estate?"

"I'll do anything you ask of me."

"You saved my life." I lean into him and then

whisper, "Thank you."

"Mine wouldn't be worth living without you."

I smile at him over my shoulder, and he presses a quick kiss to my lips.

"Now go to bed," he says. "We'll sort the rest of this out in the morning."

Gladly, I make my way to the villa.

CHAPTER TWENTY-NINE

My heart pinches as I hug Letta goodbye. "We'll be back to visit often."

She holds me tightly, not wanting to let go. It's been a week since she lost her father, and though he was a loathsome human being, she loved him.

Though I was stunned to find she'd betrayed us, the pain was fleeting. She's only seven years old, almost a baby, and only doing what she'd been told. In the end, she tried to fix the mess she made in the only way she knew how.

"You're sure you don't want to come with us to Brookraven?" I ask her again.

With tears in her eyes, Letta shakes her head. Her whole life, all she's known is the sea. I can understand why she doesn't want to leave it. At least, not yet.

I stand, making way for Milly to say her final goodbye. My friend and the girl cling to each for several moments. When they part, Letta hiccups back more tears and burrows into Grace's side.

Javid and Grace have offered to adopt the girl, to give her a permanent home. I know it's best for her, but I'm surprised to realize I will truly miss her.

As I'm blinking back tears, Aunt Camilla places her hand on my arm. She has on a lightweight traveling cloak, and several of her guards stand behind her, trunks in tow.

"I've decided to come with you," she says.

My eyes widen, and I try to conceal my surprise. "You have?"

"Someone has to keep an eye on you. I can't have my great-niece running away from another wedding." She gives me a tight smile. "Our family has a reputation to uphold, after all."

Aunt Camilla turns away, instructing the footman to make room for her things, and Irving steps behind me and whispers in my ear, "You won't run this time, will you, darling?"

I turn and clasp my hands loosely around his neck. "Not unless I get a better offer between now and then."

The day is warm, and the gardens are in full spring bloom. The winter rains are forgotten, replaced

361

by warm, balmy sunshine. It's a good day to start the sea voyage home.

Irving leans down and murmurs all the reasons no one will make a better offer than he. Just as he's about to kiss me, Barowalt interrupts.

"Save it for the wedding," my brother says.

I pull back and raise an eyebrow at Barowalt. He's one to talk. I saw him and Milly sneak off to the fountains not fifteen minutes ago.

We say the rest of our goodbyes, and a lump forms in my throat. I'll miss my distant Ptarmish family when we leave.

Queen Clara kisses both of my cheeks in farewell. "As I've said, you're always welcome here. Make sure you visit again soon."

After I squeeze her hands and promise I will, I turn to King Edlund.

I expect him to take my hand, but, instead, he pulls me into a tight embrace. "Thank you for all that you and your knights did for Ptarma."

Lastly, I turn to Kent. He's been standing quietly by his aunt and uncle's side. I haven't spoken to him, didn't know what to say.

"I'm sorry about Giselle," I whisper.

She was his wife, after all. At some point, he must have loved her.

He nods and motions me to step aside with him.

Quietly, my cousin says, "I've made mistakes—more than I can count. Giselle was one of many. We had a whirlwind romance when I went to Waldren on a hunting expedition, and we ended it with a hasty elopement. I didn't know anything about her other than she was beautiful."

He pauses and stares into a tree loaded with delicate, white citrus blooms. A bee buzzes from flower to flower, and I watch its carefree progress.

"I was too proud and stupid to admit she was using me as a means to a crown," he continues. "Once I realized how dark her heart was, I wanted nothing to do with her. Left her for weeks on end and eventually found comfort in the arms of other women. If I'd stayed close to her, treated her as a husband should despite my resentment, perhaps I would have seen what she was plotting." He lets out a slow breath. "Perhaps if I'd loved her, she would have abandoned her plans and been content to simply be with me."

I set my hand on his arm. "It's over now. All we can do is move forward."

He turns back. "I miss my father. I miss Aldus—he was born to be king, not me. Never me."

"Edlund is a good man. Listen to his guidance, learn from your mistakes, and you will be a fine king."

Slowly, Kent nods.

With a small smile, I walk back to my group.

My knights stand by the carriages, proud and strong. Their polished mail glistens in the sunlight. With us all together, I feel Rafe's absence more acutely. The knight will be missed.

I step in front of Asher. "You'll take care of the blessing, won't you?"

He kneels in front of me, his face solemn. "I swear it, Your Highness."

"Are you ready?" Barowalt asks me.

My last goodbye is the hardest. I turn to Grace, a new friend I hadn't expected to make. "Thank you for everything."

She smiles. "Don't forget to visit. I'd love to take you on a tour of Ptarma now that we don't have to worry about a shadow beast stalking our every move."

"I will," I say with a laugh. "I promise."

Javid bows, his face bright. "Perhaps we'll visit you soon. It's been a long time since we've been to the mainland."

Irving laughs. "I'll never forget the last time you toured the lower kingdoms. Remember that night we found ourselves in that seedy tavern in central Murin…?" He trails off, a wicked smile lighting his face as he glances at me. "You know what? Never mind."

I give Irving a jab in the ribs, and he laughs.

Just as we're about to step into the carriage, Letta darts away from Grace and runs to me. Tears still streaming down her face, she tugs on my hands, forcing me to kneel in front of her.

"I circled the Ludrako's lair on Grace's map," she admits pitifully, hiccupping. "Giselle told me to do it so that you'd find Milly." She's whispering, and with her tears, it's hard to make out her words. "I'm so sorry. Please don't tell Grace and Javid. If they knew, they wouldn't want me."

"Shh," I say. "Don't talk like that. It's all right."

She shakes her head, her dark curls bouncing around her face and strands of hair sticking to her tear-dampened cheeks. "It's not all right. If we hadn't followed you to the unicorns, Father wouldn't have died."

I pull her close, clenching my eyes shut as she sobs into my shoulder. "This is not your fault. Giselle was using you. Grace knows that; Javid knows that." I pull her back so she has to look at me. "We all know that."

"Do you hate me?" Her words are barely a whisper.

I look her square in the eyes. "No."

Finally, she gulps back a sob and nods. Without another word, she steps back to Grace. With a sunny smile, Javid scoops the girl up in his arms. She's really too large to be carried, but he doesn't seem to mind.

"What was that about?" Barowalt asks from my

side.

Letta looks at me with fearful eyes, terrified I'm going to share her secret.

I only shake my head. "She was just saying good-bye."

Finally, after several more last minute goodbyes, I step into the open-top carriage.

"To Vallen Harbor?" the footman says as he takes his seat.

"I have one stop I need to make first," I say, and then I give him directions.

When we arrive at our destination, I leave the others in the carriage. Alone, I walk down the trail and into the lush valley.

I'm not sure they'll come out in the middle of the day, but I sit in the meadow grass and wait. I've braided three flower chains and am just about to give up hope when a flash of white catches my eye.

The mare steps into the clearing. Her mane and tail flow behind her, and the sun glistens off of her coat.

I stay still, and she settles on the grass next to me, placing her head in my lap. I stroke her mane, and close my eyes as she replays more of my memories for me.

Happy memories of my mother and father, memories I'll cherish.

The last is of me and Irving.

"I'm going to marry him," I whisper to her.

She looks at me, but I don't know if she understands me or not.

I sit with her for the longest time, soaking up the peace that surrounds her. The others will be missing me.

It's time to go.

Sensing my decision, she rises first. Once I'm on my feet, I wrap my arms around her neck in a goodbye. In my mind, I suddenly see an image of my ring.

I step back and glance at the once-blue aquamarine. Unlike my hair, it didn't turn back. The jewel trapped the ludrako's magic, and the stone remains black.

Still, I wear it.

Slowly, the mare lowers her horn to my hand. I stand still, not sure what it is she's doing. As I watch, the stone begins to shimmer, matching the luminescence around the unicorn's horn. When she steps back, the light fades. Instead of returning to black, the stone has been restored to blue.

"Thank you," I breathe.

When I set my hand on her back, I can feel her repulsion at connecting with the ludrako's magic, but the emotion is fleeting.

I stroke her again, and then she turns to leave. I

stand in the middle of the valley and watch her disappear into the trees at the edge of the clearing.

The unicorns are safe. The threat is gone.

It's time to return home.

CHAPTER THIRTY

"Did you find it?" I demand as Milly shuts the door behind her.

She looks harried, and I'm hit with a wave of déjà vu.

The dressing room is the same, the groom is as well, but this time I'm ready to walk down the aisle. Eager, in fact.

"Why did you take the pesky thing off to begin with?" Milly asks, frowning. "It never left your finger while we were in Ptarma."

After everything that's happened, I've managed to lose my mother's ring. I know I packed it with my things. I remember wrapping it and tucking it in my undergarments.

But now I can't find it anywhere.

I turn away from the full-length mirror. My ivory gown follows me, and the train wraps around the base of the dressing table. It's not the same gown I wore all those months ago when I fled from my wedding.

Aunt Camilla commissioned this one, saying I needed something that hadn't been "sullied" with bad decisions. In fact, Aunt Camilla took care of everything on our end of things. Having her here has been a surprising blessing.

I turn to Barowalt. "I must have the ring."

He rubs his temples, probably already envisioning the chaotic event that awaits him when he and Milly are wed. They held their promising ceremony in Brookraven the day after we returned. When they announced it, Milly's parents exchanged knowing smiles.

No one was surprised.

I pace the sitting room, and Milly scurries after me, arranging my train so it doesn't wrinkle. One of the palace handmaids unpacked my things. Perhaps she tucked it into a drawer in the desk? Or a cubby in the wardrobe?

"I'm going to go look for it," I say.

"Oh, not this again," Milly says. "Ella, do you have any blue thread in your embroidery basket?"

Ella looks up. "Of course, my lady."

"Come over here and stitch a little something on Audette's underskirt."

"No," I say, backing away. "Milly, do up the bustle. I'm going."

Milly sets her hands on her hips. "If I remember correctly, we've been through this before. You can't wander the halls in your wedding gown." Then she lowers her voice, hissing, "Especially now that there are this many guests present."

Last time, only the nobles from Primewood came to the wedding, and they were here more out of duty than care. But this time, it seems as if half of Elden has arrived—and all have been personally invited by Irving himself.

Even my cousin Pippa, and her husband, Archer, arrived yesterday. Rigel and Seirsha, the young king and queen of Errinton accompanied them, and they brought a new set of drachite armor I requested in secret. I'm going to surprise Irving with it later. People from all over have flocked here to witness our wedding. According to Anwen, the woman I embarrassingly assumed was Irving's mistress, and Marigold, Irving's half-sister, all want to set eyes on the woman who finally stole Irving's heart.

"Hurry up," I say to Milly.

She growls under her breath, but she and Ella set to work on tying up the train.

"Audette," Barowalt says. "Are you sure this is necessary—" He holds up his hands in surrender when I shoot him a fiery look. "All right. Do what you will."

I poke my head into the hall, and, when I see it's clear, I hurry down the corridor. I run into a few maids and servants, and they all give me questioning looks—probably wondering if I'm running again. I don't doubt they are gossiping behind my back right now.

Hurrying, I turn a corner and nearly smack into someone. Just in time, I catch myself before I plow him over.

Irving leans against the wall, the picture of ease. He's devastatingly handsome in his wedding finery, and I suck in a breath. This is a vast difference from the wind-blown tunic he wore for our first wedding.

With a wicked grin, he holds up my mother's ring. "Looking for something?"

Holding back a laugh, I put on a stern look. "What are you doing with it?"

He pushes off the wall and stalks toward me, a smile on his face and a predatory glint in his eyes. "I knew you wouldn't walk down the aisle without it, and I was rather hoping you'd come looking for it again."

"I thought we were doing this properly this time? You're not supposed to see me before the wedding."

Irving slips his hands around my waist and pulls me toward him. "Tell me, are you from Brookraven? Are you in the princess's wedding party?"

Giggling, I try to push him away. "Stop it."

"You're breathtaking," he whispers.

He brushes a kiss just under my ear, and I tilt my head and close my eyes.

"Why go to such lengths to get me into the hall?"

Trailing kisses along my jaw, he says, "Everyone wants to meet you, everyone wants your attention. I wanted a moment with you alone, one I don't have to share."

When he makes to kiss me, I set my finger over his lips. "You'll have to wait for that."

He growls, laughing, and then hands me my ring. "You better run back to your room. We're about to start."

Unable to hold back a grin, I nod and pull away from him. Just as I'm turning away, he catches me and yanks me close again. "And Audette?"

"Hmmm?" I whisper against his lips.

He smiles, his eyes bright and teasing. "I have guards posted at all the entrances, just in case you think of running away again."

Laughing, I duck out of his arms and hurry down the hall.

When I reach the sitting room where Milly and Barowalt wait, I lean against the door and sigh. I must look particularly guilty because they both exchange a look.

"Find your ring?" Barowalt asks.

I slip it on my finger. "Yes."

"Then let's do this before one of you changes your mind."

Barowalt offers his arm and Milly unties my bustle, letting the train fall.

My knights wait for me outside the double doors that lead into the chapel. They've recently polished their mail, and Brookraven's unicorn crest shines brightly on their tunics.

Hallgrave steps forward first and kneels. "You are beautiful, Your Highness."

One by one, my knights come forward, paying their respects.

Keven is the last to kneel in front of me. With his blond hair sheared short, he looks different. Older, perhaps.

Or maybe we all look older, a little wiser after the ordeal we've been through.

When Keven takes my hand, he brings it to his forehead. Unlike the others, he doesn't speak.

"Thank you," I whisper. "For your blessing."

He nods, his eyes solemn, and he steps back into his place.

Barowalt takes a deep breath, and the doors open. Dozens of tiny girls in fluffy dresses are the first out. They throw their petals into the air with zeal. My maids and Milly follow, and then, as is the tradition in Brookraven, my elite knights. I'm glad they're here this time.

The chapel is full-to-bursting, and the audience rises as the music changes.

At the end of the aisle, Irving waits. Our eyes lock. He stands strong and solemn, the picture of nobility. Then he flashes me his crooked smile, and I fight back a laugh.

In this moment, I realize that I'm thankful I ran away the first time. This wedding is real. It's not taking place because of a promise made between our mothers. Not because of our duty to our kingdoms.

But because, as unlikely as it seems, we found love.

With Barowalt at my arm, and my family of knights standing proud at the front, I take the first step toward my forever.

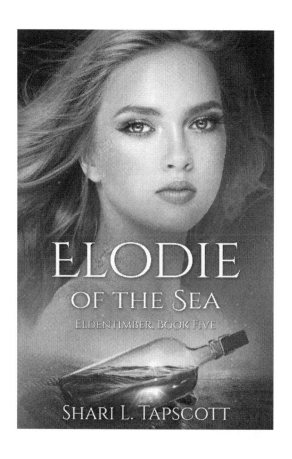

ELODIE
OF THE SEA

ELDENTIMBER, BOOK FIVE

SHARI L. TAPSCOTT

He's a king who gave up on love. She's a girl with no memory.

An entire ocean is keeping them apart.

Available March 31, 2018

About the Author

Shari L. Tapscott writes young adult fantasy and humorous contemporary fiction. When she's not writing or reading, she enjoys gardening, making soap, and pretending she can sing. She loves white chocolate mochas, furry animals, spending time with her family, and characters who refuse to behave.

Tapscott lives in western Colorado with her husband, son, daughter, and two very spoiled Saint Bernards.

To learn more about Shari's books, please visit:
shariltapscott.com

Made in the USA
San Bernardino, CA
25 June 2020